PRAISE FOR

"Jenny Hale writes touching, beautiful stories."—*New York Times* **bestselling author RaeAnne Thayne**

"I can always count on Jenny Hale to sweep me away with her heartwarming romantic tales."—**bestselling author Denise Hunter** on *Butterfly Sisters*

One of "19 Dreamy Summer Romances to Whisk you Away" in **Oprah Magazine** on *The Summer House*

One of "24 Dreamy Books about Romance" in **Oprah Daily** on *The Summer House*

Included in "Christmas Novels to Start Reading Now" in **Southern Living Magazine** on *The Christmas Letters*

"Touching, fun-filled, and redolent with salt air and the fragrance of summer, this seaside tale is a perfect volume for most romance collections."—**Library Journal** on *The Summer House*

"Hale's impeccably executed contemporary romance is the perfect gift for readers who love sweetly romantic love stories imbued with all the warmth and joy of the holiday season."—**Booklist** on *Christmas Wishes and Mistletoe Kisses*

"A great summer beach read."—***PopSugar*** on *Summer at Firefly Beach*

"This sweet small-town romance will leave readers feeling warm all the way through."—***Publishers Weekly*** on *It Started with Christmas*

BOOKS BY JENNY HALE

The Golden Hour
The Magic of Sea Glass
Butterfly Sisters
The Memory Keeper
An Island Summer
The Beach House
The House on Firefly Beach
Summer at Firefly Beach
The Summer Hideaway
The Summer House
Summer at Oyster Bay
Summer by the Sea
A Barefoot Summer

The Noel Bridge
Meet Me at Christmas
The Christmas Letters
A Lighthouse Christmas
Christmas at Fireside Cabins
Christmas at Silver Falls
It Started with Christmas
We'll Always Have Christmas
All I Want for Christmas

Christmas Wishes and Mistletoe Kisses
A Christmas to Remember
Coming Home for Christmas

Out of
the Blue

Out of the Blue

JENNY HALE
USA TODAY BESTSELLING AUTHOR

HARPETH ROAD
PRESS
Nashville

HARPETH ROAD PRESS

Published by Harpeth Road Press (USA)
P.O. Box 158184
Nashville, TN 37215

Paperback: 978-1-963483-19-2
eBook: 978-1-963483-18-5
Library of Congress Control Number: 2025934536

Out of the Blue: An Incredible, Captivating Love Story

Copyright © Jenny Hale, 2025

All rights reserved. Except for the use of brief quotations in review of this novel, the reproduction of this work in whole or in part in any format by any electronic, mechanical, or other means, now known or hereinafter invented, including photocopying, recording, scanning, and all other formats, or in any information storage or retrieval or distribution system, is forbidden without the written permission of the publisher, Harpeth Road Press, P.O. Box 158184, Nashville, Tennessee 37215, USA.

This is a work of fiction. Names, characters, places, and incidents are the product of the author's imagination or were used fictitiously, and any resemblance to actual persons, living or dead, business establishments, events, or locales is entirely coincidental.

Cover Design by Kristen Ingebretson
Cover images © Shutterstock

First printing: April 2025

CHAPTER ONE

Nora Jenkins was not in paradise. She had a view of white cinderblocks, a lukewarm chicken salad sandwich in hand, and another tough week ahead of her.

She tucked her wayward chestnut hair behind her ear and opened the text from her grandmother, June, that had pinged her phone. Under the words "Three weeks to go" was a scene of a white beach and turquoise water, palm trees dotting the edges, their green fanned leaves swaying in the coastal breeze. Nora had never been to the beach, and she had been so looking forward to her tropical honeymoon that hadn't come to pass.

Gram had been trying to convince Nora to take a summer trip. Her grandmother had even gone so far as to print out pictures of the cottage on the Gulf Coast she wanted to rent, putting them into a folder and sending them with Nora to school. Gram hadn't needed to text her anything. The glorious images of a clapboard bungalow, sitting on the pearly coastline were out of the folder and spread across her desk, beckoning her.

Nora set down her sandwich, closed her eyes, and

inhaled deeply, imagining the view from the bench swing on that sandy porch of the cottage on the edge of paradise, but instead of salty air, she breathed in the scent of dust and the unique aroma she could only compare to the rubber of a playground ball, even though there wasn't a single piece of recess equipment in her high-school counseling office.

She opened the text to reply to Gram and deliberated over what to say. Her eighty-five-year-old grandmother wasn't getting around as easily as she used to, so how could they take a trip of this magnitude? But living in Nora's cramped apartment wasn't the best for Gram either. She spent her days cooped up in that little space, waiting for Nora to come home.

Suddenly aware of the heavy tick of the wall clock, Nora stared at her sandwich. Only an hour left before dismissal—thank goodness.

After rolling her head on her shoulders and taking a bite of room-temperature chicken salad, Nora started to reply to the text, but a knock on the doorframe pulled her attention away from her phone.

"Miss Jenkins?"

Nora swallowed her mouthful, the chicken salad souring in her stomach as she took in the sight of Principal Coleman and junior Ivy Ryman.

Ivy scowled and rolled her eyes. Her shoulders were slumped and her head cocked to the side dismissively. Behind them, Nora's new teacher friend, Kim Bales made a here-we-go-again face as she crossed the hall.

Nora set down her sandwich once more. She'd spent her actual lunch break managing this unruly student, who'd enrolled at Oakland High only two months before the end of the school year. In the couple of months Ivy had been there, she'd run off the premises twice, skipped more classes than Nora could remember, and it was rumored she'd jammed the locks of a bunch of lockers, but no one could prove it.

Yet Nora had a soft spot for Ivy. After the death of the girl's mother during a routine knee surgery this past December, Ivy had been forced to live with her absent, famous music producer father, Blaze Ryman. She'd already been kicked out of two private schools, so with limited time left in the academic year, she ended up in public school and on Nora's caseload. She didn't know the girl's entire past, but she had learned that her parents divorced many years ago, and Ivy had lived exclusively with her mother in Alabama before the tragedy. The girl had a lot on her plate for a teenager.

Nora understood loss. She'd lost her parents in a car accident when she was in her twenties. Gram and Gramps had stepped in to be her support, and she couldn't have managed the grief without them. The event was originally what had drawn her to a master's degree in counseling.

Ivy first showed up in Nora's office wearing a black sack dress, hemmed higher than it should be, torn fishnet stockings, combat boots, and a scowl that showed her disdain for even having to breathe the same air as Nora. But over time, Ivy began to trust her, and she'd even gotten comfortable enough to open up about her mother, and allude to how frustrated she was with her new living arrangement. While Nora had made some progress with the girl over the last two months, she was nowhere near a breakthrough of any kind, and it wasn't her job to be the child's therapist. Nora focused on keeping the peace at school. Every time she thought they were getting somewhere, however, Ivy would act out and land in the principal's office.

When Ivy got in trouble, she sat in Nora's office to

remove the disruption from the classroom and keep the office staff free to manage their duties. It was the "Best case scenario," Principal Coleman had said, "given your background in private counseling." His way of saying he had no idea what to do with the girl.

Since Ivy arrived, Nora had been attempting to connect with Ivy's father, but they kept playing phone tag. The school principal managed to speak to him once, when he'd called Mr. Ryman to discuss Ivy's conduct. Her father had asked about collaborating with a family therapist to provide Ivy grief counseling. Though the girl had already met with someone a few times, Mr. Ryman was hoping to get counsel as to how to reach his daughter. But they hadn't heard from him since, and Ivy had told her they'd already been through a few therapists. Nora often met with the latest one after school. She was nearly ready to give up on the idea of ever getting her father to agree to a time when they could all meet. With only three weeks before summer break, her focus was more on transitioning the girl to the therapist than working through school problems.

Nora stood up, smoothing her skirt and steeling herself for another session with the disorderly teen.

"I'll let her tell you why she's here," Principal Coleman said.

Ivy slinked in and flopped down on the beanbag in the corner of Nora's office. The girl fiddled with the philodendron hanging in front of the window, the brown-edged leaves revealing Nora's neglect.

Principal Coleman eyed Nora with a loaded glare. He didn't have to say anything. It was the same story every time with Ivy. She'd probably been found in the gym's locker room, skipping sixth period or something similar.

"I'll take it from here," Nora said, resigning to her

completely inappropriate role. Whether she'd had experience as a private counselor or not, this wasn't in her job description.

With a restrained shake of his head, Principal Coleman left, and Nora turned around to face Ivy.

"Want to talk?" she asked as she sat down on the small sofa against the wall, opposite the seventeen-year-old.

Ivy blew a loud breath through her black-lined lips and piled her pink hair into a fisted ponytail before it all fell over her face when she leaned forward and hung her head.

Nora's phone pinged on her desk. Probably Gram with another tantalizing photo.

Ivy righted herself. "You gonna get that?"

"No," Nora replied. "I want to hear why you're in my office again."

"Your house could be burning down," Ivy countered, squinting at the desk. She stood up.

Typical avoidance behavior.

"If you don't want to tell me why you're here, I'll be happy to walk you back to class."

Ivy picked up one of the printouts of the cottage and ran a paint-chipped fingernail over the typed description. "Mrs. Sanderson won't let me back into class." She tossed the paper onto the pile of folders, but it caught on the movement of air, sailed to the floor, and slid under Nora's bookshelf.

"Sorry," she said, eyeing the paper, but not bothering to go over and get it. She picked up Nora's phone instead and brought it to her.

A push notification from Gram filled the screen. Nora read the first few words of the text.

> You know you need a vacation. You said it
> your—

"It's just my grandmother sending me another message about the beach that was on that paper. It's where she insists we vacation," she said, using a tactic of telling something somewhat personal to bring down Ivy's guard. She waved the phone in the air and then slid it into her pocket. "No fires."

Ivy dropped back down into the beanbag, not any more forthcoming than she had been.

"Why don't you think your teacher will let you back into sixth period?" Nora asked.

"Because I threw her stack of tests out the classroom window, and they're blowing all over the softball field right now."

Nora nodded. "And what were you hoping for with that action?"

Ivy sat up and looked Nora straight in the eyes. "I was hoping she would *see* me."

Nora cocked her head to the side. "Tell me what you mean by that."

With a huff, Ivy folded her arms and sunk backward, the beans in the bag under her hissing in response. "She never looks at me. It's like she's looking through me." The teen made eye contact again. "Like she's already made up her mind who I am."

"And who do you guess *she* thinks you are?"

"A delinquent. At least that's what I thought I heard her say under her breath once."

Nora felt for the girl. Comments like that could scar someone, and she made a mental note to speak to Mrs.

Sanderson after school to see if she remembered making the remark.

"Can you explain how throwing test papers out a window makes you less of a delinquent in her eyes?"

"One of the guys at the back was making jokes about my hair, and it was upsetting me."

"So you threw tests out the window?"

"I tried to get him to stop, but it just made his teasing worse, so I went up to Mrs. Sanderson's desk to ask if I could move seats. She kept on grading those tests, looking down at them with an irritated face, like I was the most annoying person on the planet for even coming up to her. I took the tests out of her hand and tossed them out the window to force her to look up so she could see that I had tears in my eyes."

"I'm sorry that student upset you. Would you like to tell me who it was?"

"It doesn't matter who it was."

"Why doesn't it matter? Shouldn't he face some repercussion for bullying another student?"

Ivy pursed her lips. "I can handle that guy. He just hit a nerve, that's all."

Pushing aside suggestions for all the more appropriate things Ivy could've done in response, Nora focused on the girl's feelings instead. "How did he hit a nerve, exactly?"

"He wouldn't stop joking about my pink hair. Pink was my mom's favorite color." The girl's eyes filled with tears, and her lips began to wobble. She pulled up her legs and wrapped her arms around her knees, her heavy black boots sinking into the beanbag, and hid her face.

A lump formed in Nora's throat. "I'm so sorry, Ivy." Nora understood the pain of losing your mother. Seeing that pain in Ivy brought it all back.

The teenager was so closed off, but considering what she'd been through, Nora could understand why. She'd been ripped out of her old school and thrown into a slew of new ones where she didn't know a soul. And the poor girl's mother was *gone*. Not to mention, it was tough to get her father on the phone when they needed him. Ivy had told Nora she went home to an empty house every day. At the very most, she had a person she called a "nanny," even though she was seventeen.

Nora took the weight of it all home with her every afternoon.

"Your response to Mrs. Sanderson probably wasn't perfect, but I'll talk to her, and I'll explain what was going on," Nora offered.

"Don't bother," Ivy said, her head still buried in her arms.

"It's important to express these things or change can't happen."

Ivy lifted her head. "Anyone who would treat someone like that isn't worth my effort to change them—Mrs. Sanderson *or* that guy."

"I just want to make sure your needs are taken care of," Nora said honestly.

Ivy squinted at her. "Why?"

"I want you to know there are people in your corner. If you focus on those who lift you up, and let everything else fall away, life will get easier."

"Thanks," Ivy said, her tone softening.

Another tiny breakthrough.

The bell rang.

"It's dismissal," Nora said. "You made it through the whole day."

Ivy hoisted herself out of the beanbag. "It's still going

for me. I've got after-school detention for pushing that guy's head into his locker just before class."

"But didn't he tease you *in* sixth period?"

"Yeah. After I pushed his head into his locker."

"Did he provoke you in some way?"

"Yeah. He told me nobody liked me, so I was just living up to it."

"Wouldn't you rather prove him wrong?"

Ivy walked over to the doorway. "No. He doesn't deserve to know the real me." She walked out the door.

With a sigh, Nora went over to her desk, dropped down into her chair, and squeezed her eyes shut to ward off a headache that buzzed at her temples. Four more days to go until the weekend.

CHAPTER TWO

"How was your day?" Gram asked from under the quilt on the sofa. The TV was on the news, but she raised the remote and clicked it off before leaning heavily on her thighs to heave herself into a standing position.

"Rough."

Nora hung her bag on a chair at the small dinette table that divided the kitchen and living spaces and rubbed her weary eyes. Her stomach rumbled. By the time she'd gotten back to the sandwich she'd packed for lunch, she'd worried the mayonnaise had spoiled, so she'd chucked it. She didn't have much of an appetite after attempting to talk to Mrs. Sanderson either. Ivy had been right. The woman had already made up her mind about the girl.

"This job is draining you," Gram said, folding the quilt into a perfect square of four quadrants before draping it on the back of the sofa.

"I got into school counseling with grand plans to help kids live better lives. I wanted to impart some kind of guidance for their future that would help them to learn themselves what they wanted to contribute to the world. What classes would light their fires? What jobs would be the perfect combination of passion and income? But there's too much out of my control to really help them do anything."

She kicked off her shoes and set them neatly by the door, the cool feel of the hardwoods an antidote to the confines of her work shoes. Summer couldn't come quickly enough.

"The principal wants us to focus on career planning and time management, but my kids have real problems that have to be dealt with before we can get to the lighter things."

"You're thinking specifically of the... musician's daughter?"

"Music producer," Nora clarified as she went over to the sink and rinsed out her water bottle. "She's got real control issues, and she consumes my time. I'm unable to get to any other student. I've had to cancel on three teachers this week when I was supposed to do career-guidance lessons to give them an extra planning period for the new grading system update so they can input their final grades."

"What does the principal say about that?"

"He said he understands. Of course he does. He'd rather me deal with Ivy than have her sit in *his* office."

Gram put her hands on her wide hips. "But should you be the one to deal with that behavior?"

Nora began her career as a professional counselor, holding a dual license in both private counseling and school counseling, a skill set she felt the school leaned on a little more than they should.

"No, but who else can? One of Ivy's teachers told me in confidence that Ivy was the reason she'd take early retirement. She said they don't pay her enough to deal with that behavior. Having a heart for kids is important, but we aren't all therapists. That teacher is frustrated because she doesn't have the skills to manage Ivy."

"Just because you do doesn't mean it's your problem," Gram said.

"I know. And I left private counseling, remember? I'd much rather focus on careers..." She shook her head, scrubbing her water bottle a bit too vigorously. "I feel as if I'm the only one who can still see her as something other than a troublemaker."

She'd originally taken a job at a private counseling firm, but with her knowledge of assessment she'd been used mostly as a diagnostician when she really wanted to work directly with people. While she had been able to fit a few counseling clients into her schedule, the firm had filled her caseload to the brim, causing her to spend countless hours of her own time scoring forms and writing reports. She'd taken the high-school job with the hopes of getting some of that time back during the holidays and summer break. That was the answer she told most people when they asked why she left. It was mostly true, and a lot easier than the real reason: her fiancé had been running around with one of the other counselors.

Gram patted Nora's shoulder lovingly. "I don't blame her for being an angry child. She probably feels completely out of control, so she's struggling to find that control anywhere she can."

Nora set the bottle upside down on a towel by the sink and turned to face Gram. "That scared girl hides behind the shock of her clothing choices and the brunt force of her outward expression, and I just want to hug her and tell her everything will be okay."

"You can't carry her burden for her. It'll suck your energy dry, and you'll be no help to anyone."

"Disconnecting is harder than it seems, though. I still think about her after I've left school. I can't help it."

"Have you spoken to her father? Where does he stand in all this?"

Nora shook her head. "I have to wonder if he, too, is just trying to survive. At least that's what I hope is going on. I'll give him the benefit of the doubt until I'm proven wrong."

In the silence that followed, the savory scent of spices and potatoes wafted toward her, pulling Nora from her daily strife. Her stomach rumbled again.

"Something smells amazing."

Gram waggled a finger toward the corner of the counter. "I've been simmering chicken stew in the Crock-Pot. It's ready when you are."

"Have I mentioned how thankful I am to have you?"

Gram chuckled fondly.

Last September, when Gram had a fall and broke her ankle, Nora immediately convinced her to move in. She told her that having someone else around would be helpful. Her grandmother had always been her safe place, and while she hated that a fall and minor injury brought her here, she was grateful for their living arrangements. They split the bills, which gave Nora a little breathing room financially and Nora liked the company, but the problem was that Gram was alone at Nora's most of the day.

She also felt guilty that she hadn't been the best company these last seven months of her new job. She was adjusting well at the school, but her broken heart was so fresh she wasn't doing well at masking that pain. And the entire last semester she'd been coming home more drained than usual.

Despite all this, her grandmother had been nothing but encouraging and supportive, telling her that, while Nora might not have been expecting a student like Ivy, Nora was probably the perfect person to enter the girl's life right now.

"How was *your* day?" Nora asked Gram.

"Decent. I had a doctor's appointment and then I got myself one of those big cinnamon rolls from the bakery in town."

"You never splurge on things like that. Good for you."

"I've been trying to do things I normally wouldn't. I'd say it's a midlife crisis, but I'm a bit old for that."

Nora smiled.

"Other than that, I puttered around here."

Nora lifted the lid off the Crock-Pot, the salty smells of stewed vegetables and chicken reminding her of her hunger once more. "What was the doctor's appointment?"

"Just a checkup," Gram said. "Have you thought any more about the beach trip?" Her tone was nonchalant, although the abrupt change in subject gave away her excitement about it. There had been many obvious signs she'd been wanting to go. She pulled two bowls from the cabinet, set them down, and rubbed her shoulder.

"You haven't traveled in a while," Nora said. "Do you remember how much energy it takes to do all the packing and then rushing around to get there?"

"I remember well enough." She closed her eyes and took in a deep breath. "The warm sun and crashing waves on the sand are worth all the aggravation." Her eyes opened and landed on Nora. "I don't know how many summers I've got. I'd like to spend time in paradise before I can't anymore. I'll even pay for it all."

Nora ladled the stew into a bowl and handed it to Gram. "Vacations are expensive. I don't have a lot of extra spending money, and I really don't feel comfortable using yours."

"I can't take it with me in the end. What good is it if we don't spend it?" Gram carried her bowl over to the table and sat down.

Nora followed suit. "All this talk of time and not taking things with you... Is there something you're not sharing?"

"No, definitely not. I'm not wishing away my life; I simply want to live it. None of us know how long we have, but we act as if we have an eternity. What if we don't?"

"This passion for living has come on suddenly." Nora sunk her spoon into the stew, the steam rising into the air.

Gram tucked her short gray hair behind her ears as if to ensure the intention in her wise eyes could be seen. "My *mention* of it has come on suddenly. It's been brewing for years, since Gramps died."

That was when Nora saw it: the yearning in her grandmother's face, the absolute need to get out of that apartment and do something new and exciting. And Nora couldn't deny she could probably benefit from an escape from reality for a little while as well.

"Can we even get a cottage at this point? They're probably all rented."

Gram shook her head. "I already inquired about the one I sent you. As if we have divine intervention, they have a spot next month, due to a cancellation. I just have to make sure it's still available."

"If it's available, let's do it."

Gram clapped her hands excitedly, more life in her than Nora had seen in months. "Yes! I'll book everything. Don't you worry about any of it. I'll handle it all."

"I suppose I'll need a swimsuit and some beach necessities."

"Definitely. Get yourself a beach bag, some large towels, sunscreen, and a cover-up."

"As soon as plans are set, I'll get everything we need."

"That cottage is beachside, so you'll be able to walk out the door and onto the sand. You can swim every morning if you'd like." Gram's eyes danced. "I'll watch while I sip my coffee." She put an elbow on the table and leaned forward, her spoon hanging above her stew. "All we have to do is get through the next few weeks and then everything will be better."

Nora took in a deep breath, as if she could inhale Gram's words. She knew her grandmother was right. If she could just hang on until the end of the school year, her summer break would be the time she needed to recharge.

CHAPTER THREE

"It's only Tuesday, and it feels like Thursday already," Nora told Kim Bales as they entered the buzzing school building. Kim was a ninth-grade English teacher and cheerleading coach, and she had a bubbly personality that made it difficult to have a bad day when she was around. Kim had made friends with Nora right away, and the two of them sometimes spent their planning periods chatting.

"Summer's right around the corner," Kim said brightly. "Come by my room if you need to blow off some steam." Her eyebrows bobbed playfully and she dipped into her classroom.

After dodging excitable students, hallway after hallway, Nora dropped her bag onto her messy desk, her mind on that gorgeous beach bungalow. She bent down to retrieve the printout of the cottage she and Gram would be renting that had slipped under her bookshelf yesterday, but it must have been swept up by the custodians. Oh, well. At least the floor was clean. With the year she'd had she'd barely had time to tidy anything, but today she'd make some.

She found a level spot among her paperwork to support

her travel mug full of the coffee Gram had brewed and fixed up just for her as she'd run out of the door this morning.

Sweet Gram. Nora hated leaving her, but their plans for the vacation helped.

With a sense of purpose, she began to organize her desk. She brushed the crumbs off the surface, slid them into her cupped hand and dumped them into the trash can. Then she gathered up the various books she'd bookmarked for lessons and reshelved them. Returning to her desk, she stacked the photos of beach scenes Gram had sent with her and set them on the corner of her desktop.

With her space cleared, Nora set in checking her emails, immediately seeing one from the principal about Ivy's latest bout of misconduct, downloading a virus onto one of the biology lab computers yesterday during detention. She scanned the message, her eyes falling on the phrase *possible expulsion*, and then focused on the email from her upcoming appointment: family therapist Janine Swarovski.

In his one phone call to the principal, Blaze had asked if Nora could meet with the woman to discuss Ivy's progress at school and ways they could transition from Nora to a family setting with Janine off school grounds. Nora had agreed.

It had been clear to Nora early on that Ivy hadn't fully dealt with the grief of losing her mother or the major transition of moving in with her father. Neither issue was in Nora's domain as a school counselor, so she was happy to meet with Janine. But Ivy wasn't connecting with her family therapist, so the administration told Mr. Ryman it might be a good transition to bring the therapist into the school regularly, so she could discuss with Nora the techniques and responses that seemed to work best for Ivy.

While Nora had yet to speak to Ivy's dad personally, he had signed the paperwork online for them to continue.

The problem was, the therapist wasn't at all the person Nora would've chosen for Ivy. The woman's natural demeanor would never work for the girl. She wasn't warm enough, and she seemed set in her diagnoses instead of hearing people. Had Blaze screened people at all, or had he plucked someone off the internet? It wasn't Nora's job, however, to choose a family counselor; she just had to tell Janine what worked for her at school.

Today the topic with the therapist just happened to be Ivy's connection to her father. Blaze was a top music producer, working between Nashville, New York, and LA, and it wasn't clear what, if anything, he was doing to help his daughter. Nora worried that he'd left helping Ivy up to the therapists.

She scanned Ms. Swarovski's confidential message in her inbox.

> Blaze has already gone through a string of caregivers. Ivy ran them all off. The most recent one stayed the longest—three days.

Ivy needed a mother, not a twenty-something who could be her big sister. The teen had no one to grieve with, no one around her who even knew her mother. And Blaze needed to be present for his daughter, but he hadn't made a single school meeting. In his defense, he hadn't had time yet to structure his busy lifestyle around Ivy. But Ivy had been with him for a few months now, so he needed to figure it out.

"Hello," Janine said, coming in with a flourish and offering a handshake—something she did every time they met.

Nora stood up and shook her hand, then offered her a seat. "I was just reading your message about Ivy's caregivers."

"Yes." Janine neatly arranged her ballpoint pen on top of her clean notepad and then folded her hands. "Any new developments on your end before we discuss family dynamics?"

"Principal Coleman emailed Ivy's dad this morning. She has detention again today. She didn't want to take her biology exam, but the teacher forced her to, so she downloaded a virus onto the computer, jamming all the programs and erasing everyone's scores, including hers."

Janine narrowed her eyes, her gaze roaming the tiled ceiling. "So she has a fixed mindset."

"Sorry?"

"She's focusing on how she's going to perform instead of what she might need to learn."

Nora tried to maintain a neutral gaze. Janine hadn't really hit the mark, as usual—this was about attention, about feeling seen—Ivy had said it herself. If Ms. Swarovski was ever going to get through to Ivy, she had to understand the girl. Her blanket judgments weren't entirely correct. While Nora didn't want to overstep her bounds as a school counselor, she felt compelled to make this woman understand.

"I think, deep down, Ivy wants acceptance. She's hurting inside and she needs people to give her a break."

Janine's face wrinkled. "What does a computer test have to do with acceptance?"

"Even though Ivy puts up a hardened front, I have to

wonder if she really does care what people think about her. She's more sensitive than she looks."

Janine wrote the words "school counselor believes Ivy is sensitive" on her paper and then underlined it. She asked Nora, "Why do you think that?"

"Because she got emotional when another child teased her about her pink hair."

An incredulous laugh burst from Janine's chest and she set down her pen. "But if she was worried about what people thought about her, why would she choose to stand out with pink hair?"

Had this woman had any training at all?

"She craves *emotional* acceptance," Nora clarified. "She told me her mother's favorite color was pink. Dying her hair her mother's favorite color is a cry for help. She's calling out, 'Someone pay attention to my grief.'"

Janine gave her a placating smile, making Nora's skin prickle. Nora wanted to shake this woman by the shoulders. No wonder Ivy wouldn't listen to her. She had no heart.

"Miss Jenkins, I fear that pink hair and acceptance might be a stretch to explain Ivy's downloading a virus onto a school computer. Her hair color is up to her, but the school's property is another matter. And I'm just not seeing the connection."

Nora swallowed the lump of irritation that rose from her chest. She'd have to spell it out for the woman. "Ivy's behavior is not related to getting a poor grade in biology. She's trying to tell everyone that, given her circumstances, biology doesn't matter to her. All she wants to do is process her sorrow, which is something no one has helped her do, to my knowledge. She goes home every day to an empty mansion of a house where there *might* be a glorified babysitter a few years older than Ivy, who has no experience in managing the death of a parent. She desperately needs her father, but he's working all the time. She's alone when she requires people around her who can talk about more than her *fixed mindset*." She'd spit out that last bit through gritted teeth. It had come out before she could reign it in, and she clamped her mouth shut before she said any more.

With measured movements, Janine picked up her notepad and pen and slid them into her bag. "You must be having a hard day," she said through tight lips. "I don't think we're going to get anywhere, given your demeanor." She got up and walked out.

Nora didn't bother to stop her.

Great. How was she supposed to explain to Principal Coleman and Ivy's father that she'd run off the family therapist?

She rubbed the pinch in her shoulder. As she stared at the empty doorway, she knew she'd done them all a favor. That woman wasn't going to help Ivy.

THE REST OF THE DAY, Nora tried to fit in as many of her regular activities as she could, working through her planning period to catch up on all the reports and paperwork she'd missed, all the while thinking of ways to repair her blunder with the family counselor somehow. Then after school, she'd spent an hour going from classroom to classroom, rescheduling the lessons she'd missed this week due to Ivy's antics. The teachers had all heard about Ivy and were very understanding and flexible, which had been a big help.

By the time she'd finished, she had an idea.

She made sure she was outside the classroom when

Ivy's detention let out. She needed to talk to Blaze before she told the principal what had happened with the therapist that morning so Ivy's father could hear the explanation from her mouth, not Janine's.

Nora crossed the hallway to greet the girl.

"Hey," Ivy said under her breath. The girl looked down the hallway in both directions as if scouting out who would see if she talked to a teacher. The coast clear, she made her way over. "What's up?"

"Ms. Swarovski came for a visit this morning," Nora told her.

"I saw her in your office, on my way to math class," Ivy said, rolling her eyes dramatically.

Nora bit her tongue when she really wanted to side with Ivy on this one. "I'd like to talk to your dad about my meeting with her *and* your biology stunt."

Ivy blew a deep breath through her lips.

"I'm not calling your dad to get you in trouble," Nora assured her. "I'm calling to tell him how I think I can help you."

"How?"

Nora nodded down the hallway to get them out of range of the detention room. Ivy complied, the two of them exiting through the double doors by the gym and into the late spring sunshine and the sidewalk that lined the parking lot.

"What if I was the one to find your next counselor, and you helped me do it? We could meet right after school a couple times a week until the end of the year and see how it goes together. Once we have someone you connect with, the two of you could meet during the summer. We'd have the next three weeks to work on it."

"Could I get out of class?" Ivy asked.

"Well, I'm not sure I have enough pull to excuse you from classes." She actually did. She'd spoken to Principal Coleman about it, and he was fine with anything at this point that was the lesser distraction for the other students. "But I thought... hopefully you won't, but if you get another detention I can ask you to serve it in my office instead."

A glimmer of what looked like hope sparkled in Ivy's eyes. "Are you allowed to do that?"

"I have no idea," Nora said. "But I want to do what's best for you. Think we can call your dad and get him on our side?"

"Maybe." Ivy pulled her phone from the drop-pocket of her leopard vest, dialed the number, and held it to her ear while a couple of baseball players climbed into an SUV after practice, their laughter sailing over from the open windows as the vehicle drove away.

It occurred to Nora she'd never heard Ivy laugh.

The girl clicked off her phone. "He didn't answer."

Figures. "Think he's at home?" Nora asked.

Ivy shrugged. "Maybe. He's not supposed to leave for New York until this evening."

"Any idea when he'll be back from New York?"

"No."

"Do you know what he'll be doing in New York, exactly?" It wasn't her place to ask, but come on. This guy was not parenting his daughter.

"There's a Broadway actress who sings country music, apparently. She's originally from Georgia, and a video of her singing one of her songs went viral. Dad said he wants to see if he can get her to Nashville to cut a demo and meet with 'some people.'"

"I have no idea how long that takes," Nora said.

"Neither do I."

While Nora didn't want to enter the murky divide between business and personal, if she didn't see Blaze before he left, she might not connect with him for a couple of days at least, and she needed to let him know what had transpired with Janine and how she planned to fix it.

"Do you mind if I follow you home to see if I can catch him?" she asked Ivy.

"I guess."

"Okay, I'm just here." She pointed to her Honda on the edge of the teacher's lot.

"That one's mine." Ivy pointed to a wreck of a car, pieced together from various scrap parts, all different colors, a dent in the fender.

This is the car of a millionaire's daughter?

When she surfaced from her thought, Ivy was glaring at her.

"Before you say anything, I wouldn't let my dad buy me a car. I wanted the one my mom bought for me. We bought this one with just our money. We didn't need Dad's money." Her lips turned downward in a defiant pout. "I still don't. Money is the root of all evil—my mom taught me that."

"Fair enough." She had to give it to Ivy—she valued honor over appearances, which was more than Nora could say for a lot of students at Oakland. "I'll pull around to you and follow your lead."

"Okay."

The two parted ways, and Nora got into her car. She started the engine and backed out of the parking spot. When she drove over to Ivy, the girl wasn't in the vehicle. Instead, she was outside it, door open, kicking the tires.

Nora put down her window. "Everything all right?"

Ivy turned to her, tears pooling along her bottom, black-lined lashes. "The car won't start." She marched around to the front and lifted the hood, securing it with the safety bar and then fiddling with various pieces of the engine. Then she unhooked the bar and banged the hood shut.

Even her car had let her down.

"Why don't you try to call your dad again?"

With a huff, Ivy slammed the car door and pulled out her phone. The wind blew her pink hair back, revealing her milky skin. Her face was usually covered, as if she could hide behind her locks, but in this moment of defiance and frustration she seemed to have forgotten that anyone would see her.

"Dad?"

A rush of interest shot through Nora, and she leaned over the open window.

"I'm at school... I had detention." Ivy rolled her eyes and let the phone drop by her side. Then she picked it back up, holding it away from her. "I know... That's not even why I'm calling." She held the phone in front of her mouth and barked, "My car won't start." Then she put the phone back to her ear. "No, I don't have any *friends*... Miss Jenkins is here with me."

Nora put her hand on the door handle, poised to open it. Could she hop on the phone right now and talk to Blaze?

Ivy leaned away from the phone. "Dad's busy and wants to know if you can take me home."

"Um..." Nora wondered whether she was supposed to drive a student in her car. But if she said yes, she could have a word in person with Blaze. "Sure. Hop in."

Ivy put the phone back up to her ear. "I got a ride."

She ended the call and climbed inside Nora's car, lumping her canvas bag between her combat boots. Without a word, she pulled up a map on her phone and started the route. Then she set the phone in the center-console cup holder so Nora could view it.

Nora followed the directions, left school, and turned down a side road leading away from the city. As they drove, Ivy put down her window, the breeze blowing in. The girl leaned away from it, and Nora couldn't help but compare her behavior with the boys she'd seen earlier. With Ivy's fingers delicately laced in her lap, her thin frame relaxed, Nora could almost imagine her as a little girl, before her world had fallen around her. As they drove, her usual scowl softened, the tightness between her brows released. It was as if she was calmer knowing no one from school could reach her now.

The two of them drove in silence, allowing Nora's mind to move to their destination. She was about to enter the grounds of one of the most influential music producers in Nashville.

She'd looked up Blaze online once. He was incredibly handsome—a thick crop of dark hair and gray eyes with flecks of brown, like seawater at low tide. He looked almost her age, in his mid to late thirties, which meant he and his ex had Ivy young. He seemed tall, at least compared to the group of musicians he was standing next to in the photo.

His client list read like a who's who of music royalty. What had stuck out most was his reputation for honesty, kindness, and impeccable work. The articles made Nora wonder why he hadn't offered that same attention to his daughter.

She found it interesting that Ivy had never really talked about her father when they were together. Clearly, he worked a lot, but what was he like?

"How is it, living with your dad?" she asked the girl now.

Ivy looked out the open window as the Tennessee hills slid past, and shrugged.

Nora glanced at her, waiting for more, but nothing came. "Surely there's *something* you've connected on."

"He's never home."

Nora couldn't argue with that statement.

"We do have something in common. I'm not sure he even knows it, though."

"What's that?"

Ivy held back her hair, a few whisps escaping across her cheek. "We both play guitar."

"Really?"

Ivy nodded. "I've never told him I play."

"Why not?"

"He's never asked *what* I do."

"Maybe you should tell him? Extend an olive branch."

Ivy looked back out the window.

"Do you have any good memories of him playing guitar? You could start there."

Her frown relaxed. "When I was really little he'd sit by my bed and strum until I fell asleep."

With a statement like that, Nora couldn't help but have optimism for the two of them. "That's a wonderful memory."

"That's about all I've got of him—a few memories."

Not wanting to pry, but wondering what had happened between Ivy's parents, she said, "Maybe you'll get to make more memories now."

"Kind of hard when he's absent every single day." The words came out as if they tasted bitter on Ivy's tongue.

"The two of you have to have been in the same spot at some point." She came to a four-way stop and waited for the light to turn. "You've never gone to the movies, had a meal at home, anything?"

One corner of Ivy's mouth twitched upward. "We did make dinner one night."

"What did you make?"

"More like what did we *try* to make."

Nora peeked over at her.

"When I first came to live with him, we didn't really feel like going anywhere, and there was nothing in the house, so we tried to make lasagna with the ingredients we had. We pieced together different recipes from the internet to make our own version, but it came out of the oven like a cinder block. Dad almost broke a steak knife trying to cut it."

Nora laughed. "How is that possible?"

"That was my question exactly!"

For the first time since Nora had met the girl, Ivy broke into a gorgeous smile—a wide grin with perfectly straight, white teeth. It dawned on Nora how beautiful she was when all that angst was stripped away.

"So what did you two end up doing?"

"We tried to eat it, and there was no way, so we decided to go out. But going out with my dad is difficult because everyone in Nashville knows him, and they won't leave us alone."

Nora followed the map, turning in at a gate that led to a neighborhood full of mansions sitting like giant pearls in their manicured lawns on top of the rolling hills. She pulled to a stop at an ornate wrought-iron neighborhood gate that kept all the grandeur secured.

"The code is 77665," Ivy said.

Nora put down her window and typed in the numbers. The gates slid open.

"So what happened when you went out?" she continued.

"Dad knew this little hole-in-the-wall called Cappy's. It's famous for its pickle burgers: burgers with these spicy fried pickles on top—so good. It's where all the stars go because you can get in through a back door in the alley. We went there."

"And no one saw you?"

"Nope. Which is perfectly fine by me. Talking to random strangers is annoying." She let out a little chuckle. "It's sort of become our spot. Whenever he's home, we go there to dinner."

The softness in Ivy's voice gave away how much those dinners with her dad meant to her.

"This one." Ivy pointed to a sprawling estate at the end of the street.

The home sat on a hill and had a six-car garage and windows the size of skyscrapers. Nora drove her Honda up the hill and onto the intricately patterned circular driveway. When she parked, Ivy got out, and the two of them walked up to the arched double doors. Ivy typed in a string of numbers on the keypad and the latch clicked open.

"Dad?" she called into the airy two-story entryway with nothing but marble tile glistening under the light of a ten-foot-wide glass-and-iron chandelier. Through the large windows at the back of the house that were visible through the center of the space, a bright blue swimming pool with fountains glistened.

"Da-ad!" Ivy's voice carried through the expanse.

She pulled out her phone. "I'll text him. It's easier."

Ivy fired off a few lines to Blaze while Nora gazed at the wide, curling staircase. What would it be like living in this huge, cold house? The entry alone felt like a hall in a grand museum.

"He had to leave to fly out," Ivy said. "Guess that's why he was busy." Her eyes were still on her phone, her fingers moving a mile a minute.

"Okay," Nora said, putting on a smile for Ivy's benefit. Now what would she do? "Are you going to be all right here on your own?"

"Yeah, Lucia's probably here somewhere."

"Lucia?"

"She's the housekeeper. She's here until five."

"And then you'll be alone?"

"Well, she lives in the guest suite out back."

"No nanny?"

"I think we're 'hiring,'" she said, throwing up air quotes around the last word as she smirked deviously.

"All right." Nora turned to go, but then stopped. "How will you get your car?"

"I'm ahead of you." Her shoulder's slumped forward, an outward expression of her irritation. "I just asked my dad that question. He's getting it towed. And I have to ride the bus tomorrow. Ugh. I hate all the kids on the bus."

"How often have you had to ride the bus?"

"I haven't ever ridden on it."

"Then how do you know if you hate the kids on the bus?"

"I don't have to know them to know that I'll hate them. The way they look at me when I drive past the bus stop is enough."

Despite her empathy for the girl, Nora gave her a firm look. "Don't make a ruckus on the bus. Promise?"

Ivy looked up at Nora through thickly mascaraed lashes, her lips set in a straight line. "Never."

"You'll never make a ruckus or you'll never promise?"

"I'll never promise. If they act like idiots, I'll have to retaliate." She slipped her phone into the pocket of her vest.

"Or, if you ignore them and get to school without incident," Nora said, making her way toward the door, "I'll pull some strings and let you hang out with me during first period."

Interest lit up the girl's face. "I can skip geography? How?"

Nora had heard all about her distaste for the geography teacher. "I have connections."

A smile twitched at the edges of Ivy's lips. "Fine."

As Nora opened the door, a look of solidarity filled her those gray eyes like her father's. If anyone could help this girl, it was her. But could she get Ivy to a good place before she took off for the summer?

CHAPTER FOUR

"You're later than usual," Gram said when Nora came into the living room.

"I had to drive Ivy Ryman home after school. Her car wouldn't start."

Gram closed her novel around her finger to hold her place. "I don't really think that's your job, is it?"

"Definitely not." Nora lumped her bag on the floor.

"Her millionaire father couldn't fire up one of his sports cars to come get her?"

"He wasn't home. He was flying to New York."

"So what would the girl have done if you hadn't driven her home?"

Nora pulled a throw pillow from the corner of the sofa and sat down, hugging it in her lap. "I have no idea." She twisted around into a lying position and stuffed the pillow behind her head. "And I think she'll be in that big mansion all alone for the night."

Gram's eyes rounded. "That man left his seventeen-year-old at the house all night by herself?"

"As far as I can tell. The housekeeper lives in the guest-house, apparently, but there's no one in the main house to watch over her."

"That's unbelievable." Gram opened her book back up, dog-eared the page, and set it on the table. "Do you have her number to check on her or anything?"

Nora shook her head and closed her eyes. "No. But she's coming to my office during first period, so if she doesn't come to school for any reason, I'll know right away."

"That's not going to help her tonight, though, is it?"

"I don't know what I'm supposed to do about it. Ivy's after-school activities aren't my place. You said yourself that I shouldn't bring my work home with me. And I have to draw the line with what's appropriate." The words were easy to say, but she couldn't shake her worry for Ivy.

Gram clapped her hands together. "You're right." She stood up. "Come to the kitchen table with me. I want to show you what I've got planned for our trip. It'll be the perfect way to take your mind off work."

Nora swung her feet around to the floor and stood.

"I got us the cottage," Gram said, bringing the laptop to life at the table.

Nora rooted around in the fridge and pulled out an apple while Gram pulled up the online listing. "You haven't seen all the pictures of this place."

Nora sliced the apple on a plate and added a dollop of peanut butter. Then she took it over to the table and pulled up a chair beside Gram. Her grandmother scrolled through the photos of serene beach images, one by one. The white bungalow on a beachside hill was the epitome of relaxation with its wide porch on stilts and cushioned porch swing. Nora could almost hear the softly lapping turquoise water on the white sand beaches as she nibbled her apple slices.

Gram tapped the photo of a white porch swing full of

pillows with a view of the Gulf of Mexico. "You can pile all your favorite books on that little table next to this swing and read to your heart's content."

The location seemed secluded; the nearest cottage was a couple of minutes' walk down the beach. It would be the perfect place to recharge.

"It looks absolutely amazing." Nora couldn't wait to feel the sand between her toes and fill her lungs with briny air, leaving all her troubles behind.

"And there's a crushed seashell path leading right down the hill to a patio full of Adirondack chairs that overlook the water," Gram added as she showed her a photo. "It even has a fire pit. We could make s'mores." Her eyes glittered with anticipation.

Nora dipped an apple slice into the peanut butter and scooped some up. "When do we leave?"

"The day after school ends."

"And you've got it all reserved and everything?"

"Yep." Gram flashed a wide smile. "It'll be the perfect retreat for the two of us. We can make ice-cream sundaes, carry cocktails down to the beach... I'd like to start packing right now."

Nora laughed. "How long's the rental?"

"Well, the cancellation they had was a two-week wedding and honeymoon—the couple decided to elope in the Bahamas instead."

"Two weeks?"

"Yep."

"That's a long time. Are you sure you want to spend that amount of money? That cottage isn't cheap."

"You can't put a price on relaxation," Gram said, taking Nora's hands. "We'll spend our days basking in the glorious sun until we doze off. We'll read books, drink wine, and sit on the porch until the stars fill the sky. I want that as long as I can have it. No matter the price."

"It will be so nice to spend time with just the two of us," Nora said, getting excited. "We could hunt for seashells, browse the beach shops, and play cards like we used to on holidays."

"That's the spirit." Gram stood up and scooted the laptop toward Nora. "You keep browsing all the fun things we'll do. I'm going to get a bath and put on my nightgown. My shoulders are aching, and I need to soak them."

"Are you going to have dinner?"

"I ate early," Gram said. "But I did leave you the rest of the pizza. It's in the fridge."

Nora's face lit up. "You made pizza?"

"I did. And it's your favorite—the sourdough with three cheeses."

"That sounds delicious." Nora rolled her head around. "I might eat and then come in after you."

"You should." She put a hand on Nora's arm. "Don't overwork yourself in these final days of the school year. Just wrap things up and get your mind into summer mode."

"Okay."

When Gram left, Nora tried to follow her grandmother's advice. She chewed her lip in thought as she slid the pizza in the microwave. It would've been easier to put a finishing touch on things if she hadn't run off Ivy's family therapist. Now she'd somehow managed to put herself in charge of finding the girl's next therapist.

The microwave beeped, and she added the warmed slice to her plate of apple, returning to the laptop at the table.

Ivy was like high tide, that swell of water that could overtake Nora. She couldn't wait for the summer when she could wade into the warm months slowly and bask in the calmer pace of life. But she'd never get to that point if she didn't get Ivy's therapy squared away. She needed to speak to Blaze. How should she approach him?

She took a bite of savory pizza and focused on the laptop in front of her. While the water ran in the bathroom down the hall, she clicked off the cottage and opened her social media, then typed "Blaze Ryman" into the search bar. His public page came up. Her eyes widened at the number of followers: 104k. How many people was he following? Twenty-six. Sheesh.

His most recent post was a photo of him and a tall, thin, doe-eyed redhead with perfectly pouty lips, her arm draped around him. The caption read: *Stealing the fabulous Kasey Miles, Broadway sensation, and bringing her to Nashville. New York, I might let her come back... #risingstar*. That must have been the singer Ivy had mentioned. The woman's sequined mini-skirt, oversized dangly earrings, and stilettos were a far cry from Nora's cotton blouse and wide-legged trousers. She turned her attention to Blaze, with his massive watch that peeked out from the sleeve of his high-end suit. A couple of half-empty champagne glasses sat on the table next to them. Even in a photo there was an air of confidence about him that made Nora feel small. He seemed so sure of himself, almost superior or self-important. Was he that stylish in real life? Or had he put on his best in an attempt to impress Ms. Miles?

She'd find out soon enough. She needed to know when he was coming home so she could schedule a meeting. With another bite of her slice, she scrolled through a few more posts, looking for any clue as to when he'd return. A photo of him at the airport came up—a selfie in front of the window with a view of the plane. The caption read: *Headed to the stars. Back soon, Nashville!*

Nothing helpful.

She continued. There was a photo of him with Dolly Parton, the two of them laughing together, and another of him fist-bumping Willie Nelson. He certainly knew the best in the business. He probably dated the best too. She tore her eyes from his kind smile and rugged good looks and tried to focus on her task. She went into his stories to see if she could find anything there. The first one was a video of him in a taxi, filming the New York streets. "Here I am, in the Big Apple. It's looking gorgeous, don't you think?" He turned the camera around and offered a goofy, cheesy smile, making her laugh.

She clicked to the next frame: his feet, walking along the sidewalk during the day. He had some kind of designer sneakers... "I'm starving," his smooth, deep voice said through her laptop speakers. "I'm probably going to have sushi to impress a client, but I really want a slice of pizza and a beer..."

She stopped, mid-chew, feeling a small bond with him just then. But pizza wasn't exactly a unique preference. She took another bite.

In the next story, he tossed his suitcase onto a hotel bed. "Made it! I'm off to meet a talented singer tonight." He turned the phone around. "I'm so excited to get her into the studio. I love giving new talent a shot. We all start at the beginning, don't we? Wish me luck!"

After a few more videos, Nora landed on one where he'd put on a fur coat in a designer shop. He filmed himself in the mirror, looking absolutely ridiculous. "What do you think? Is it me?"

"Definitely not," she said.

He slipped it off and handed it to the store clerk. "I'll think about it." He made a face into the camera.

She chuckled.

Blaze Ryman didn't seem as intimidating as he had in the glossy photos on his timeline. She preferred hearing him talk. He had a personable, casual way about him, and she could see why he was so popular. But no matter how successful he was—he was doing something most people would give their right arm to do for a living—he should be home with his daughter. At least more often.

She refreshed the feed, and a brand-new story popped up. She opened it.

"After a full day, I'm heading to the airport tomorrow! Back home I go," he said. "Another amazing day."

Perfect.

Nora channeled her determination to get ahold of this man as soon as he landed in Nashville.

CHAPTER FIVE

Ivy showed up no worse for the wear after her night alone, and for the rest of the week the girl came to Nora's room during first period without incident, which was good because Principal Coleman hadn't had to stop by her office. And now Nora was about to get two glorious days off for the weekend. Except she still had the counselor issue hanging over her head.

Nora sat at her desk, drumming her fingers, her office phone pressed to her ear.

"Hi, Mr. Ryman, this is Nora Jenkins again. I wanted to see if we could touch base on a time to meet. Give me a call at the school at your earliest convenience." Nora left the call-back number once more and hung up the phone.

She'd left messages since Wednesday with no response.

"Hey, girly!" Kim said, poking her head in. "Ready for the weekend?"

"I am."

Kim frowned. "You don't look like you're ready. What's stressing you out?"

"Is it that obvious?"

"Definitely."

Nora sighed. "For the last three days, I've tried to get Blaze Ryman, Ivy's dad, on the phone to no avail. I've left message after message, and I'm starting to worry."

Did Blaze have any regard for people other than himself and his clients? His social media feed was overflowing with his daily goings-on, yet he couldn't pick up the phone even once to return her calls?

"You can only do what you can do, Nora. Don't take it personally."

"It's tough not to."

"If you need a sounding board, come by my room later. I'm free fourth period because of the assembly."

"Thanks."

At least Ivy hadn't done anything monumental recently. She'd ridden the bus all week and been a perfect angel. Nora had let her skip geography, as promised, but made her go today, reminding her that it was Friday, and she could do anything for one day.

Ivy had also been serving detention for the biology virus stunt in Nora's room each day after school. The girl seemed to look forward to it. She enjoyed being with Nora. She'd even stopped by that morning to ask when the end-of-year pep-rally was going to start, a question she could've posed to her homeroom teacher. Nora got the sense Ivy had been looking for an excuse to touch base.

Nora was happy the girl had had a better week, but she wasn't any closer to resolving Ivy's situation. And while she tried not to take baggage home with her, she always did. Even with her trip getting closer. Gram had piled their bathroom counters with sunscreen, aloe vera gel, and travel-sized bottles of shampoo, gotten Nora a new sunhat, and even left her laptop open to swimsuits so Nora could order a new one. But Nora struggled to get excited about the trip. She had too much to do in the next two weeks. She had to make sure Ivy was okay before she left so she could enjoy herself.

Just when she'd gathered up a stack of paperwork she needed to file before Ivy showed up for detention, her office phone buzzed. She picked it up.

"Hey, it's Joyce," the office receptionist said. "I've got Blaze Ryman on the line for you. Can I transfer him?"

Nora's mouth dried out and she lowered herself at her desk. "Of course."

As the line beeped three times to alert her the call was being transferred, Nora set the papers on top of her keyboard and braced herself.

"Hello, this is Nora Jenkins."

"Hi. Blaze Ryman. I'm returning your call."

Calls. Plural.

"Hi, Mr. Ryman. Thank you for calling back," she said through gritted teeth. *Glad you could grace us with your attention.*

"I'm so terribly sorry," he said. "I've been a complete jerk."

Nora sat up a little straighter. *This is unexpected.*

"My schedule has been absolutely slammed. I've been trying to squeeze six months into the last four weeks so I can try to figure out how to be there for my daughter." He let out a breath. "I can come in next week, if you're free."

He sounded sincere. How quickly she could forgive him.

"That's fantastic news," she said. She decided to wait to tell him about the family counselor until they met in person. "What are you doing on Monday?"

"My schedule's open. What time works best for you?"

"I can do ten o'clock. That way you and I can talk before Ivy gets out of class. Then she can join us during fourth period."

"Perfect," he said. "I'll bring some paperwork about a few programs I'd like to get her involved in this summer."

He's planned activities this summer?

"There's a young creatives group I think she'd like, and I also have information from Youth on a Mission, since I know she enjoys helping underprivileged people."

Nora cocked her head to the side. "She does?"

"Yeah. At least she did when she lived with her mom."

This news initially shocked Nora, but then again, she could see Ivy having a heart for people who didn't have a lot, given her need to separate herself from her father's money.

"Well, I'll see ya Monday," he said.

"Okay. Thanks again for calling me back."

"Thank *you* for your patience. Losing Candace hasn't been easy for me either."

Another surprising admission.

Nora said her goodbyes and hung up the phone, then stared at her black computer screen, still processing the call. She felt a tiny bit lighter, knowing she might finally be able to make some small difference with Ivy and her dad before removing herself from the situation over the break.

She clicked on her computer and focused on her work until the final bell when Ivy arrived for detention.

"Hey," Ivy said, coming into the room right on cue and dropping her sack of books onto the table. "Last day."

Nora checked the time on the wall clock. "The bell only just rang. You're earlier than usual."

"Yeah. Trying to win student of the year." Ivy smirked.

"What kind of student were you in your old school?"

she asked, standing up and moving over to Ivy. "Were you different?"

Ivy's gaze dropped to the bag of books. "Yeah, I was different."

"How so?"

"I didn't get into trouble as much."

"Why do you think that is?"

Ivy's face dropped. "I was too busy being happy." The girl went over to the window and leaned against the white-painted cinderblock ledge, the sun shining on her hair, making it a lighter pink, like cotton candy. She squinted toward the football field. A few kids were running around the track that encircled it.

"Thank God for summer," she said, making her way to the corner of the room where she dropped into the beanbag and started braiding a lock of her hair. "I can't wait to get out of here." She looked up. "No offense."

"None taken." Nora sat across from the girl. "I'm excited for school to end too. Remember that day when my grandmother was texting me about the beach? I'm going to go with her."

Ivy's eyebrows rose, and she nodded.

"What makes *you* excited for summer? Have anything planned?" Nora asked.

Ivy shook her head. "No, but I can do what I want. Dad won't be there to tell me I can't."

Had Blaze gotten information on the young creatives group and mission work to keep Ivy busy since he wouldn't be there? Were the activities a form of babysitting?

The girl stared at Nora for a tick before she said, "Not all of us get to run off to the beach."

"It wasn't my idea, but I'm not complaining. It will be nice to get away."

"When are you leaving?"

"The day after school gets out."

Ivy smiled politely and shifted her gaze. Nora suspected the girl wasn't as excited about her summer as she made out to be. If her dad didn't follow through on the activities he'd planned, what would her days be like, all alone for eight or more hours at a time? As much as Ivy hated it, she needed the routine that school brought. What kind of trouble would she get into unsupervised all day?

They were down to two weeks. Two weeks to find a suitable family counselor to take over.

"You said you can do what you want this summer," Nora said. "What *do* you want to do?"

"Probably sleep in and then..." Ivy frowned, and for the first time her hard outer shell crumbled, a vulnerability took over her features, and tears welled in her eyes. "I don't know." Her voice broke on the last word. "Nothing, I guess." She closed her eyes, and flopped back onto the beanbag chair, throwing her arm over her face.

Nora felt for Ivy. She could see that, deep down, a little brown-haired girl with big gray eyes like her father's was inside this teen, frantically building walls to protect herself from any more pain.

"What are you doing the rest of today?" Nora heard herself say.

Ivy peeked out from under her arm. "Nothing. My dad's at work and my car's still out of commission."

"Want to help me organize my office for the summer?"

Ivy sat up and grimaced. "No. Why would you do that?"

"I need to go through my cabinets and get things packed away for the break, when the custodians wax the floors. You're welcome to just hang out while I organize, if you'd like. I think there's a special Friday coffee station in the teacher's lounge. There were baskets of snacks. I could see if they have any sodas."

She really needed to keep to school hours with Ivy, but the girl's despair was heartbreaking, and it had hit a nerve. Helping people to love life had been her original goal in getting a counseling degree. She was drawn to Ivy because the teen had a need that Nora could fill. The need just didn't fit within her job description.

Ivy pulled out her phone, her thumbs flying across the surface. After a ping, she looked up. "Dad says it's fine with him."

They spent the rest of the detention period cleaning up Nora's office for the weekend and getting ready to tackle her two large rolling cabinets.

"What do you think you'll do at the beach?" Ivy asked as she sorted class papers by teacher and filed them.

"I'm not sure," Nora replied. "Probably read."

She expected the girl to scoff, but she seemed interested.

Ivy dropped the last of her stack of papers into its file, shut the drawer, and asked, "What kind of books do you like?"

Nora stapled packets for her lesson with Mr. Atkins' class. "It depends on my mood. But I'm guessing I'll grab a couple beach reads and some mysteries."

Ivy moved to the white board and erased the old lists on it at Nora's request.

"What do you like to do to pass the time?" Nora asked, licking her thumb to gather up another stack of papers.

Ivy shrugged.

"I won't let you off that easily," Nora said. "I told you I like beach reads and mysteries. I also put an herbal mud mask on my face in the evenings. It's supposed to have antioxidants that will keep my skin looking young."

Ivy snorted.

"What? You think it's not working?"

Ivy fluffed a pillow on the sofa in the corner. "I think you don't need it."

"But maybe that's because it's working," Nora countered.

Ivy let out a little laugh. The sound filled Nora with happiness. She finished setting out the papers she'd need for Monday's lessons and her meeting with Blaze.

"What are you going to tell my dad when you have your meeting?" Ivy asked, eyeing the discipline forms on the corner of Nora's desk.

"What would you like me to tell him?"

"That school is pointless. I can learn everything they teach in ten minutes on the internet."

"But would you?"

Ivy opened the first cabinet and made a face at the disorganized mess. "Would I what?"

"Would you actually spend the ten minutes—or I'd argue longer—to teach yourself all the subjects you learn in a day?"

Ivy wrinkled her nose. "Probably not."

"Then school isn't pointless." Nora reached around her, pulled two overflowing bins from the cabinet, and set them on her table.

Ivy shuffled after her, hooking a finger under the elastic band on her wrist and pulling it off. She piled her hair into a ponytail and secured it, then rummaged around in the bin. "What is all this?"

"Papers I never look at, but should probably keep."

Ivy rolled her eyes. "Do you have any file folders?"

"Yep." Nora retrieved a new pack from the other cabinet and removed the cellophane wrapping. She handed them to Ivy.

"What are you really going to tell Dad?"

"Probably that in order for a family therapist to be beneficial, they have to be a good match." She went around to the other side of the table and began sorting the papers in the second bin.

"I don't think any of them will be good matches," Ivy said, adjusting her ponytail.

"How do you know? Have you tried them all?"

"Therapy's just not my kind of thing."

Nora sorted the papers into three piles: keep, trash, and not sure. "Having someone to help you work through your emotions can be beneficial in your healing process."

Ivy shook her head and looked out the window.

"Hey, are you thirsty or hungry? Want to check the teacher's lounge for goodies? You can go in with me."

"All right," Ivy said.

They walked down the hallway to the lounge that was usually off-limits to students. But with Nora, Ivy floated right on in. The girl put her hands on her hips, her mouth hanging open.

"Y'all get all this stuff and we have to eat chicken nuggets that could pass for small rocks?"

"This is just a special treat, since it's Friday."

"Right, but we got the chicken nuggets on a Friday, so…" Ivy scooped up a handful of mini candy bars and dropped them into the pocket of her vest. Then she perused the coffee selection.

"Are you allowed to have coffee?" Nora asked.

Ivy rolled her eyes again and laughed. "I was a barista in

the evenings last year, and I get coffee every morning on my way to school."

Nora put her hands in the air. "Just checking."

But Ivy had already passed. "There's nothing good." She opened the lid of the ice box on the table and dug around in the melting ice, pulling out a can of soda. "This'll do. Want one?""

"Sure. I'll take one of the decaf drinks."

Nora grabbed herself a bag of chips, and she and Ivy walked back to the classroom. Ivy popped the top of her soda and took a sip.

"It's 4:57. Won't that keep you up all night?"

Ivy shrugged. "I don't sleep very well anyway." She entered the office, set her chips on the table, and dropped into one of the chairs.

Nora sat across from her, the piles of sorted papers between them.

"Why don't you sleep well?"

"I don't know." Ivy tapped her black-painted nails on the table, her attention on the bag of chips. She reached over and grabbed it, tugging at the edges until the bag tore open.

"Have you always had trouble sleeping, or is the issue recent?"

"Just since my mom died." Ivy inspected the chips in her bag before pinching one and popping it into her mouth.

"I'd definitely mention that in therapy once we find you a family therapist."

"Sure," she said, as if it tortured her to say the word.

"Being open-minded is the first step, you know," Nora said.

Ivy took out another chip, the bag rattling. "Some therapist isn't going to help me sleep."

"They might offer strategies to calm you so you can drift off more easily."

Ivy took a drink of soda.

"I'm serious," Nora said. "What's the worst that could happen if you actually tried a therapist's suggestions? They might not work for you, right? That's it. So what do you have to lose?"

"It's a waste of time. So I lose time." Ivy took another drink and licked her lips. "Besides, I'd rather just talk like you and I do. Why do I have to do all these strategies and things?"

"The strategies might surprise you."

"You surprised me."

Nora tapped her chest. "I did? How?"

"You weren't like the other teachers or that crazy counselor. You're easy to talk to."

"I'm glad." Nora scooted a pile of papers out of the way and opened her own snack. Then she stood up and nibbled while she sorted.

Ivy fell in line as well, the two of them working together in silence. Ivy probably liked the quiet space where she could have Nora's support without the busy atmosphere of the school day. Nora didn't mind having Ivy there either. She went over to her desk and stacked up a few things. Every now and again, she stole a glance at the girl. Ivy alternated between sips of her soda and scrutinizing various papers to determine where they should be filed.

"It's about time to stop for the day," Nora said. The dinner hour was quickly approaching and they both needed more than a bag of chips. "Do you mind taking these books down to the library and dropping them off? I'll get everything put away."

Ivy set down her papers and came over, taking the stack of books from Nora. "No problem."

While Ivy ran her errand, Nora collected all the unsorted papers and got them back into her bins, placing them into the cabinet—quite a job in itself, but they'd gotten more done than she'd expected. When she finally finished, she filed the folder Ivy had created with the papers they'd been able to sort and then put the finishing touches on the things she wanted to have ready for Monday.

After quite a while, Ivy hadn't returned, so Nora went to check on her. She walked the hallways until she came to a stop outside the library. She peered in through the window. Ivy was browsing the fiction section. The girl crouched down to get a book off the bottom shelf, and she looked a lot less menacing than she often did in a school setting. She sat down cross-legged on the floor, her head bowed over the open novel in her hands. She looked up and caught Nora's eye. By her pause, her mind seemed busy. She put the book back on the shelf and met Nora at the entrance.

"What were you thinking about?" she asked the girl.

"Just how maybe I don't want school to end after all."

CHAPTER SIX

"What's this?" Nora eyed two plates of chocolate chip pancakes—her childhood favorite.

"I know you're nervous about your meeting with the big music producer today. I could see it on your face all weekend."

The weekend had gone by in a flash. While Gram sorted through her drawers for clothes she planned to donate to a secondhand shop, Nora poured herself into mapping out the final weeks of school and getting ready for her meeting with Blaze.

But also she'd worried about what Ivy had said outside the library: that she didn't want school to end. That worry and her preparation for her meeting with Blaze had prompted Nora to use the weekend to try to secure a family therapist for the Rymans. She'd found one who seemed promising named Emma Simpson, and she'd sent the woman an email. She planned to bring up Ms. Simpson's name in today's meeting.

"Sit," Gram said lovingly.

With twenty minutes to spare before she needed to

leave for school, Nora took a seat at the table, and Gram poured her a glass of milk.

"Ivy is all-consuming. I don't really know how to help her in my capacity, but she seems to connect with me." Nora picked up the syrup and drizzled it over the steaming pancakes.

"You might not have been expecting Ivy, but you know firsthand what it's like to lose a parent. You're in the unique position to help her through something similar while encouraging a stronger relationship between her and her dad. I'd focus on that with her father today."

Nora cut a piece of pancake. "It's not really ethical to spill the beans about my past, but maybe it wouldn't hurt to give Ivy a little bit about myself if it'll help in some way."

"You'll know just what to do when the time comes." Gram patted her shoulder.

"Thank you for breakfast."

"You're welcome, dear."

Two weeks to go and then two weeks of paradise. She could do this.

OVER THE WEEKEND, Nora had completed all the end-of-year documents that she could, put in her recommendations for classes for a few on her caseload, and even made herself a ten-day check-off sheet with a picture of the beach cottage at the top to mark the days she had left. When she'd got to school she'd posted it by her desk and immediately marked off day one with a red marker.

The morning went on without incident, until it was time to prepare for Blaze Ryman's arrival. The reality of who she was meeting with set in, and her nerves got the better of her. She walked around her office, breathing in deeply for three, holding for three, and exhaling for four in an attempt to slow her pulse. The calming strategy worked just as he knocked on the doorframe.

"Miss Jenkins?"

Nora spun around to find the uber handsome and impeccably dressed Blaze Ryman in the flesh. His shoulders were broader in real life, and his eyes more vivid. He came in with the kind of smile that only a model could offer, and she swallowed then cleared her throat to remind herself that she was still there, standing in front of him and not floating around in some dream. Behind him, two teachers in the hall craned their necks to get a glimpse of him. She forced herself out of her starstruck daze and shook his hand.

"Nice to meet you." She offered him a chair at her therapy table and shut her door, closing off more discreet onlookers. "Please, have a seat." She sat down across from him, in front of her paperwork about Ivy.

"I'm sorry again that it took me so long to meet with you. Trying to rearrange my schedule is a nightmare. I usually need a six-month lead."

He flashed that smile that sent her pulse rising. He probably used his charm on everyone, but it wouldn't have the same impact today.

"I've been working around the clock to keep things going while attempting to clear out my schedule to have more time with Ivy," he said. "It probably doesn't look like it, but I'm trying."

She cleared her throat again. Why did she keep doing that? "Well, I wanted to meet with you to talk about some of the behaviors we've seen from Ivy and our suggestions for how to best meet her needs in the time we have before summer break." Nora slid the conduct report toward him.

"I've been actively trying to support Ivy, but she has shown aggression toward other students, and she's been accused of destruction of property..."

The million-dollar smile melted away, and lines of stress formed on Blaze's forehead. In that moment, he looked like any other parent who'd just viewed a long list of behavior issues from his child.

"I don't think this list is indicative of who Ivy is," Nora added, wanting to stand up for the girl. "If I might be candid, personally, I see her actions as less to do with defiant behavior and more as a cry for help. I think she misses her mom, and she wants the company of her father—it's as simple as that."

He rubbed his forehead, the weight clear. Air filled his chest. "I'm not very good at this. I'm better at putting in eighteen-hour days, on the phone to agents, flying back and forth across the country to scout talent, or working in the studio." He shook his head. "I've made a lot of mistakes that I can't undo..."

"I understand." But she didn't. She had no idea what it took to do what Blaze did or the mistakes he might be referencing. She didn't want to know. Her goal was to secure a stable environment for Ivy before the end of the school year.

Those gray eyes landed on her, full of remorse.

"I don't know how to be a dad," he said. "I tried to get her nannies, but she runs them off. I'm hoping this family counselor will be helpful."

A pinch formed in Nora's neck. "On the topic of the family counselor," she said, her mouth completely dry from the turn in conversation. "I've met with the one you chose several times, and I really don't think she's a good fit for Ivy."

His gaze met hers with near desperation.

"Not to worry," she said, pulling out the list of counselors she'd made. "I've found a few who I think would be more suitable and one in particular I'd like to try first. I emailed her to find out if we could fit into her schedule for an initial meeting to see if she connects with Ivy. Her name is Emma Simpson."

His shoulders relaxed. "Okay."

He seemed completely relieved that she'd done the legwork for him in finding another counselor. While Janine's departure had been Nora's fault, Blaze didn't know that. Did he expect someone else to do all the work for him? Did he even care who Ivy's counselor was? Did he realize what Ivy was going through at all?

"You know, I lost my parents in my twenties. I can't imagine what it would be like to go through that kind of loss at seventeen."

A palpable shame fell upon him, down-turning his features.

It wasn't Nora's place to judge him, and she shouldn't have offered up such a personal bit of information anyway. She needed to focus on Ivy and the school setting. She passed him the document she and Principal Coleman had built for in-school support.

"Ivy seems to respond to visits to my office. It's a quiet place away from the pressure of school and her peers, and she trusts me. So until the end of the school year, we're building in time with me as a reward for good conduct."

She tapped the goals she'd listed for Ivy. Blaze looked down at them, but he seemed miles away.

"We'd like to see her engage in less destructive behavior and begin to apply more appropriate coping strategies. I've listed the ones I plan to use with her here." Nora uncapped her highlighter and drew over the strategies she'd included. "If you can support her at home by suggesting she use these coping strategies, that would be great."

"All right." He chewed on the edge of his lip, his gaze still on the paper. "I've got to finish these few big projects that were already planned. There are millions riding on them—I can't let them go. After that, I've cleared some of my schedule, and I can spend more time with Ivy in the evenings."

Nora leaned on the table, trying to find some spark of parenting ability in this man. She wasn't supposed to offer child-rearing advice, but he wasn't getting it.

"She might need more than evenings," she said as kindly as she could, but still directly.

He stared at her, vulnerability swimming in his eyes. That confident man she'd seen on social media was nowhere to be found. He was regarded by so many as a powerhouse in his industry, but right now, he just seemed broken.

"I know," he whispered, the words pained.

An uncomfortable silence sat between them.

Then, he pulled out his phone and opened a calendar app. "I'll wrap up the last one this week." He scrolled a bit, dragging little boxes around with his finger. "Can you hold on a second?"

"Of course."

He dialed a number and put the phone to his ear. "Hey, Monique. Could you check with Bianca and see if she can do the Chip Morgan run?" He nodded, his gaze roaming around as he listened. "Great. And then move the Mike Richards project over to Susannah's schedule. I'll explain to Mike."

He said his goodbyes and ended the call, setting the

phone down on the table. "When I finish this current project, I'll have a gap in my schedule."

"That's wonderful."

"I don't know how to… comfort her," he admitted.

"I'm not your family counselor, so you might want to speak with her for strategies once you get someone offering regular therapy. But I can say that I'm hopeful that with the right interventions, we can get Ivy to a more stable emotional state. She's a good kid."

He nodded.

"She's going to need some fatherly support this summer, though."

"Yeah." He stacked the papers and looked into her eyes again. "Thank you for all you do for Ivy. I know she's been a handful."

She offered him a consoling smile. "We'll get there."

His gray eyes met hers once more. She could get lost in those eyes. Couldn't everyone?

When the class bell rang, she stood up to break the spell. "Ivy should be heading down at any minute."

He rose and there was an uncomfortable air between them as they waited in silence for Ivy to arrive. Blaze wandered the room and began leafing through a copy of *The Great Gatsby* that one of her students in Mrs. Ellison's fifth period had left accidentally.

"Would you believe I've never read this?" He held up the book. "What's it about?"

"It's about a man named Nick who intermingles with a millionaire named Jay Gatsby."

Blaze turned the book over and scrutinized the back copy. "So it's about a rich guy?"

"Well, kind of. And his fixation on reuniting with his lover."

"Millionaires and lovers..." Blaze said with a huff of disbelieving laughter.

Nora's cheeks heated up when he made the little joke. While the word "lovers" was absolutely not something she thought would filter into the conversation; his comment made her wonder how many lovers he'd probably had, which was not a thought she wanted to entertain. But given her ex-fiancé's infidelity, her mind just went there.

Blaze didn't seem as affected. He set down the book. "So Ivy tells me you two stayed after school last week."

"Yes. I'm doing what I can to help her fill her afternoons."

He peered over at her. "Thank you."

Whenever he answered her, he looked directly into her eyes with absolute attention, making her feel as if she was the most important person in his world. She wanted to like how he did that, but she also didn't trust it.

"Ivy tells me the two of you have some interests in common," Nora said.

"Oh?"

"Hey." Ivy came into the room. She lumped her bag onto one of the desks and gave her dad a flippant salute.

"I was telling your dad that you two have some similarities," Nora said.

Ivy went over to her favorite beanbag. "I don't know what you mean."

"Want to tell him about your... instrument?"

Ivy's gaze bore into Nora. "Maybe later."

Fearing she'd crossed some sort of imaginary line that would create a divide in her carefully curated connection to Ivy, Nora let it go.

"What instrument?" Blaze asked.

"It's just something I used to do with Mom. It's not

important." Ivy folded her arms. "So what are we here to talk about—the locker incident or my computer-hacking skills?"

"Neither," Nora replied. "Your dad and I were talking about the counselor, his schedule in the next few weeks, and your plans for summer."

"There's a creative camp I thought you might like," Blaze interjected. "It's for young adults who have an interest in the arts."

Ivy's face glazed over in boredom.

"It might be fun," Nora said.

Ivy tapped her heavy boot on the floor. "Then you go."

"I also found a place you can do mission work," Blaze said, coming over to her.

To Nora's surprise, he sat down on the floor cross-legged, and she worried for an instant about the state of his designer trousers.

"You can stay in the city or fly to different countries to help dig wells, build schools, teach kids—whatever you like, they have lots of options."

Ivy brightened just a little at that, but decided to pick at her nail instead of responding.

"And until the summer, we can work with the family therapist together to make sure we've found one that fits you."

"Why can't you just be my counselor for the summer?" Ivy asked Nora.

"Because that's not what I do for a living."

Ivy squinted at her. "But what if it's off school grounds? You don't work in the summer, right? Lots of teachers have other summer jobs."

Nora sat on the sofa opposite Ivy and her dad. "I'm going to be on vacation for two weeks, so even if I could do it, I couldn't offer consistency. But I'll be here until school gets out."

Ivy didn't look convinced. "We're not going to find a counselor who's worth anything."

"How do you know?"

"I just want you to do it."

Blaze looked between Ivy and Nora. Nora eyed him helplessly. Why wasn't he stepping in for support? He'd admitted he didn't know how to be a parent, and from what she could see now, he wasn't far off. Shouldn't he back up Nora and tell Ivy his plans for the summer? But it was obvious that apart from clearing his schedule and considering a few activities, he hadn't devised a strategy at all.

The bell for the end of class rang.

"Well, you're free," she said to Ivy with a smile.

Blaze stood up and brushed off his trousers.

"I'll walk you all to the front office so your dad can sign out."

Nora was deflated after having seen the look on Ivy's face, but she was doing the right thing—after all, she was a high-school counselor, not a family therapist.

NORA LIFTED another heavy box of Gram's clothes into the trunk of her car to take them to the secondhand shop that afternoon. When they'd gotten them all loaded, Gram buckled herself into the passenger's seat of Nora's car, and they drove into town to donate them.

"So how did the meeting go with Mr. Music Producer?" Gram asked.

"It was interesting," Nora said, turning onto Hillsboro

Pike as Blaze's stormy eyes came to mind. She gripped the steering wheel and focused on the road.

But Gram's laugh distracted her.

"What?" She glanced at her grandmother.

Gram chewed on a smile. "That good, huh?"

"I didn't say it was good or bad."

"The fire in your cheeks says another thing entirely."

"Oh, please." She willed the flush from her face. Why was her body reacting to the mention of Blaze?

"Is he as handsome in reality as he is on screen?"

She peered at her grandmother. "When have you ever seen Blaze Ryman on screen?"

"I might have peeked over your shoulder while you stalked him online."

"Stop it," she said with a laugh as she made a turn at the stoplight. "I wasn't stalking him."

"Call it what you like," Gram said with another laugh. "You didn't answer my question. Please tell me seeing him in real life wasn't a letdown, and he's actually short and pasty."

Nora tried to block the memory of Blaze's chiseled face and broad shoulders. "He's more handsome, actually. No photo doctoring at all going on…"

Gram sucked in a breath. "Oh, to be young and fit again… You should make up an excuse to get him back into your office. Tell him you'd like weekly check-ins about his daughter or something. Maybe there could be fireworks." Her eyebrows bounced suggestively.

Nora laughed. "One, I doubt that very much. And two, I'd never date a student's parent. I've dated someone in the workplace, and you know how that turned out."

"Carson wasn't right for you anyway."

"You could've told me that before I got engaged to him."

Nora had been in a three-year relationship with Carson Jennings, one of the counselors at her last job, and they were only engaged for a few months before he called it off. He'd told her he'd fallen for another of the counselors, a new colleague by the name of Molly Davis. Nora had asked him how he could possibly know already that he cared for her enough to call off his and Nora's engagement. By the shifty look in his eyes and his ghostly white face, it became clear something had already happened between them. In a matter of months, they were engaged. Even though everyone at the office had wanted Nora to stay, she couldn't bear the thought.

"It wasn't my place," Gram said, pulling her back to the conversation, "but now the relationship has irrevocably fallen to pieces, I can tell you my true feelings."

Nora turned into the parking lot of the secondhand shop and got out. She popped the trunk, and she and Gram each pulled out a box.

"You'd never date a student's father? Even if he was Blaze Ryman?" Gram pressed.

"I would absolutely never cross that line," said Nora. "And although this school year turned out to be more challenging than I anticipated, I'm loving the staff and the location of the school, and I want to stay there for as long as they'll have me. I'm not going to jeopardize my job, and I only want what's best for Ivy. Which would certainly *not* be dating her dad."

CHAPTER SEVEN

The entire morning had gone as planned. Nora had made it to all her classroom lessons, she'd picked up Casey Ferguson to go over her electives for next year, and she'd met with Bobby Jacobs and his mother to finalize his schedule. Emma Simpson, the counselor she'd emailed for Ivy, had even replied to let her know she had an opening in her calendar, and she'd be able to come by today after school to meet Ivy.

Just as Nora considered whether she might sail through the last two weeks of school, Principal Coleman knocked on her doorframe, interrupting her thoughts.

"What have you done?" he asked, coming into her room.

"What do you mean?" Had he heard what she'd said to Janine Swarovski? She geared up to explain herself, but he began speaking, so she snapped her mouth shut.

"Ivy hasn't made a peep in class. She's coming in, doing her work, and not bothering a soul. What magic did you perform?"

"I have no idea." Nora capped her pen and stood up from her desk. "Maybe the before- and after-school meetings with me are helping?"

"She seems to like you."

"I have the time to listen to her. And I'm including her in finding a family therapist that can take over this summer."

"What about Ms. Swarovski?" he asked.

"Ivy didn't connect with her," she explained. "But we've got everything under control. I even met with Ivy's father."

"I heard. The office staff haven't stopped talking about it since he arrived." He chuckled and straightened his belt line around his protruding belly. "Whatever you're doing, keep it going. It's working."

The end-of-school bell rang, and he turned around and walked out of her room, raising his hand to say goodbye as he left.

Nora felt positively calm. And when Ivy came in for her meeting after school, Nora was already at the table waiting.

"Hey," Ivy said, dropping her bag of books on the desk like she always did.

"Well, hello, stranger." Nora offered a hospitable smile. "I haven't seen you all day."

"I'm laying low so I can get out of here in a few weeks without having to do any summer school or anything." She pulled a paper out of her bag. "I got an A on my geography test." She turned the paper around.

"Wow, that's fantastic, Ivy." Nora gave her a high five.

Ivy set the test on the desk next to her bag. "I used to get good grades in school before my mom died."

"I can imagine how insignificant school must feel in comparison to losing your mom." Nora offered her a chair at the table.

Ivy sat down. "Yeah. You nailed it. It all seems pointless."

"When I was twenty, my parents were both killed in a

car crash. I went from having a family to having no one but my grandmother, so I understand."

Ivy cocked her head, her eyes focused, showing her surprise.

"Losing the people you love is a huge thing to deal with," Nora said.

Ivy's eyes instantly brimmed with tears, as if they'd been waiting for the green light. She blinked them away.

"You don't have to keep it all in, Ivy. There's no weakness in being sad."

A tear escaped down Ivy's cheek, and she brushed it away. "I don't know any other life than the one with my mom. We didn't have a lot, but we were happy, you know?"

"Was your dad not involved at all?"

"We lived with my dad until I was about four. But when they divorced, Mom didn't want him to be involved."

"How come?"

Ivy fiddled with the corner of her test paper. "When they split up, the tabloids called Mom trailer park trash, and said she was out to get Dad's millions. I looked it up. It was just some rag mag in LA, but she hated being in the public eye—she was a private person and she didn't want anyone making her look bad. So she took me to Alabama and wouldn't let Dad give us anything."

"He didn't try to fight that? Did he try to see you?"

"I don't know. I don't think so."

Ivy's explanation didn't sit well with Nora.

"Knock, knock." A female voice broke through their conversation. A small woman with a light brown bob and a friendly smile stood at her door.

Nora got up and Ivy followed suit.

"I'm Emma Simpson." The woman came in and shook

Nora's hand before turning to Ivy. "And you must be Ivy Ryman."

The woman held out her hand to Ivy, but the girl didn't shake it. Instead, she focused on putting the geography test into a folder and shoving it into her school bag.

"Who's that?" she asked, not taking her eyes off her bag.

"I'm a family therapist," Emma said, her gaze fluttering over to Nora for guidance.

"I called her," Nora added. "She's one of the therapists I personally recommended. I thought you two could meet today."

Ivy flashed a betrayed look at Nora.

"Feel free to call me Emma." The woman walked over to them.

Ivy nodded, and it appeared as if she was working overtime to suppress that ever-present eye roll. She struggled to get the folder back into her bag, jamming it in over and over to no avail.

Nora leaned into her space to help her and whispered, "Just give her a chance." She held the bag for Ivy to get the folder in.

The woman continued with pleasantries, asking Ivy a few surface questions about herself, such as which school subject was her favorite and what did she like to do for fun. The whole time Ivy's arms were crossed, and that wall she'd had when she'd first arrived at Oakland had slid right back up.

When Ms. Simpson left, Nora handed Ivy her bag and they prepared to leave for the day. "What did you think of Emma?" Nora asked.

"I think she's like the rest of them."

"The rest of whom? Counselors? Teachers?"

"Everyone who thinks they can fix me." She pulled her

pink hair free from her bag's shoulder strap. "I don't like how they treat me."

"How do you feel they treat you?"

Nora clicked off the office lights, and they walked down the hallway to the parking lot.

"Like I'm a walking list of answers, some code they have to crack to reprogram me into this perfect little student who does what she's supposed to."

"They're just trying to figure out how best to help you."

"But I don't need help. I've been fine the last few days."

Nora held the door open for Ivy, and they walked into the sunshine. "Your tears tell me that you might not be as fine as you think. They just want to help you process your grief."

Ivy squinted at Nora and shook her head. "You said yourself that it's okay to be sad."

"It is. And knowing that is one of the first ways you can begin processing what you've been through."

"I don't need a random person to help me know that I'm sad about my mom dying, that I had to give up my friends and my old room back at my house and live in a place the size of a small airport that's always empty."

"Your dad did tell me that once he finishes up this last project, he'll have more time, and he plans to spend it with you."

Ivy shrugged.

"It sounded like you two had fun at that restaurant with the alley access. What was it called?"

"Cappy's."

"Yeah, Cappy's. Maybe the two of you could do more things like that."

Ivy strode beside her without skipping a beat. "That's cool. But this will never be home. And that Emma lady isn't going to make it feel any more like home by asking me my favorite color."

A black Maserati pulled up, and Blaze put the window down.

Nora offered a wave.

"All go well today?" he asked as Ivy went around and climbed into the passenger side of the car. When Ivy didn't answer, he questioned Nora.

"Ivy got to meet the family counselor, but she isn't quite sold on her yet."

"I'd rather just meet with you," Ivy said, leaning across her dad to speak through the open window.

"We can absolutely meet until the end of the school year, but you'll need a different kind of counselor for grief and family counseling over the summer."

"No, I won't," Ivy said. "I'll be fixed by then. You'll have asked me all my favorite numbers and stuff, and I'll magically be better." She fell back against the seat.

Blaze seemed confused.

Nora wanted to explain Ivy's sarcasm, but it probably wasn't worth going into right now. They all needed to head home.

"Well, thanks for today," Blaze said.

Nora offered a weak smile.

Blaze put up the window and waved as they drove off.

When Nora got home that night, she tried not to ruminate on her issues with Ivy. Finding just the right counselor personality for the girl was going to be a challenge.

"It's late. You're still up?" Gram asked.

"I'm getting ready to go to bed," Nora said.

"Look what I got." Gram held out a brightly colored cover-up. "It's the perfect shade to go over my swimsuit."

"It's pretty." Nora reached over and fiddled with the soft fabric. "I should get one too."

"Yes." Gram sat down on the sofa and draped the garment across her lap. "In no time at all, we'll be sitting on that glorious front porch, with our morning coffees, listening to the sound of waves, and chatting away."

"It sounds like paradise. I'm going to take a blanket out onto that porch swing in the mornings, curl up with a good novel, and read the hours away until you want to go into town and do a little shopping. And we'll buy seashell trinkets and postcards with beautiful beach scenes..."

"I'm ready to go right now," Gram said. Then she sobered.

"What is it?"

"Oh, I wish your grandfather would've been able to see it. He always wanted to go to the Gulf Coast."

Nora could only imagine what her grandfather would've wanted to do in paradise. "He'd have made coffee every morning for all of us, then taken his newspaper out on the porch, spread it all over the tables, organizing the sections he wanted to read first, and then just as we got comfortable, he'd finish reading and want to go for a bike ride or something."

Gram laughed. "Yes. He was the fastest reader on the planet. I used to swear he would absorb an entire page of the paper in one go. It was as if he didn't need to read it line by line."

Nora breathed in a long breath as the memory of her grandfather settled upon her. "I used to think he was superhuman."

Gram smiled. "To me, he was."

"We'll do all the things you think he'd have liked to do," Nora suggested.

"I'd love that." Gram stood back up. "I'll start making a list."

Nora yawned. "I'm planning to go to bed. You could always make a list tomorrow."

Gram shook her head. "Seize the day."

"The day is over. I'm heading to bed. You should too," Nora said with a laugh.

"There's never enough time, is there?" Gram asked, thoughts behind her eyes that Nora couldn't decipher.

Guilt pinged around inside Nora. Gram probably felt alone while Nora worked all day. She wanted to stay up with Gram and spend time with her, but she was absolutely exhausted.

Gram kissed her cheek. "Don't mind me. I'm sentimental in my old age." She fluttered her hands in the air. "Get some sleep. I'll see you in the morning."

Nora gave Gram a hug. This trip couldn't come soon enough.

CHAPTER EIGHT

She'd made it through the entire week, and Ivy had been on her best behavior, only coming by in the afternoons to complete her school coping-strategy checklist. She hadn't been late to a single class, and she'd gotten a couple more A's on her end-of-year assessments.

In a strange way, Nora missed seeing Ivy during the day. She tried not to let her absence impact her, however. The girl's willingness to participate in school was a good thing. Even though things felt quiet without her, and she found herself getting excited to hear about Ivy's classes, she had to look forward to her summer with Gram. Gram was all Nora had, and she couldn't wait to escape for a while. She just had to get through the end of school.

Ivy hadn't wanted to meet with Emma again—she'd really dug in her heels—so they were back at square one with a family counselor. Ivy was doing well with only the afternoon meetings with Nora, but Nora worried that Ivy was masking her issues in an effort to lay low until summer.

With one more period to go until the teen came for her after-school session, Nora worked on her student forms.

"Miss Jenkins?" her intercom sounded.

"Yes?"

"I have Blaze Ryman on the phone. Can I put him through to you?"

She sat up straight. "Sure."

Her office phone buzzed. She mentally prepared herself for the shift from the task at hand and answered the phone.

"Hello, this is Nora Jenkins."

"Hi, Nora. This is Blaze." His smooth voice came through the phone.

"Hi," she returned.

"I wanted to let you know that I think I've found a family therapist."

"Oh, really?" Had Blaze found a counselor himself? Wow.

"Yeah. Her name is Blythe Coats and she can start once school's out."

Nora toyed with one of her pens, drawing little lines on a pad of sticky notes. "Has Ivy met the counselor?"

"She spoke to her on the phone last night. She said the counselor was 'decent.'" A huff of humor escaped through the phone line, making Nora smile in response.

"That's a step in the right direction," she said, surprised Ivy was willing to go so far as to call anyone *decent*.

"Well, it'll be tough to replicate the rapport you have with her, that's for sure. But Ivy's willing to give her a chance."

Absentmindedly, Nora scratched B-L-A-Z-E on her notepad and then realized what she'd written and scratched through it.

"I'm not sure why she connects with me," Nora said.

"It's a natural thing. You have just the right personality

for her. You're a quiet force, and a lot like her mother, Candace."

Her pen stilled. "I didn't know that."

"Yeah, it's true. I'd love to have a conversation about Ivy and her mother with you. Would you be willing to meet me for coffee?"

She dropped her pen. "Um. What?"

"I also need some tips and advice on things I'd really rather not discuss in front of Ivy."

Meeting a parent off school grounds?

"I'd come in after school, but I thought it might be nice to treat you to a coffee instead, since you'd be on your personal time anyway."

Before she could finish a thought, he was giving her his personal phone number. She quickly wrote it down on the sticky note.

"Why don't we go to Java House near Music Row?" he suggested. "It's out of the way, and most people know me around there, so they'll leave us alone."

"When did you want to go?"

"Would you be willing to meet tomorrow afternoon? My treat."

Saturday? Her wild doodling stopped once more.

"I won't keep you. But I want to make sure I'm responding to Ivy correctly, and I'd like to figure that out sooner rather than later. I'm out of my element here."

Would meeting Blaze on the weekend be crossing any lines? She was uneasy about it, but the teachers she knew did all kinds of things after hours for kids, and she'd do a favor if it meant making things better for Ivy. Given how difficult it was to get Blaze to meet, if his schedule had opened up it might be worth working outside school hours. And, really, did people tell Blaze Ryman no?

"I'd be happy to meet," she said. She jotted down the time and got off the call just as Kim walked in.

Kim leaned against the doorframe. "I was in the office when Blaze Ryman's call came in. I had to come get the scoop."

Nora gestured for her to come in and shut the door.

Kim tucked her long dark hair behind her ear and sat down at Nora's table. "Dish."

Nora filled her in on Blaze's suggestion for coffee tomorrow. "Kind of weird, right?"

Kim propped her feet up on the bottom of the chair in front of her. "I mean, he's one of those creative types. They work any time they want to. He probably isn't thinking that you'd care what day it was or that there were any rules to your workday."

Nora sat down opposite her and Kim pulled her feet back.

"To be honest, I don't really mind," Nora said. "It's just coffee. I'd get coffee on a Saturday, right?"

Kim waggled her eyebrows. "Unless..."

"Unless what?"

"Unless he's choosing Saturday because he really just wants to get coffee with *you*."

Nora threw her head back and laughed. "I seriously doubt that."

"Not all of us get weekend coffee requests from a famous producer dad. You know he made *Nashville Magazine*'s 'Most Eligible Bachelor' last year? I'd think you'd welcome the idea that he'd want to take you out."

"I do *not* want to date anyone, especially Blaze." If a regular Joe like Carson could have a wandering eye when dating her, spending time with Blaze and all his glittery distractions certainly wouldn't end well. She was sure that if Blaze did have any interest in her, he'd realize in about ten minutes she wasn't anything special.

Nora checked the time. The bell was about to ring, and Ivy would show up any minute.

Kim stood. "All I'm saying is that I'd be sure to have on your mascara and a little extra lip gloss." She giggled on her way to the door. "I can't wait to hear what happens—Oh! Our monthly teacher happy hour is next Friday. Tell me then! I'm sure everyone will want to hear."

"Nothing is going to transpire except discussion about Ivy," Nora assured her.

"Are you going next Friday?"

"I'd planned on it."

"Great! I'll make sure my whole night is free for this conversation."

"There will be nothing to tell," Nora insisted.

With a hopeful shrug, her friend left. Would the meeting with Blaze look like a date to others? Was she doing the right thing, meeting him? Why couldn't they chat on the phone or have another meeting on school grounds? Surely this was about Ivy... Right?

Ivy appeared in her office when the bell rang.

"We made it to Friday," Nora told her. "That means we have fewer days until summer break." She opened her laptop to the slides she'd made on school coping strategies and pulled out Ivy's paper checklist they'd been using from her desk drawer, setting both on the table. "Aren't you even a little bit excited about summer?"

"It's not sandy beaches and ice cream for all of us." Ivy dropped into the chair.

"You might be surprised how refreshing the time off could be. Maybe you could buy one of those novels you were looking at in the library and sit by the pool." Nora handed her the checklist.

Ivy shrugged as if the Olympic-size pool with fountains in the back of her house was the furthest thing from inviting.

Nora considered asking the girl what she thought an entertaining summer looked like, but that was the wrong question.

"What was summer like with your mom?" she asked instead.

Ivy chewed her lip, visibly falling into better times. "When my parents split up, Mom and I moved back to her hometown of Fair Hope. She worked as a server in a restaurant, and she got off pretty late, since she worked the dinner shift, but she said it was worth it because the restaurant was the best one in town, and the tips were enough to keep us afloat. I was little—only four—so I'd stay with a neighbor until she got home, but once I got older I stayed by myself. Summers were her busiest season because that was when the out-of-towners came in."

Ivy scooted her checklist out of the way and rested on her forearms. "In the summers the restaurant would cook way more than usual to manage the big crowd. Mom would bring home all the leftovers from the dinner shift and put them in our fridge. The two of us would each have one meal ourselves as a treat, but that was it. She'd heat up the rest of the food, and we'd take it down to the women's shelter in the next town and serve the ladies. They'd all mostly gotten out of rough relationships and things like that, and my mom being a single mom would talk to them and listen to their stories while I played with the kids, doing kickball or helping the girls braid their hair. That's one of my favorite memories of summer."

"What did you like specifically about that time with your mom?"

"It was just the two of us, and we were a team. Mom and I could feed a whole place and make everyone happy. We'd talk about it all the way home."

Ivy's story warmed her. "That's a wonderful memory. You know, your dad mentioned possibly getting you involved with mission work this summer."

Ivy rolled her eyes. "You're both missing the point."

"How so?"

"Yes, I like to help others, but it was the time I spent with Mom that kept me going. Dad wants me to do mission work on my own when he should want to do it with me."

Ivy had a point. And there was nothing Nora could do about Blaze's choice not to participate, even though she wished he would. She leaned in. "But what if your mother has given you exactly what you need to carry on her work? She didn't have anyone to help her get started. She followed her heart and did what she thought would help. What if it's your turn now?"

Ivy sat silently, gazing around as if digesting this new idea. "I didn't think of it that way."

"So armed with a new perspective, maybe it's time for you to choose what's calling your heart. What mission would you be most passionate about?"

"I'll have to think about it."

"Maybe that can be your homework for the next two weeks: decide what you want to do to honor your mom and fulfill yourself."

"You make everything feel so easy," Ivy said.

"Maybe you're just easy to talk to when you let people in."

Ivy didn't answer, but the small lift at the corners of her lips told Nora she understood.

LATER THAT NIGHT, after her evening conversations with Gram had dwindled and they'd retired to their rooms, Nora lay in bed, her mind buzzing with what she was going to say to Blaze over coffee tomorrow afternoon. Her mind was so busy, she was unable to sleep, so she got up and typed notes into her phone about how she planned to advise Blaze, assuming she had an idea of the exact topics he wanted to discuss. She was guessing he wanted information for the counselor about specific strategies she'd used, so she was listing them and retrieving various scenarios from her memory to support each one.

Once she'd made the list, she opened a social media app and typed in Blaze's name. His page came up, and she clicked on it to see if there were any new posts. Of course, there were. He was sitting in what looked to be a recording studio, next to some woman she'd never seen before with perfect skin and pouty lips.

The caption read: "Keep an eye on socials for this album to drop. It's going to knock your socks off."

She tapped the photo and the tag came up: Gracey Lane. She clicked over to Gracey Lane's page and the woman had one hundred thousand followers. The same photo was on her page as well, with the caption: "Blaze Ryman is the real deal. My career just exploded under his watch."

She couldn't help but wonder if Blaze found the woman attractive. Surely he did; she was beautiful. But Nora checked herself. Blaze could find Gracey Lane attractive if he wanted to. It was none of Nora's business.

And why did she feel completely inferior, looking at the woman? She didn't want to admit it to herself, but Carson's infidelity had wrecked her self-esteem. She wondered what had been so wrong with her that she hadn't been able to keep Carson's attention. Why had he even bothered to propose? Was there something about her that he hadn't known prior to the proposal, but little by little, as more of her authentic personality came through, she'd driven him away? She'd tried to talk to him about it, but he had no answers. Not having an explanation was worse than getting one; she didn't know if there were flaws in her personality she needed to fix or if she was just generally not as interesting as other women.

She went to Blaze's other pages and clicked on his stories, thoughts of Carson floating away. Blaze was barefoot, head down, by his pool, strumming a guitar. It was impossible to pull her eyes from the video. His fingers moved effortlessly over the strings, creating the most serene music she'd heard in a long time. It was so good she wondered if he'd ever considered playing music instead of producing. When the song finished he looked straight into the camera and smiled, sending heat through her cheeks. It was as if he could see her right through the screen.

Even less drowsy now after seeing that, she clicked off her phone and tossed it onto the floor. Then she stared at the ceiling, willing herself to sleep, but she continued to toss and turn. She flipped the pillow and yanked the blankets closer to her chest. The whole time she wriggled around she couldn't shake her disbelief that she was going to have coffee with *The* Blaze Ryman tomorrow. What in the world?

CHAPTER NINE

"You've changed outfits three times now," Gram said as Nora walked into the living room, wearing a pair of linen trousers and a flowy tank top. "I liked the sundress."

"I worried it might be too coffee-dateish."

"Isn't that where you're going—a coffee date?"

"A working meeting," she clarified. "The sundress wasn't professional enough. I'm trying to look Saturday-casual while also maintaining an air of professionalism. It's harder than it seems."

Gram laughed. "Do you think Ivy's father is putting as much effort into his outfit?"

"He's got it easier; he's not the school counselor. And his star power gives him unwritten permission to do whatever he wants." Nora put Ivy's paperwork into a folder and slid it into her bag.

"You're overthinking it. It's just coffee. No one will be weighing in on your choice of attire."

"Hopefully not. What if someone takes a picture of us?"

"It's Nashville, not LA."

Nora laughed. "How do you know the difference in

Nashville versus LA when it comes to the rich and famous?"

"I see the country stars getting coffee all the time around here, and no one bats an eye."

Nora slipped her bag onto her shoulder and slid on her flats. "Well, Ivy told me herself that people bother Blaze. He's a very popular producer."

"Or maybe onlookers will simply think you're catching up with a friend for coffee. Your hair looks nice, by the way."

Nora ran her fingers through her curled locks self-consciously. "Thank you."

"Just be yourself, and you'll be fine."

That comment didn't really help things.

"Love you," Nora said to her grandmother.

Gram blew her a kiss, and Nora was out the door.

The entire drive, Nora tried to recount specific instances of success with the items on Ivy's checklist. Nora had committed each one to memory and by the time she'd pulled up at the coffee shop, she was ready to explain them to Blaze.

His black Maserati was already parked right out front, and she willed her heart to quit thumping. There was no need to be nervous. This was just a parent meeting—whether he was drop-dead gorgeous or not. Nora grabbed her bag of files, and went inside.

When she entered, Blaze waved and stood up from a nearby table for two. He had on an unfussy pair of jeans and a casual short-sleeved button down. It fit him loosely, as if he were headed to the beach after their meeting. An expensive-looking pair of sunglasses sat on the table next to his phone.

Nora meandered through the growing line and went

over to greet him.

"Pick your poison, my treat." He waved a hand at the chalkboard menu.

"Oh, I'm happy to get my own, thank you," Nora offered, keeping it all business.

But Blaze was already shaking his head. "Nope. I insist. You're meeting me outside of your regular hours, and it's the very least I can do."

"All right."

He gestured for her to go first and led them toward the line that had grown with the addition of a group of girls and was now snaking through the tables. She squeezed past a small space and sucked in a tiny breath as Blaze's hand lightly grazed the small of her back to guide her through. Her heartbeat resumed its drumming once more.

"I hope I didn't interfere too much with your weekend plans," he said.

She faced him in the small space. "No, I was only hanging out with my grandmother, and she's in an organizational phase at the moment, so she's been cleaning out closets." Nora gave him a pretend-horror grimace.

Blaze laughed, and her stomach did a flip as his gray eyes sparkled.

"She's welcome to come my way when she's done. My housekeeper, Lucia, draws the line at closets."

Nora smiled, trying not to be smitten by the fact that he had a live-in housekeeper out back of a mansion yet might have messy closets. "I'll bet your closets are perfect."

"With my recent travel schedule, definitely not. I lump my dirty clothes from one suitcase on the floor and pack the next one. I'm looking forward to being home for a while but not necessarily doing laundry," he said.

The line moved a few people, and they shuffled forward.

"Do you have any summer trips planned, or will you be home all summer?" Nora asked.

"Probably staying home. Ivy tells me you've got a trip coming up. You're going to the beach?"

"Yes," she replied. *Blaze Ryman knows my summer plans?* "My grandmother wants to go, so we're spending two weeks along the Gulf Coast. I've never been to the beach."

His head tilted, and he looked at her as if she were some rare bird. "You've never been?"

She shook her head, and tried to laugh lightly, but it stuck in her throat. Was she boring? All the insecurities born from her relationship with Carson reared up and snared.

Just then, the line moved, and the barista was waiting for Nora's order. She chose a house-made honey and lavender latte, and Blaze put in his order for a double shot espresso with a splash of milk. When he spoke, the barista's shifty eyes and nervous smile gave away the fact that she recognized him. The girl kept looking over at Nora as if trying to place her.

Don't worry. I'm nobody special.

When they got their coffees and settled back at the table, Blaze put down his porcelain cup and saucer and folded his hands. Sitting across from him, she couldn't deny how attractive he was. A few people had also noticed and were stealing glances at them. Nora pulled out her file and opened the notes app on her phone, focusing on Ivy.

"Let's jump right in. Here's what I've been doing with Ivy in our after-school sessions."

She went through the checklist, trying not to focus on the little lines that formed between Blaze's eyebrows or how adorable he was as he intently listened to her as if she were some important wealth of knowledge. Given what she'd seen of his inattention to Ivy, she didn't trust his sincerity. He might be able to swoon those up-and-coming stars with that charming act, but Nora was a tougher nut to crack.

"This is all really helpful." He picked up his small mug and took a sip. "I've been flying by the seat of my pants. I know she's grieving, and I've been out of state so much."

"Connection is key. She needs to feel the support of those around her. I'm not sure she does right now."

"I text her all the time, and I've tried to connect on video call every night before she goes to bed. I've even cut some of my trips into two, coming home for a day just to spend a little time with her."

"She needs to know that she comes first," Nora said bluntly.

Blaze took in a slow breath, his gaze dropping to the table. "I know it isn't perfect," he said, looking back up at her, "but it's the best I can do right now."

"Given your success at work, I'll bet you can surprise yourself if you put that attention entirely on Ivy."

He shook his head, his stress clear in the downturn of his features. "I... haven't been great at relationships. I can do the superficial work relationships, but when it comes to anything more..." His brows pulled together. "It's a puzzle to me."

Nora was treading outside of her job description once more. The whole meeting had her uneasy. This family needed a therapist, not a coffee date with the school counselor. "Relationships are about small steps," she offered.

"She isn't receptive," Blaze said. "I'm putting in effort to get as much time with her as I can, but when I come home she barely speaks to me. I'm actively trying to give her more, although I'm not sure my presence will be helpful if she doesn't want to see or talk to me. That's why I wanted to meet with you. I was hoping for some suggestions."

"I think just showing her you care and continuing to show up is the best you can do right now." Nora took a drink of her sweet latte. "I'm happily surprised that you want to be an active part in her life."

He flinched with her use of "surprise," but maintained a neutral expression. "I always have."

Nora set down her cup, confused. "Ivy said she didn't think you tried to see her in the past. She said her mother didn't want you to be involved."

"The second half of that is true. Candace didn't want me to be involved."

Nora nodded, taking another drink of her coffee and offering a listening ear. It wasn't her place to get involved in their family drama, but she did feel he should know what Ivy thought.

"When Ivy's mom and I first divorced, I wanted to see Ivy regularly, allowing for my work commitments, but Ivy's mom found ways to plan things that interfered with my scheduled time."

"Why?"

"When Candace and I met, we were really young and both dirt poor. All we had was each other. We worked our fingers to the bone, until things took off for me. For a while we thought we'd made it, but as my work picked up I spent less and less time with her and Ivy."

He ran his finger around the handle of his mug and lifted it to his lips. Then he set it back down, pensive. "I became the provider. I was good at it, suddenly, but the job required an incredible time investment. In Candace's mind, I was choosing work over her. But I didn't mean to. She was angry about the long hours I put in. Ivy was a baby, and Candace was exhausted at the end of every day, managing everything." His eyes filled with guilt.

"She got the groceries, did laundry, cooked, cleaned, sent off the bills, and took Ivy to all her infant doctor appointments. I didn't know how to balance my insane work schedule with the demands of my growing family. All I knew was that if I kept going, Candace and Ivy wouldn't have to go to bed hungry anymore. I could provide them with *lavish* things. But over the next few years, Candace became angry. My career was a source of tension. With my rise in status, I was pulled in every direction. When I got home at night, dog-tired, we argued, and she told me any chance she got what a terrible husband and father I was."

He bowed his head, his back rising with a long breath before he looked up again. "She wasn't wrong. But I didn't know how to fix what I'd broken. I had to work so hard to provide for us financially; how could I continue at that pace and give my family what they needed emotionally as well? By the time she wanted to leave, she told me I wouldn't ever be able to make them happy, and I believed her."

The buzz of the coffee shop faded away with the revelation of the broken man in front of Nora. The very picture of stardom, the man from social media, a farce.

"When we split up, the tabloids out in LA called her trash, and said she was out to get my millions, which she bitterly resented, so she took Ivy to Alabama and wouldn't let me give them anything. I threatened to take her to court. She begged me not to put her and Ivy through that. After they left, I wondered if Ivy would be better off without me."

While Ivy had painted her mother as a loving mom, Nora could see that Candace might not have been entirely fair to her ex-husband.

"I think you should sit Ivy down and let her hear your side," she suggested.

"She loves her mom. I don't want to put Candace in a bad light."

"Fair enough, but there are two sides to every story. Acknowledge what Ivy's mother felt and then give her your point of view. Let Ivy decide how to feel."

"That's what I'm worried about. She's had a long time to hear her mother's side of things. Ivy turns away anything to do with wealth—and I get that, given how she was raised. But I have been putting away money for her every month for her entire life, and I'm saving it in an account that she can access when she's eighteen."

"You should tell her that too. Maybe if she doesn't want the money, you can let her decide what she wants to do with it. She and I talked a bit about the mission work, and I think she might be on board with it. At least some of that money could be a nice investment in something she can be proud of. Offering her the decision would also give her a little control."

"That's a great idea."

Just then, a man with a scruffy gray beard and bootcut jeans over his Luccheses came over and clapped Blaze on the back, interrupting them. "Good to see ya, Blaze."

"Oh, hey, Buddy," Blaze returned, that self-confidence surfacing once more.

"Any new talent on the horizon?" The man eyed Nora and then landed back on Blaze.

"Always." Blaze gave him a good-natured grin.

The man's attention moved back to Nora. "You courting one right now?"

"Not unless she wants me to." Blaze consulted Nora. "You don't sing, do you?"

"Um, no. Definitely not." Nora hid behind her coffee mug.

Blaze laughed, sending a flutter through her chest. "This is Buddy Gibbons. He's the owner of one of the record labels."

"One of the record labels?" Buddy scoffed playfully.

Blaze grinned. "He owns Big Sky Entertainment. They signed four of the most recent top-ten artists in country music."

"And three of those four worked with your coffee date, here," Buddy added.

Nora smiled, but she wanted to crawl under the table for two reasons: she was actually carrying on a conversation with a famous producer as if it were the most normal thing in the world, and Buddy had called their meeting a "date." While he probably didn't mean a thing by the term, it struck that nerve.

"Well, I'll let y'all get back to it," Buddy said. "Good to see ya."

"Sorry about that," Blaze said once Buddy had moved out of earshot. "We managed to get through quite a while before we were interrupted."

"Ivy tells me that happens when you go out." She sipped her latte.

"Yeah. Out here, it's mostly locals who actually know me, but in downtown Nashville I'll get a lot of people trying to give me demos and network."

"That must be hard to deal with."

"It can be, but being interrupted comes with the job. And it also has its perks."

She smiled from behind her coffee. "What are the perks of the job?"

"It pays rather well," he said. "I know money isn't everything—believe me, I didn't grow up with any—but it can help get things done, like sending Ivy on whatever missions she wants to do. I just want to help her figure out who she is and what she wants."

He took a drink of his espresso. "So you lost your parents at twenty, you said?"

"Yeah. To a car accident. They were coming home from a wedding in a driving rainstorm. My dad lost control of the car, and they went off a steep embankment."

"I'm so sorry to hear that." But then he backtracked. "That was a typical response—I'm sure you get it every time you tell someone."

"It's okay."

"It's not, really, which is what makes a response so difficult. How did you manage?"

Nora set down her cup. "I was in college, so keeping up with my academics while I worked through the loss was the hardest part for me. I understand what Ivy's going through because of that. She's getting good grades again, which is wonderful, but I worry she's having to push aside her grief to do it. Eventually, it will come back to bite her when she isn't expecting it to—in the form of anxiety, depression, panic attacks, you name it."

"So how did you process your feelings? You don't seem affected—are you?"

"I had the support of my grandparents. They were a guiding force for me, stepping in when I wasn't able to manage and filling in the gaps that my parents left. They had a role a lot like yours. The difference was, I ran to them with open arms. We have to get Ivy to trust you and to turn to you in times of emotional need. Hopefully, the counselor you found will help her learn how to process her feelings."

"How do I get her to trust me?"

"Tell her your story about her mother. Ask her opinion on the matter, give her open-ended questions and listen to her answers. You're great at listening—I can tell just by the way you listen to me when I talk."

The corner of his mouth twitched upward. "You're a pretty good listener too."

"Thank you." She fiddled with her cup. "I don't want to betray Ivy's trust, but I do know something she hasn't told you that might be a good way to get her attention."

He eyed her with interest. "What's that?"

"She remembers when you used to play guitar for her before bed. She, too, plays guitar. For whatever reason, she's holding on to that and won't tell you."

"Why?"

"Probably a subconscious grab for control. She might be afraid to allow herself to be vulnerable by telling you something she likes about you—she's got her guard up to protect herself from the grief and stress from the upheaval of her mom's death. But you could organically play for her." The picture of him by the pool swam into her mind, and she pushed it away to focus on him now. "When did you learn to play?"

"I was twelve."

"Twelve?"

"I cut grass for extra money and saved up for an old guitar I'd found at the secondhand shop. I couldn't even play yet, and my parents told me it was a waste of money, but something about that guitar called to me—I still couldn't tell you what it was."

"Once you bought it, how did you learn to play?"

"I felt my way around the strings. It was a little like learning a second language. I wanted to play melodies, and matching the chords to the notes took time, but eventually I remembered where they were and began to pull sounds together to replicate songs I'd heard."

"How long was it before you could play a whole song?"

"A couple of months."

"Wow."

"It's funny. I hated school—I was a terrible student—but I loved learning if it had anything to do with a guitar. I played it all day, every day."

"I love that you found your passion. You're lucky."

"Lucky is right. I have no idea where I'd be if I hadn't picked up that guitar."

"How so?"

"I got pretty good, and began playing in the park after school. People around town began to take notice. My music teacher got wind of it and asked me to bring my guitar to his class during study hall. He taught me the correct finger placement for chords. So I got lucky having him too."

"The right people always seem to come into our lives, don't they?"

Interest sparkled on his face. "Indeed, they do."

There was something in his gaze that made Nora want to get up and leave.

"So if you loved playing guitar," she continued, avoiding whatever that look was, "and you were good at it, did you ever join a band or anything?"

He chuckled. "I did. In rural Alabama I didn't have many options for bandmates. I got a few friends together, but we didn't have a lot of talent between us, so I had to work really hard to select the right material that would showcase what talent we had and then arrange the songs for our demos to get the most out of them. I loved that part of the process. What I didn't realize at the time, was that producing was my true talent."

"How did you get to Nashville?"

"At eighteen, Candace and I packed up and moved to Nashville with nothing but a tent and one suitcase each. We camped in the woods on the edge of the city, lived on gas-station food, and we showered at our local gym until we got jobs. I worked at a discount store in town, and Candace got a job waitressing."

Again, Nora considered how the man in the fur coat on social media was a far cry from the struggling teen he spoke of. Did people know what Blaze Ryman had to do to get to where he was now?

"That must have been hard," she said.

"It was, but we were young and happy then," he said. "That's how I got the nickname Blaze—I blaze a trail wherever I go." He smiled.

"What's your real name?"

He produced a crooked grin that almost took her breath away. "Timothy."

She laughed.

"What?" he asked, humor glittering in his eyes.

"Weirdly, you look more like a Blaze than a Timothy." She took another sip of her coffee, all her attention on this interesting man in front of her.

"Good thing the name stuck then."

"How in the world did you get into Nashville's music producing business? I'd think that would be incredibly hard to do."

"While I worked at my day job I arranged songs and consulted small bands that were trying to break into the music scene. We were all broke, so they couldn't pay much, and I had no experience, so I couldn't charge a lot either. But I loved what I was doing. Sometimes, if I thought a band had incredible talent, we split the cost of the studio and called it even so I could have credit for production. As bands began to get deals, people started to take notice of my work, and my schedule filled up, until I was barely sleeping trying to get it all done. I upped my prices and quit the day job."

"That's an incredible story. I assume it all went up from there?"

"Well, by nineteen I was able to afford an apartment, and we stopped living in our tent. Candace and I got married in a little chapel off Broadway. We thought we'd really made it. But as my popularity grew, I was working around the clock—weekends, late nights... I threw everything I had into this career. And then Candace told me she was pregnant. In the later months of her pregnancy, she struggled with long shifts on her feet, and I had to work even longer hours. But those longer hours produced incredible opportunities for me, and I eventually began making enough money for her to quit waitressing."

"That's incredible."

His light expression fell. "Not entirely. Candace had an instance where she went into what she thought was preterm labor, and she couldn't get a hold of me. She had to drive herself to the hospital."

"Oh, no."

"I was in the studio and not near a phone. I still remember the agony of knowing I'd let her down in the worst way. The song I'd produced that night hit the *Billboard* top ten, but I couldn't enjoy a single minute of it, knowing what the success had cost me." He leaned back in his chair casually and propped his arm up on the back of it.

"Things didn't get any better after Ivy was born. I was building a client list and if big names came my way I had to find time to work with them no matter what because I needed to have their talent on my roster. Now, people depended on me."

"And that eventually led to your split with Candace?"

"We managed for about four years after Ivy was born, and then she snapped. She told me it wasn't the life she'd wanted at all, and if she had to go back to living in a tent, she'd choose that version of me. I wanted time to be with her and Ivy, and I begged for her patience, but she said I'd never slow down. By the time she left, I was convinced they were better off without me."

Nora took in the vulnerability on his face as the two fell into a quiet lull.

He looked uncertain for a moment. "I'm sorry I unloaded all that on you. Maybe I shouldn't have... I'm not a great parent. I guess I just wanted you to hear why."

"None of us are perfect," she said.

Her comment didn't seem to ease his mind, and he looked at his watch. "I know I've taken way more of your time than I should have on a Saturday, talking about myself when you're here to help with Ivy."

She shook her head. "No, it's fine. I asked you the questions."

"Maybe we can grab another coffee at the end of the school year, and you can get me up to speed on Ivy before her counselor starts. And then I can give you a chance to talk."

"Oh, there's not much to tell on my end, but I'd be happy to chat about Ivy."

"Everyone has a story." He tipped up his mug and drank the last of his espresso. Then he gathered their cups and took them over to the dish return.

Nora stood up when he returned. "Thank you for the coffee."

"Of course. Any time. You've got my direct number in case you need to get a hold of me for Ivy."

As they made their way to the door, the public around them came back into Nora's focus. She could see people were discreetly eyeing them when they left.

"One more question," she said, looking up at him through the blinding sunlight. "Is Ryman your real last name?"

His eyes glittered with interest as he peered down at her. "Yeah."

"Do people ever think you're related to the namesake of the Ryman Auditorium?"

"I have had a few people ask."

She nodded.

"I'll check in soon. About Ivy," he said, before slipping on his designer sunglasses and heading to his car.

She waved as he got in.

Nora headed home with mixed feelings. On one hand, she felt confident that Blaze and Ivy would be fine because the girl had a loving father who was willing to try. But she dared not spend another coffee date with him. She was way more interested in him than she should be.

AFTER A FULL AFTERNOON of organizing the house to appease Gram, they'd watched a movie together, but Nora hadn't really seen any of it. Her mind had wandered back to her coffee date with Blaze. Nora had only brushed over the meeting with Gram, not wanting to tell everything for fear that might make her face things about herself she didn't really want to face. But now her issues were swirling around in her head instead.

All the talk about Ivy's loss had Nora thinking about her parents. After Gramps died four years ago, she didn't have anyone left in her family but Gram, and the thought of what she would do when her grandmother passed on almost paralyzed her with fear. She scolded herself for even thinking about Gram going anywhere, but one day losing her grandmother would be a reality. Was this apartment and this job what Nora was meant to do?

And what would she tell Blaze about herself if they met again? Her life wasn't nearly as exciting as his. Was that her own doing? Maybe she should take some risks in life the way Blaze had. For goodness' sake, he'd lived in a tent. And while his personal life hadn't panned out quite the way it probably could have, look at what that risk had gotten him in terms of a career. But Nora couldn't come up with any risks she wanted to take. Her destiny wasn't as clear for her as it had been for Blaze. Why was that? Was she just cruising along without a real purpose or mission? Or had she found it, and her life just wasn't as noteworthy as his?

Gram was asleep in the chair, her closed book in her lap. Nora rubbed her tired eyes. She quietly got up from the sofa, and roused Gram. Then she washed her face, and climbed into bed. Her mind still full of questions, she lay there, unable to sleep. After a few more minutes she reached for her phone on the nightstand and scrolled to Blaze's social media. She clicked his stories to see what he'd posted today. But there was nothing new. Just the same photos of him and the music industry up-and-comers.

He didn't seem to have time for a personal life, but he had made time for coffee. His choice of location was an unusual way to meet regarding a student, but she had to believe that his motive was entirely Ivy. While Nora found him wildly interesting and handsome, she definitely wasn't

Blaze Ryman's type. She didn't actually know his type, but given the flashy people he hung out with, she'd bet a million dollars she wasn't it.

Why, then, had he wanted to hear her story? What did her past have to do with working with Ivy? Certainly, he'd only been trying to be polite. And that was exactly the way she wanted it. The very last thing she needed was to muddle up a perfectly fine position at the school by mixing business with pleasure.

Not any closer to sleep, she fell into the internet, eventually looking up Ryman Auditorium to learn more about the last name Blaze shared with one of Nashville's most famous venues. According to the internet, the auditorium's namesake, Thomas G. Ryman, wasn't a musician at all. He was a sea captain. He invested all his money into his dream of constructing a church that later became the Ryman Auditorium. Blaze, too, had navigated choppy seas, and he'd put all his money and time into his dream. Was Nora the captain of her life? What seas was she navigating? Or was she just coasting along?

Every time she tried to clear her mind to sleep, thoughts of her life floated back in. Was her subconscious trying to tell her something? Was there more to her life than what she'd been living?

CHAPTER TEN

"If you could be thirty-five again," Nora said to Gram over Sunday breakfast, "knowing what you know now, would you have done anything different?"

Gram scooped up a forkful of scrambled eggs, her face contorting in deliberation. "I don't know. I suppose there are a few small things I'd change, but what if changing them would alter the entire course of my life? I don't know if I'd want to. It's been a pretty good one."

"But what if changing your life had given you an even better life?"

"Where's all this coming from?"

"I don't know if I've made the most out of my life." Nora nibbled a piece of bacon.

Gram looked thoughtful. "Well, if that's true, it's good you figured it out now. You do still have quite a bit more life to live."

"I don't know what to do, though. I don't really have any talents."

Gram set down her fork. "Of course you do."

"What are they, then?"

"You have an innate ability to connect with people. You find the positive in almost everything, and when you can't, you work like the dickens to figure out how to make things better. You're caring. You give of yourself without ever wanting anything in return—"

"Yeah, but what about *tangible* talents? I don't play an instrument or make or produce anything at the end of the day."

"Produce...? As in the music producer?"

Her quick connection surprised Nora.

"You've been quiet ever since you came home from that coffee meeting. I didn't press you on it, but I think now I should. Want to tell me what went on?"

"While he isn't great at being a family man, Blaze still has such an inspiring story, and he's gone through a lot himself. He worked really hard for what he has and built it all from nothing." She told Gram about how Blaze had come to Nashville with only a dream. "I haven't worked for anything like that."

"Your journey isn't going to look like Blaze's. You'll have your own trials. How about having to be entirely on your own at twenty, when you were still finishing college? And you did it. You graduated, found a job, and got yourself on your feet financially, without any help. That's working for something."

"I guess so. But he has so much passion for what he does."

"Do you feel that kind of passion when you work with kids?"

"I do with Ivy—I want to make a difference with her. But not as much with the other students. I'm not quite as keen on study skills and career path development."

"Maybe you should go into private practice again."

"I could, but this job is so good. I have great benefits, I get shorter hours, I've made friends..."

"You don't have to go around chasing a struggle. Just see where your gut takes you. Your life will lead you."

"I guess."

"And in a week, life will take you to the coast and a relaxing retreat where you and I can talk until the sun sinks in that gorgeous pink sky I sent you in the photos." Gram's eyebrows bounced up and down.

"You're right. And we'll bury our toes in the sand and reset."

She'd leave everything here in Nashville, and put all her focus on relaxation and spending time with Gram.

"YOU'VE ORGANIZED yourself down to bare essentials, and you've almost got me doing the same," Nora told Gram after they came home from dropping off the last of their used books at the secondhand bookshop in town. "Our apartment is spotless and ordered." She waved a hand around their tidy little space.

"I know." Gram flashed a wide smile.

"It should make packing for the beach much easier," Nora said.

"Indeed." Gram opened the sliding door to the small veranda off their living area. "And where we're going, the scenery will be much better than this." She nodded toward the view of the parking lot.

"Nashville's finest," Nora teased.

Gram laughed.

The ping of Nora's phone interrupted them.

Nora let out a little gasp of surprise when she viewed the screen.

Gram's eyebrows rose.

"It's Blaze." She opened the text. "He's thanking me for meeting him for coffee, and he wants to set up another time to meet next week before we leave for the beach."

"Maybe Friday after school, then?"

"I have my teacher happy hour on Friday." Nora's finger hovered over her phone screen.

"Go Saturday morning," said Gram. "We don't fly out until 2 p.m."

Trying not to read too much into the message, Nora texted back:

> How's Saturday at 9 a.m.? Same place?

The notification that Blaze was checking her text bubbled onto her screen, and the pictures of him on social media flashed through her mind. She held her breath, her heart pattering. Why was she getting worked up over this? It was a parent meeting. And there happened to be coffee. That's it.

His text pinged through.

"I guess I'm meeting Blaze on Saturday morning." She hit the thumbs-up emoji and closed the screen. "Now, I have a week to create an exciting life."

Gram chuckled. "Just be yourself."

"Absolutely. I'll give him all our organizational practices. That should definitely impress him." She wrinkled her nose at Gram.

"You're trying to impress him?"

Nora opened her mouth in an attempt to backtrack but had nothing.

Gram threw her head back and laughed. "You said it, not me!" She patted Nora on the shoulder before heading over to her chair and sitting down.

Nora went into her bedroom to turn her focus to her vacation packing list. With her closet cleaned and all her old clothes purged, she could see exactly what she needed to include. She ran her hands along her sundresses, their pastels calling to be worn on the coast. She rearranged them, putting all the dresses she wanted to take with her on the right of her closet. Then she moved her wedge heels and her sandals under each dress, getting them ready to go into her suitcase next week.

As she ticked off the items that she'd set aside, she pictured herself walking along the wooden boardwalk, a fruity cocktail in hand, the turquoise water at her side. She imagined what it would feel like to actually be there, and she couldn't wait to experience it. Perhaps all those great adventures she was missing in life would start with this trip. She could only hope that they would.

CHAPTER ELEVEN

Monday afternoon, Ivy pulled out a chair and straddled it, leaning her forearms on the back. "My dad played guitar with me last night."

Happiness swam through Nora. Blaze had taken her advice.

"How was it?"

"Good. We started writing a song together."

Nora took a seat in another chair, facing Ivy. "That's exciting. I didn't know you wrote songs."

"It's something I started after my mom died." Ivy dug around in her bag that was in a lump on the floor. She pulled out a black, leather-bound notebook and handed it to Nora.

Nora opened it, revealing lines of scratchy handwriting in ballpoint pen. She read the first few.

> *Sometimes I pretend you're still here.*
> *Sometimes I pretend you didn't leave me.*
> *I walk our old haunts and hear our old songs*
> *And everything's just as it should be.*

"Is that about your mom?" Nora handed the book back to Ivy.

"Yeah. Dad's helping me with the tempo."

"That's wonderful."

"He told me that once we get the song arranged and the notes all good, he'd introduce me to some people at a couple of the labels."

"Is that what you want?"

Ivy shrugged. "Maybe. I haven't really thought about it."

"It could be a promising prospect. Especially if songwriting is something you're interested in. And, either way, it sounds like a great opportunity to get to know your dad a little better."

Ivy shrugged again.

"He wants to be there for you," Nora said gently.

"He could've been there for me for the last seventeen years, but he barely was." Ivy returned the notebook to her backpack and resumed leaning on the back of the chair.

"Have you voiced your feelings about that to him?"

"No."

"Why not?"

"Because it's weird." Ivy huffed. "What do you want me to do, say, 'Hey, Dad. I'm kind of angry with you for never showing up in my life and only being there because you had to when my mom died.'?"

"You could ask him why he wasn't there. He might have an explanation."

"I can't imagine what else it could be besides the fact that he put work over me and my mom."

"I encourage you to talk to him, Ivy."

Ivy cut her eyes at Nora. "Why are you so persistent?

Did he tell you something? What did you all talk about over coffee the other day?"

"I'm sure he'd tell you, if you asked him. He's your family, so it might make more sense to get him to answer your questions. I'm just the middleman."

"So, what—you and my dad are friendly now? Is he trying to get on your good side, schmooze you so you side with him and not me?"

"Not in the slightest."

"Then what?"

Nora went over to her desk to collect a few sheets she'd pulled out on alternative coping strategies to manage school bullying, in case they needed them, and Ivy's checklist. On one side of the checklist, she'd included some of the things Ivy had done to get in trouble. On the other side, she and Ivy had come up with coping strategies that might have helped that circumstance work out better for Ivy. Beside each coping strategy, she'd included check boxes for Ivy to document which strategies she'd used that day. From the list, they were able to get a "Top Three" group of strategies Ivy used most. Those were her go-to strategies in times of stress. Once they'd collected enough data, Nora planned to pass the sheet along to Ivy's family counselor.

"I don't like that you talk to my dad without me there. It's like you're going behind my back," Ivy said.

"I'm doing nothing of the sort, I can assure you."

Nora set down the papers on her back table and gestured for Ivy to come over. Ivy came, seemingly begrudgingly, and Nora slid the checklist toward her.

"Then give me the gist. What did you talk about with him?" Ivy folded her arms on the table, ignoring the checklist completely.

Nora offered her a pencil, but Ivy didn't take it, so Nora set it down in front of her.

"You're *my* counselor. You have to tell me."

"Ultimately, as I said, if you want to know what your dad and I spoke about, you need to ask him. But I promise you, it wasn't anything terrible or life-shattering."

"Do you always see your students' parents outside of school hours? Like a date?"

Ivy was clearly trying to push Nora's buttons. Nora didn't get ruffled, but the girl was hitting a nerve. Nora willed her face not to flush as her thoughts of Blaze's sideways grin fluttered into her mind.

"It was definitely not a date. And it was entirely in your best interest."

"It wouldn't be the end of the world if it was a date," Ivy said, eyeing Nora.

Nora tapped the checklist. "It wasn't a date," she said again. "I simply discussed with your dad the best way to help you. Now, can we get back to business?"

Ivy tipped her head to the side and all but tuned out for the rest of the session. When they finished, the teen left the office sulking.

Nora quickly pulled out her phone and texted Blaze to give him a very quick recap of what had happened. He replied and told her he'd give her a call when he was free tonight.

She stared at the screen. He'd give her a call tonight? What would Ivy think of that?

GRAM HAD ALREADY TURNED in for the night, and Nora was sitting in her bed, with her end-of-school forms strewn around her, when her phone went off on her bedside table. She'd forgotten all about Blaze's text saying he was going to call her when he got a chance. She checked the time: 10:08. *That's late.*

"Hello?"

"Hey, sorry to call at this hour, but I was waiting until Ivy went to her room for the night."

Nora piled her papers into a stack on her bed. "No problem."

"How are you?"

She peered down at the stack, but the view didn't register. Blaze Ryman had just asked how she was as if they'd known each other for years.

"I'm fine."

"Did I disturb you?"

"No, I was just finishing up a little work, but it's getting late and I needed to stop anyway." She got up and put the papers in her bag.

"Ivy's not happy with me," he said, his smooth Southern accent sliding into her ear.

"I tried to encourage her to talk to you, but she thinks you abandoned her and her mother, and she doesn't want to ask you anything."

"I don't know how to approach her. How do you talk to teenage girls?"

"Just be honest with her, and see if she'll listen."

"You make it all sound so easy."

"It's nothing you can't handle, I'm sure."

Nora felt his smile in the tick of silence on the other end and she had to fight a plume of happiness that she'd flattered him.

"Ivy did mention that you played guitar with her and

you were working on a song together. That's a step in the right direction."

"We've got a long way to go."

"She wanted to know why you'd asked me to have coffee. Use her curiosity to bait her into a chat."

"That's a great idea."

"I think she feels betrayed by me for meeting you, so she sees the two of you on different sides. You want to try to become her ally."

"How do I do that?"

"Well, she felt an alliance with me, and I formed that with her by listening and by treating her as an individual. Do you have any opportunities of forced proximity to get her to open up?"

"Her car will be done Friday. Maybe I can bring the topic up on the drive to the mechanic when we go to get it."

"That sounds like a plan." Nora crossed her legs on the bed, the ten o'clock call and her socked feet making her feel a bit like a teenager on the phone with her crush. She had to admit it was easier than expected to imagine having a crush on Blaze.

"What will you do?" he asked. "Ivy's not happy with you either, and it's my fault for asking you to coffee."

"I think she'll come back around. You telling her your side will hopefully help."

"Thank you for taking time out of your night to talk to me. I really appreciate it."

"No problem."

She ended the call and fell back onto her pillow. Thank goodness she only had a week to go, and then they'd have a long break. Ivy would hopefully build a rapport with her new counselor, and Blaze wouldn't require any more help.

He was too easy to like, and she didn't need to like him as much as she already did. She had enough to figure out about herself without bringing unnecessary feelings into the mix.

CHAPTER TWELVE

"Do you know what today is?" Gram asked, putting her hand to her heart.

Nora gathered her things for her last day of school. The week had been a busy one with all the end-of-year paperwork, finalizing schedules for the next school year, and boxing up her office. She was beat, but tomorrow she would head off to paradise, so she could do anything for one more day.

"Friday?" Nora said.

"Well, yes, but it's better than just any old Friday."

"What day is it?" Nora leaned into the fridge and pulled out her packed lunch, tucking it into her lunchbox.

"It's your gramps's birthday."

Nora's happy buzz instantly disappeared. "Oh, wow. You're right."

"I've been missing him a lot lately. He keeps coming to mind, but not in the usual way."

"What do you mean?"

"Yesterday, I could've sworn I heard him whistle the way he did when he was working on something. Remember he used to whistle little tunes while he fixed a broken door or changed out a light switch?"

Nostalgia filled Nora as the forgotten memory floated back into her consciousness. "I do."

"I actually got up to check if he was in the kitchen." Gram's eyes became glassy. "And a few weeks ago, I swore I heard him whisper 'I love you' just as I was falling asleep. My eyes sprung open and clicked on the light, sure I'd see him."

"Why do you think he's coming back to you so often?"

"I don't know, but that's why I wanted to go to the coast. I swore; he asked me to go."

Nora stared at her grandmother. Firmly grounded in her knowledge of how the brain worked, Nora had a very difficult time believing that Gramps was anywhere near them or that he'd asked anything of Gram.

"What made you think he asked?"

"I heard his voice on the wind as I took my morning walk around the apartments."

"So this whole trip is because of Gramps?" Nora resumed packing her bag, the time getting away from her.

"Pretty much. I feel he wants me to see it. You know, he was planning a trip there when he had his heart attack."

"Wow. I didn't know."

That was why the trip had come to Gram: she missed Gramps and, subconsciously, she wanted to be closer to him, so she decided to act on his wish. Her mind had played tricks on her, and she'd wanted to hear his voice so badly she'd actually conjured it in her mind.

"You don't believe that I heard him," Gram said.

Nora slid her bag onto her shoulder. "I believe that you believe you heard him." She kissed her grandmother on the cheek. "Gotta run. See you tonight!"

Gram's disappointment shone in her eyes, but she smiled at Nora all the same. "See you tonight, my sweet girl."

The unfinished conversation weighed on Nora all the way to school.

"HEY," Ivy said, coming into Nora's office at the end of sixth period.

Kim, who'd stopped by during her planning period to catch up, eyed the girl on her way out of the room. Nora had asked Kim's opinion about her second coffee meet-up with Blaze, but she should've guessed that Kim's motivations were less to do with work and more with Blaze's fame. When Ivy walked in, Nora still didn't feel any surer of her decision to meet him.

"Thanks for letting me come early," Ivy said.

"It's no problem at all. I figured you wouldn't want to stay after school on the last day."

Ivy shrugged. She slipped off her vest and hung it on the chair. The temperature already climbing outside, the hallways were warm.

"I got my car back," the girl said.

Nora maneuvered around a stack of boxes full of her office materials—all packed up for the break. "I'll bet you're excited to be able to come and go on your own."

"Yeah." Ivy moved to Nora's desk and picked up the lone paper next to the pencil sharpener: her checklist. "And Dad told me about your meeting with him."

"Do you feel any better after talking to him?"

"I guess. He says he's meeting with you tomorrow too."

"That's right."

Ivy seemed okay about Nora and Blaze chatting this time.

"He thinks the same way about you that I do," Ivy said.

"Oh? What do both of you think about me?" Nora grabbed two pencils from one of the packed boxes and sharpened them. Then she handed one to Ivy and set the other one on the table.

"That you're great at what you do." Ivy sat down at the back table and wrote the date on the top of her checklist before marking which strategies she'd used today.

"I'm glad you both feel that I'm doing a good job."

"Definitely." Ivy looked up. "I'm going to miss our time together over the summer."

Nora sat down across from her. "That might be the best thing I've ever heard you say."

"You're happy about me floundering around without you?" Ivy allowed a small smile.

"You've come a long way in the last few weeks."

Ivy tucked her pink hair behind her ear. "It's because of the time we worked together. You treated me like a normal human being."

"You're definitely a normal human being," Nora said with a laugh.

"Is there any way to see you this summer before school starts again?"

"I'm sure we could work something out."

"What if I need you before then?"

Nora looked into Ivy's gray eyes. "Your dad found you a counselor, right?"

Ivy sunk back in the chair.

"Don't discount her. Treat *her* like a 'normal human being' and she might surprise you," Nora said.

"I doubt it."

"Give her a chance like you gave me."

Ivy smirked. "I sort of accidentally gave you a chance. You just have a different vibe from the other teachers." She held up her coping checklist. "I need to add 'See Miss Jenkins' to this list because when I feel overwhelmed, coming to your office helps."

Ivy's honesty was refreshing.

"We'll add it on for next year."

The teen's expression dropped. "The summer's going to be awful." She picked at her black painted nail.

"I'm sure it will be better than you think. You'll get to do mission work, if you want to, and you can write songs. Put all that pent-up emotion into your songwriting and you might pen an entire album's worth. In this town, your songwriting might take you places you never thought it would."

The bell rang and a streak of fear flashed across Ivy's face. She stood up but didn't go anywhere, her lips parting as if she wanted to say something more. She finally pressed her lips together and grabbed her vest off the chair.

"You can keep your checklist," Nora said. "Take it home so you can access the strategies whenever you need them."

"Thanks." Ivy opened the door, lingering in the entry to Nora's office. Then she pulled her car keys from her front pocket.

Nora wished she could do something more for the girl, but she'd already done all she could. It was time to step away and let someone else take the reins.

Ivy turned and stepped through the door.

"Have a wonderful break," Nora called after her as the halls filled with whooping, excited students, ready to be out for the summer.

Ivy looked over her shoulder and produced a half smile. Were those tears in her eyes? "See ya."

Then she disappeared into the crowd of students.

ONCE A MONTH, a group of teachers from Nora's school got together for happy hour at a Nashville bar. Most of them had been meeting up for years, but they'd welcomed Nora with open arms when she'd started at Oakland High. Tonight was the last hurrah before they all went their separate ways for the summer.

Nora walked down Nashville's busy Broadway in her cut-off jean shorts and flowy top, ready to let off some steam. She meandered through the crowds, music from all the bars spilling out onto the sidewalk. The summer warmth had already taken hold, and a warm breeze wrapped around her. Kim was in front of the bar, waiting.

"Everyone's inside. It was so hot in there I needed some fresh air, so I figured I'd come out here to wait for you," her friend said when she walked up. "You look so summery!"

"I'm slowly getting into my beach mode." Nora linked arms with Kim as they went inside.

"When do you leave?" she asked over the music.

A fizzle of excitement swam through Nora. "Tomorrow."

"You're so lucky. I'll be here, frying like an egg in the heat." Dramatically, Kim fanned her face with her hand.

They reached the table of women who already had their drinks and were laughing together. They cheered over the band that played on stage in the corner when Nora and Kim walked up, and Melissa Edmunds, the chemistry teacher, pulled out a chair for Nora.

"Glad you could come," Melissa said loudly while she

pulled her curly locks into a messy bun and secured it with a ponytail holder.

"Me too."

"Oh, oh! Nora's here," Sheila Rodgers, the orchestra teacher, said as Nora sat down. "We're all dying to know the latest on Ivy Ryman."

"She's actually doing quite well. By the end of the year she was following rules and settling in. There's not much to tell in the way of drama." Which was good because they were having to shout over the music.

The waitress came by and Nora pointed to Sheila's pink cosmo. "I'll take one of those."

"There absolutely *is* drama." Jill Bryson, the P.E. teacher, leaned into the group, putting her forearms on the table, her eyes wide. "You've had meetings with Blaze Ryman! We want to know all the details!"

"Blaze is soooo handsome." Melissa tipped her head back and rolled her eyes in ecstasy.

"I heard you went to his house," Sheila said over her cosmo. "What's it like?"

"Big," Nora said. But there was so much more to him than a big house and good looks. She already felt she knew him so much more than these women did.

"She's meeting him for coffee tomorrow," Kim said.

There was a collective gasp at the table.

"I'm just helping him transition to their family therapist and giving him a few pointers. That's all."

Jill lifted her martini. "I'd like to give him a few pointers…"

The women erupted in laughter as the band kicked into high gear, the drumbeat thumping in Nora's chest.

The waitress returned and set the cosmo in front of Nora. She took a sip of the sweet pink concoction, the alcohol immediately relaxing her. The warmth seemed to affect everyone in its path. The whole atmosphere—her joyful friends, the fruity drink, the heat—made her already feel as if her vacation had started, and she hadn't even left Nashville yet.

As the night went on, the ladies got up to dance. Nora joined in, forgetting all about school and immersing herself in the lighter atmosphere. She'd switched to lemonade and was feeling positively giddy about what the summer would bring, when out of nowhere, a hand caught her arm.

"Nora?"

She turned around to find Carson with Molly, the woman he'd left her for. Carson blinked repeatedly as if the sight of her was completely incomprehensible.

"I'm surprised to see you on Broadway," he said. "This isn't your usual hangout."

"It is now. Hi Molly," she said.

Molly smiled uncomfortably while Carson continued to look baffled.

Nora said, "My new teacher friends chose the location. We go to happy hour together once a month."

"Ah," Carson said.

Molly excused herself to go to the ladies' room. She tucked her designer clutch under her elbow and straightened her form-fitting mini-dress on her way—an outfit Nora would never have chosen. This spiked her insecurity, but she didn't let it show.

Carson leaned in. "Hey, I'm really sorry."

Nora stopped him. "No need to apologize."

"Yes, there is. I didn't mean to—"

"If we were meant to be, we'd be."

She didn't want to admit that they would still "be" if he hadn't decided she was unfit to be his wife. She squared her shoulders. As she looked into his eyes, she realized she didn't see anything anymore. There were no fireworks. A new wave of insecurity washed over her: she hadn't noticed until this moment that she didn't love him either.

"I feel terrible," he said.

"Look, our relationship was good on paper, but you and I both know we didn't have enough to sustain a lifetime together. You were just the first one of us to act on it."

He nodded, relief flooding his face.

"I hope you're super happy with Molly," Nora said.

"Thanks."

Maybe Nora had romanticized her parents' relationship, and that was what had kept her from seeing the breakdown of her relationship with Carson. The reasons she'd started dating him in the first place were now overshadowed by the suspicion that she'd been ready to settle for something when she could do better.

When Molly returned, and she and Carson walked away, Nora couldn't help but feel relief that she'd been spared the heartbreak of a failed marriage. She turned back to the dance floor, focused on the band, and tried to get back into her summer mood.

CHAPTER THIRTEEN

Java House was buzzing already as Nora pulled up next to the familiar Maserati. Blaze waved from the table as she entered, and she walked over to him. His hair was still a little wet, and he was clean-shaven, wearing a pair of casual jeans and a T-shirt that stretched over his biceps and pectoral muscles as if it had been tailored just for him. He held the handle of his mug of black coffee.

"Same table as last time?" Nora said.

The corner of his lips twitched upward. "I guess it's our table now."

She gave him an obligatory chuckle, but it certainly wouldn't be their table since they weren't planning to meet again after this day.

Blaze stood up, leaving his mug and leading the way to the counter. "Pick your poison. My treat."

"No, no." She shooed him off. "I'll get my coffee this time."

"Please." He gestured toward the counter. "I insist on treating because I'm going to have to drag you down the street to the recording studio for a quick favor. I tried to get out of it, but it's an emergency."

"Oh?"

"It's only for a few minutes and it's just around the corner. I can run over and then come right back, but as it's a gorgeous day you could come with me if you want to take a walk."

Feeling summery, Nora put in her order for a vanilla bean sweet cream latte and paid the cashier before Blaze could. "Make the coffee to go, please." She turned to Blaze. "A walk sounds nice," she said, as the woman wrote the order on a paper cup and the barista began packing grounds into the portafilter.

"It does," Blaze agreed. "Mm. Those blueberry muffins are looking really good right now." He leaned onto the counter. "I'll have two of your muffins—one for me and one for the lady—and another black coffee."

The woman grabbed the muffins and placed them in a bag, before handing it to Blaze. Then she rang him up, and he tapped his phone for payment.

"What if I didn't eat blueberry muffins?" Nora asked lightheartedly.

"I'd have had to eat two." He pretended to wipe sweat off his forehead.

She laughed, but quickly drew herself back in to remain professional. He was definitely a charmer.

The barista eventually placed their coffees on the counter. Blaze retrieved the two cups, and handed her the latte. Then he led her to the door, opening it and allowing her to exit into the morning sunshine.

"What can I help with today?" she asked as they stepped onto the sidewalk.

"Ivy let me tell her my side of the story when we went

to get the car, but she seems skittish. I wonder if she believes me, and I'm not sure how to get her to trust me."

"It might take her a little time. For many years she's only heard her mother's side of things. She believed her mom. But it sounds like you're doing the right thing by trying to talk to her. Just keep doing that. Be yourself, and your transparency should eventually sway her."

"I'm also still unsure how to respond to her grief over her mom." He nodded to the right, and they turned the corner onto Music Row. "I mean, I hadn't seen Candace in years, but I struggle myself with the fact that she's gone. A couple of times, I thought about approaching Ivy to talk about her mom, but I teared up. It's unbelievable that the woman I'd loved enough once to marry, and the mother of my child, is gone." He cleared his throat and took a drink of his coffee, his emotion evident.

"Grief is a very complex thing. You'll both have ups and downs for a long time," Nora said.

They passed RCA Studio B, where stars like Elvis Presley and Dolly Parton had recorded their hits. The rectangular buildings of larger corporations dotted the landscape between old bungalow houses-turned-music-studios—the signature of Music Row. She and Blaze continued along the shady sidewalk, Nora's handbag swinging on her shoulder, the warm coffee in her hand, the topic of loss still hanging between them.

"I've actually been thinking a lot about my own parents lately," Nora confided.

"You have?"

She nodded, Gram's admission about hearing Gramps coming to mind. "I wonder where they are. Can they see me? Do they know what I'm doing?"

"What do you think happens to us when we go?" he

asked, the two of them striding in unison down the sun-streaked pavement. "Do we just hang around, or do we get to fly to some other place? Or... are we just no more?"

"None of us know for sure, do we?"

"I guess that's where faith steps in," Blaze said. He stopped at a gray bungalow with a banner that had the headshots of three country music artists out front. "I'd love to think there's a heaven," he said, ushering her up the three steps to the porch.

He opened the door, and they went inside. The place was quiet. They stopped outside a closed door. Blaze knocked, put his ear to the door and then opened it, revealing an empty room containing a wide panel of buttons.

"What is all this?" Nora asked.

He offered her a stool and she took a seat, feeling completely out of her element.

"It's where we edit, mix, and master the sounds coming from in there." He set down his coffee and muffin and pointed past the glass to another room with musical instruments and microphones.

She scanned the array of sliders, buttons, computer screens, and lights. "It looks like the cockpit of an airplane."

"Watch this." He flipped a few switches and then tapped a couple of buttons on one of the computers. Music began to pour through the speakers in the room. It was a low beat with a quick tempo.

"I like that."

He frowned, the skin between his eyes wrinkling. "I think it should be slower." He moved a couple of the slides up and down until the tempo decelerated. Then with a few clicks on the computer, the tinkling of bells came in underneath the sound. He lowered the volume.

"It sounds like summer," she said, goosebumps forming on her arms.

Blaze closed his eyes. "Music is like painting. It has layers, and what you put in those layers, changes everything." He moved a slider up, and a dark, hollow hum squeezed out the summer and caused her heart to thump with the drama.

"Wow."

He rubbed his hands together; his passion clear. "Enough playing. Let me create a few samples so we can get out of here." He began moving buttons and typing at warp speed, recording clips and loading them onto the computer in front of him. "I'd have done this before we met, but I got the call on the way to the coffee shop." He didn't look up from the workstation, his entire attention on it.

"It's fine," she said, curious about his work.

With a few more clicks, he had three samples. The first one was softer, more romantic. The second, happier. The one after that so bouncy she wanted to get up and dance.

She sipped her coffee. "You make all this look effortless."

"Ah, the workstation is like an instrument itself. You just have to know how to play it." He met her eyes. "We were talking about heaven. This is my heaven." He saved the clips to the computer and turned toward her. "Do you actually think there is a heaven?"

"I think so, yes."

He nodded, pensive.

"My grandmother swears she can hear my grandfather sometimes. I don't know if that's true, and the field of work I'm in tells me it's probably her brain coping with the grief of losing him, wishful thinking on her part. But a tiny piece of me believes it might be true."

"Only a tiny piece?" he asked, interest in his gaze.

"Do *you* believe in heaven?"

He frowned, clearly thinking it over. "For Ivy's sake, I hope so. It would be nice to know she'd see her mother again one day." He opened the bag and handed her a muffin. "I'd say I believe more than I don't believe."

Nora gently pulled the muffin paper from the side of the cake and pinched a small bite. She dared not admit that she wished with every fiber of her being that there was a heaven and that her belief in a higher power meant something. But the world, and even Carson sometimes, could paint the picture that she was a fool for trusting in her faith.

"What makes you believe?" She popped the sugary sweet confection into her mouth.

"I suppose that even as great as it is here on earth..." He waved a hand at the workstation. "This can't be as good as it gets." He flashed that handsome grin of his.

Nora liked that answer. His response was a ray of clarity in the darkness she'd been in recently.

He set down a few napkins on a small bit of counter in front of them.

"Have you ever asked Ivy if she'd like to see all this?" Nora said. "Knowing where you are all day and what you're doing might be helpful."

"That's a great idea... If I can motivate her to get in the car and come in with me. In fact, Miss Coats was wondering if you had any suggestions to motivate Ivy?"

"She's most motivated internally, when her thoughts and feelings are validated. But aren't we all?"

"Right." He took a bite of his muffin. When he'd swallowed, he said, "I still think you somehow have a magic touch."

"I don't think so. It's just my version of this." She waved a hand at the workstation.

"What do you mean?" he asked.

"The way you can make music and naturally have a plan in your head for what works, I'm the same when it comes to reaching people."

"You're definitely skilled at it. I listen to Ivy and I think I validate her thoughts, but she doesn't respond the same way to me as she does to you."

Nora peeled more of the paper from around her muffin. "It's a little different as the parent. She's going to have her guard up around you because you make the rules."

"You made rules for her, too, though," he countered.

"Yes, but in the end, if you wanted to pull her out of school and away from me, it would be your call."

He chuckled lightly as if her comment were ridiculous. "I'd never do that."

"But you could. You have a lot of power in your relationship. She subconsciously knows this."

"So what do I do about it?"

"Be consistent and honest, like I said. Acknowledge her feelings and explain why you're making your decisions. She might not agree, but she's a reasonable person, and when she has time to consider your choices, she'll probably come around."

He fell into a contemplative silence, and she allowed him to work on the task at hand. Did he believe her? He continued to work, tempos rising and falling, instruments filtering in. She zeroed in on his strong hands as he typed, the roundness of his shoulders and the ease in which he communicated. He had a confident yet casual way about him that was undeniably attractive, and she could see why he'd been on eligible bachelor lists. Just sitting with him made her question ever dating Carson in the first place. There were better guys out there. Why had she almost sold herself short?

"Let me just double-check the beats made it to the internal server so the band can access them from home. Be right back." He got up and went into another room.

She watched him go. A woman like her could never have someone as charismatic as Blaze Ryman, but it was fun to imagine what it would be like to have him walk into a room and make a beeline to her.

She needed to get a grip. She'd done her job and helped Blaze with his questions, but now it was time to get on with her summer before she made a fool of herself.

When he returned, she picked up her cup. "I hope I've given you enough to pass on to the counselor. I should probably get going."

"You haven't finished your muffin."

"I can wrap it up." She folded the paper around the leftover portion and rolled it in the napkin. "I'm leaving for the coast today, so... I need to head home to be sure I've got everything packed for my flight."

"I remember." His lips parted again as if he wanted to say something, his body restless.

She retrieved her handbag from the floor and slipped it over her shoulder. She stood up and balled her half-eaten muffin in her fist.

He rose, the stool groaning loudly on the hard floor. "Ready to walk back to the cars then?"

"Okay."

They left, passing a few people in the hallway. Blaze gave each of them a friendly nod. He opened the door for her, and they stepped back into the sunshine.

"It's getting hot already," he said, switching his coffee

and muffin to the same hand so he could retrieve a pair of Ray-Bans from his shirt pocket. He slipped them on, looking like a rock star.

With her simple outfit and flats, she paled in comparison.

Even after spending time together, walking next to him was surreal. Nora had seen him online, conversing with the biggest stars in the country, and yet they made their way to their cars as if he lived a totally normal life. But while he could play the part of a star—he was extroverted, charming, and walked with a kind of confidence that set him apart from the average person—he was also down to earth, kind, and easy to talk to.

She was still thinking about it when they arrived at their cars.

"Well, you have my number. Text me if you need anything this summer: concert tickets, coffee suggestions..." His gaze lingered on her.

Why was he doing that? It was probably fear that he'd have to navigate the summer with Ivy with little help because the new counselor didn't know Ivy the way Nora did. But with his levelheadedness and kind demeanor, he'd be okay. She was nearly sure of it.

"Tell Ivy I hope she has a wonderful summer," Nora said.

"I will."

"And you too."

He nodded. "Enjoy your vacation."

"Thanks." She opened her car door and climbed inside. Tossing her muffin on the passenger seat and slowly sliding her coffee into the cup holder in the center console, she stalled until Blaze had started his engine and was backing up. When the view of his car in her mirror finally faded away, she exhaled and rested her head on the steering wheel.

An undefinable feeling formed in her chest—a heavy emptiness. It was a faint version of the same feeling she experienced in the year or so after her parents died, a sense that some part of her was missing after they'd gone and she had the burden of having to live with it. Why would she be getting this feeling now? While she found Blaze far more interesting than she wanted to, she had to wonder if she was reacting to the fact that she'd no longer be a go-to for Ivy. The girl had seemed so emotional on their final day together, but Ivy would settle with her new family counselor—the person most equipped to handle what Ivy was going through. Then, after the summer months of counseling, Ivy might not need Nora anymore. And after that, Ivy would graduate, and off they'd go...

Nora had to shake the feeling. It was summer. She had a wonderful trip planned, and she'd be in paradise in a matter of hours. With a shake of her head, she pulled out of the parking spot. She drove off, the moment with Blaze sliding away, getting smaller and smaller in her rearview mirror.

CHAPTER FOURTEEN

The salty coastal breeze blew in through the open windows in the rental car as Nora and Gram made the last leg of their trip to the cottage. After a quick flight and a fifteen-minute drive from Panama City Beach, the villages gave way to empty land that stretched out to the Gulf of Mexico on one side and the tree line on the other. The late-afternoon sun came in at a slant, casting a bright beam on Nora's legs. She held her hair back with one hand and drove with the other, whisps escaping her grip and tickling her cheek.

Gram was quiet. She peered out the window, taking deep breaths, and smiling every so often as if she were having an unspoken conversation. Her shoulders were relaxed, her hands folded in her lap, and Nora was glad she'd decided to do this for Gram.

Nora recognized the clapboard bungalow sitting right on the coastline from the photos Gram had given her. She pulled into the sandy drive and put the rental car in park.

"We made it." She popped the trunk and opened the door.

Gram got out on the other side and put her hands on

her hips, facing the turquoise water of the Gulf. "It's like a dream."

"It definitely is." Nora pulled their suitcases out of the back and set them in the sand. "Why don't we get you settled, and I'll find the market where I can pick up some groceries?" Nora suggested.

"I've already thought of that." Gram pointed to a couple of paper bags on the front porch.

Nora shut the car door and picked up two of the suitcases. "What are those?"

"I called a grocery delivery company, told them when we'd arrive, and had them deliver groceries from the local market. I paid for it on my credit card." Her eyebrows bobbed and she looked proud of herself.

"That's amazing. What did you get?"

"I got the basics, plus your favorite granola cereal, fresh bread, pizza, and piña colada mix."

"But we don't have rum."

"Yes we do. It's in my carry on. I got it at the airport when you were in the bathroom."

Nora laughed. "You've thought of everything."

They stepped onto the wooden porch, the light gray paint on the boards peeling from the salty air and the grit of sand. Gram checked her phone and input the door code, the latch clicking. She pushed open the door and Nora set the suitcases inside then grabbed the groceries and carried them into the kitchen. She dropped the bags on the small counter, distracted by the view through the sliding glass doors opposite them. She pushed the gauzy curtains to the side and opened the door to the back porch.

The wind was stronger on this side of the house. She tucked her brown hair behind her ears and sat down on the bench swing, the ropes that suspended it creaking with her weight. The waves lapped quietly on the pearly shore. The sand was so fine it appeared to be powder, and she couldn't wait to get down there and sink her toes into it.

"I will definitely relax here," Gram said, lowering herself next to Nora.

"That's for sure."

With the rocking swing and the shushing of the waves, Nora *almost* felt as if she could leave the last year behind. The only thing she couldn't quite shake was that final day with Ivy, when she swore she'd seen tears in the girl's eyes. She took in a deep breath of the briny air.

After getting the rest of their bags and putting away the groceries, she and Gram sat together for quite a while. As they rocked, Nora worked to clear her mind and slowly let her thoughts go—Ivy, Blaze, Carson, and his new fiancée, and even some of the pain from losing her parents that had been dredged up by working with Ivy.

"Should we see if we can find the blender?" Gram asked. "I'd love one of those piña coladas."

"Sure," Nora said, finally on the cusp of relaxation. "That sounds fantastic. I'm ready for dinner. I'll put the pizza in the oven as well."

Gram hoisted herself off the swing. "I'll dig out the rum. I wrapped it in my cardigan so it didn't break on the flight."

With the drinks made and the pizza in the oven, they stepped down the wide wooden staircase and onto the beach. Nora sipped the pineapple-coconut drink as she padded through the soft sand. It felt just as powdery as it looked, the warm smoothness of it soothing her feet after her travel. It was hard to believe she'd been at a coffee shop in downtown Nashville with Blaze just this morning.

"Whatcha thinking about?" Gram asked as they made their way to the water.

"Nothing, really." She pushed Blaze from her mind, promising herself not to allow him to creep in again. "I'm just drinking in this view. The water seems to go on forever."

They stepped up to the quiet surf, the shades of blue striping the water taking Nora's breath away. The waves were small today, barely more than ripples—just enough movement to create a sparkle on the horizon.

Gram stepped forward, the foam gurgling over her toes, making her laugh. "The water's warmer than I'd thought. I'd like to get my swimsuit on and float around in it, but I'll wait until I'm not so tired. In this state, I'm liable to fall asleep and float out to sea."

"Maybe we can come out first thing tomorrow."

Gram held up her drink. "Yes. It's a date." She linked arms with Nora. "I can't wait to spend two weeks with you—just the two of us."

A sense of excitement filled Nora. "It's going to be great."

GRAM LAID DOWN A YELLOW FOUR. "UNO."

As they sat at the small table on the back porch, the sky had exploded in bands of pink and orange, the Gulf's light turquoise turning a deep green. Condensation dripped down their piña colada glasses. They'd switched to just the mix after their pizza, saving the rest of the rum for another day, but Nora's cheeks were still warm from the earlier alcohol and the salty air.

Nora dropped her last card, a yellow six, onto the pile. "I'm out."

"I demand a rematch." Gram picked up the discard pile

and shuffled it with the remainder of the deck. "Best out of three?"

"You're on."

While Gram divvied up their cards, Nora turned her face toward the water.

"It sure is peaceful out here. There's not a soul but us."

Gram wriggled a finger down the beach. "And that cottage over there."

"It's far enough away that they can't hear a word we're saying. Unlike our apartment back home."

Gram raised her eyebrows in agreement and flipped the top card over—a blue two. "You go first."

Nora studied her hand and then dropped a blue four onto the table.

"Gramps would've loved it here," Gram said as she added a card to the pile.

"I think so too." Nora took a drink from her glass, the sweet pineapple-coconut flavor going down easily in the warm weather.

"Your grandfather was always preaching to live life to the fullest. I thought his wild ideas were silly until one night I realized they weren't at all."

"What ideas did he have?"

"He wanted to take me here, and skiing in the mountains, he wanted to go on an African safari!" She squeezed her eyes shut and shook her head.

"Well, I'll fulfill his wish to go to the beach, but I might not be a great safari companion."

"Why not?" Gram asked, chewing on a grin.

"I prefer vacations that don't involve wild beasts that could have me for dinner."

Gram let out a loud laugh and dropped a card onto the

pile. "Your go." She seemed more animated tonight than she'd ever been, and they'd only just arrived.

"What do you want to do tomorrow besides float in the Gulf?" Nora asked.

"I want to get up early, sit on that porch swing with my book and a cup of coffee, and read until the sun comes up. Other than that, it's your call."

"Maybe we could go into the villages and peruse some of the little shops."

Gram took in a contented inhale, her eyes closing. "Yes. The village names here are something out of a storybook: Rosemary Beach, Santa Rosa Beach, Watercolor, Seaside..."

"I know. The whole place is a picture book." Nora moved her feet gently back and forth on the old wooden boards, the remnants of sand carried on the wind making a scratching sound under her toes. "I can't believe people get to live here."

"Going back to the apartment will be difficult, for sure, but we can always return. Where do you want to go shopping tomorrow?"

"I'd like to go into Watercolor. I saw one shop on the drive in that had beautiful paintings in the window."

"That sounds like the perfect way to spend the day."

Nora laid down another card. "Should we also do something in honor of Gramps? What would he have wanted to do?"

Gram rolled her eyes. "Well I'm certainly not smoking cigars and drinking whiskey."

Amusement bubbled up in Nora at the memory of Gramps in his favorite chair.

"What?" Gram asked.

"I just got an image of Gramps with a cigar between his fingers and a splash of whiskey in his tumbler on the table beside him while he flipped through the news stations, complaining about how no one actually reported the truth anymore."

Gram laughed. "That memory surfaces because it was what he did every evening." She set her hand of cards onto the table face down and leaned on her forearms. "But when we were alone, he liked to dance with me."

Nora's eyes widened. "*Gramps?* Danced?"

"He'd turn on the old radio in the living room, take my hands, and pull me off the sofa, and then he'd pull me into his arms and spin me around the room." Gram closed her eyes. "If I try hard enough, I can still smell his Brut cologne and the bite of whiskey."

"Wait here."

Nora put down her cards, got up, and went into the kitchen. She made a beeline to the old radio she'd seen when they'd first arrived. She'd wondered if it had been there for use during storms, when cellular service was out. She grabbed it and brought it to Gram.

"Let's see if it works." Nora plugged it into an exterior outlet and flipped the switch.

A fuzzy squeal and then a buzz came through the speakers. Nora tuned the knob until she found a station and when a song began to filter through, Gram gasped and reached across the table, grabbing Nora's arm.

"That's 'Something' by The Beatles." Her eyes became glassy. "He used to sing that to me." Gram put her hand to her heart. "He's here with us. I can feel him."

The lyrics filled the space between them. What were the odds that the old radio would work and *that* song would be playing?

"You don't think it's just a wild coincidence?" Nora asked, not ready to fully believe that Gramps could be dancing around them right now. If that were true, surely her parents were there as well, and if so she might break down into tears.

Gram shook her head. "It's definitely not a coincidence. I've come here, the place your gramps always wanted to go, and we were just talking about him. He's telling us he's here."

Nora's heart pattered and she looked around for a flash of light or a glitter of something in the distance, but there was nothing. She couldn't believe it. Gramps being with them would be too wonderful.

She picked up her cards. Gram's fanciful ideas had rubbed off on her. But in a way, she was glad. She'd never known Gramps had been a secret romantic. She only hoped she could grow old with someone like that one day.

CHAPTER FIFTEEN

"I could get used to the sound of seagulls in the morning," Nora said as she gripped her coffee mug on the porch swing the next day, a new novel nestled in the folds of her yellow sundress that was spread across the seat.

She'd slept surprisingly soundly, and waking early without an alarm had restored her. Excitement over the days ahead must have propelled them because both she and Gram had come into the kitchen before dawn. They'd made coffee and sat out on the porch until the sun had made its way past the horizon. Then they got dressed and took their books out to the porch swing to enjoy the cool breeze coming off the water.

Nora's laptop and cell phone had been in the living room since last night, and she'd not even touched them. She couldn't even believe she'd bothered to pack her computer. There was no need for any communication with the outside world, and she was just fine with that. She had everything she needed right here.

Gram closed her novel around her finger and peered out

at the Gulf. "That view makes the whole world go away, doesn't it?"

Nora set her novel and mug on the small table next to the swing, fluffed her dress, and leaned against the outdoor pillows, closing her eyes. "It's amazing how quickly the real world disappears. It's almost instantaneous." She wriggled into a more comfortable position and rearranged the cushions behind her back, the swing shimmying with her movement. "What time do you want to go into the villages today?"

"Maybe around eleven and then we can spend the later afternoon swimming? What do you think?"

Nora turned her face toward the sun, the warmth of it making her skin tingle. "That's a great idea. And I'd like to go for a walk on the beach before heading out."

"That sounds divine." Gram took a drink from her mug. "I might not be able to keep up with you the entire way, but I'll definitely walk down to the water and—"

They were interrupted by a sound at the front of the bungalow.

"What was that?" Nora asked, sharpening her hearing.

With the sound of the waves, it was hard to be sure, but they had both heard something. Then, Nora thought she'd heard it again.

"Was that a knock at the door?" Gram asked.

"I doubt it. We're in the middle of nowhere. Who would be out this way?"

Knock, knock.

Gram's eyebrows pulled together as she tipped her head toward the screen door between them and the house. "Well, something's blowing in the wind at least. We should probably secure it."

"I'll go see what it is," Nora offered.

She got up and went inside just as another knock came through from the front of the cottage. She peered through a window and froze at what was in the driveway: Ivy's beat-up, old car. Nora flung open the door to find the girl in a pair of flannel pajama pants and a concert T-shirt, with no makeup and her pink hair pulled back into a ponytail. A canvas bag was slung over her shoulder and an old suitcase covered in stickers sat at her feet.

"I'm so sorry. I know you're on vacation..." Ivy's gaze dropped to her combat boots.

Nora took a step back. "Come inside." She ushered the girl into the kitchen.

"I can't live with my dad. I thought about going home to Fair Hope, but everyone there would send me back to him, and I didn't know where else to go." She locked eyes with Nora. "I don't have anyone who understands."

The real world collided with this dream world, and Nora forced herself back into counselor mode. "Let me get you something to drink. Want a cup of water? Juice?"

"Do I smell coffee? I need some. I've been driving all night." Ivy stifled a yawn.

"I can make some."

The back screen door opened, and Gram walked in. "I thought I heard talking." She offered a questioning glance to Nora.

"Gram, this is Ivy Ryman. Ivy says she can't live with her father, and she drove here." Nora rinsed out the coffee pot and refilled it with water before pouring it into the reservoir. "How did you know where I was?"

"Remember the sheet with the rental information that was on your desk? I knocked it off and it went under the shelf in your office." Ivy climbed onto one of the stools at the small counter.

"Yes."

"After school, I came back to your room and grabbed it when the custodian was sweeping the floor. I got it in case I needed to get in touch with you over the summer. I figured I might because my dad doesn't have a clue how to be a parent." She put her elbows on the table and picked at her fingernail, frustration evident in her pout. "I knew it was nuts to crash my school counselor's vacation, so I folded up the paper and shoved it into my dresser drawer, not planning to actually use it unless there was an emergency. I thought if things got stupid, I'd get the number and call or something."

Nora pulled a mug down from the cabinet. "How long was the drive?"

"Seven hours. I left around midnight. I waited for Dad to go to his side of the house. He went into his office to work on some songs."

"At midnight?" Gram asked.

"That's when he does his best work, he says."

Nora filled the coffeemaker with grounds and hit the button.

"While he was working, I snuck out through the side entrance, got in my car, and left," Ivy said.

"So your dad still thinks you're in your bedroom?" Nora asked.

Ivy nodded.

"Gram, do you mind pouring Ivy a cup of coffee? I'll be right back."

Ivy jumped to her feet. "Don't tell him I'm here."

But Nora was already halfway to the living room before Ivy had finished her plea. She grabbed her phone. She could see she'd already missed a text from Blaze, asking if she'd seen Ivy.

"Don't call him." Ivy surfaced at the doorway to the living room.

"Ivy, I have to. He's your legal guardian, and he needs to know where you are." She clutched her phone and walked over to the girl. "But I promise, I'll try to help with whatever it is you're going through."

Gram summoned Ivy back into the kitchen, and Nora called Blaze. He answered, his voice sounding as if he were on speaker phone.

"Hello, I got your text," she said. "Ivy's here."

"I'm on my way now. At around three in the morning I looked up from my work and went to check on her. I guess I had a hunch that something was off. Her bedroom was empty, so I checked her location on my phone. She was halfway to Florida. I've been following her route. I've got about four more hours or so. The traffic's picked up."

"Okay, well, take your time. She's here with us and safe. I'll let her get comfortable, and when you get here we'll figure out what to do next."

When she got off the call, Nora joined Ivy and Gram in the kitchen.

Ivy looked up from her mug apprehensively. "What did he say?"

"He's on his way."

"Ugh." Ivy slumped and rolled her eyes. "Why?"

"Because he cares about you."

"No, he doesn't," Ivy said through gritted teeth. "I'm just another task that he has to fit into his schedule."

"He worked in his office until three in the morning and then realized you were gone. He's been driving since then— I doubt very seriously he's slept at all. That doesn't sound like he's fitting you into his schedule. He cares about your wellbeing enough to risk his life driving on no sleep."

Ivy rolled her eyes.

"Did something prompt this?" Nora asked.

Ivy blew a breath of frustration through her lips. "He gave me a summer schedule, and every hour of every day was full. He's got me doing all this charity work and camps... He's trying to keep me busy. So I saved him the trouble and got out of his way."

"I think he's trying to entertain you and keep you out of trouble. He's doing the best he can at being a dad when he hasn't had a chance to do that until now."

"He had his chance, and he left my mom."

Gram fluttered her hands in the air. "Well, we're not going to solve this now, so we might as well have breakfast. Ivy, welcome to paradise. Do you like eggs and bacon?"

"Yeah."

"Great. Nora, do you mind cutting the watermelon and the cantaloupe? I'll get started on the eggs." She puttered over to the old radio from last night and flicked it on. "Oh, perfect. The Drifters."

Ivy and Nora looked at each other.

Gram shook her head with playful irritation. "You two don't know 'Save the Last Dance for Me'?" She did a little twirl. "Well, you're going to get an education today."

As the music played, Gram made more coffee and encouraged Ivy to help cook, asking her to be in charge of the bacon. Every now and again, when a song came on that Gram liked, she'd take Ivy's hands and give her a spin, making the girl laugh.

As they sat down at the porch table with their plates of food, Ivy said, "I doubt my dad would cook like that—dancing and all."

"Well, we'll just have to show him how," Gram said with a twinkle in her eye.

After breakfast, Nora got Ivy settled on the sofa inside the cottage. She'd driven all night, and her exhaustion had begun to show during breakfast. Before they could even clean up the dishes, the girl had fallen asleep. Nora and Gram spent the next thirty minutes hand-washing everything, drying the frying pans, and putting away the plates.

"There are a couple of beach chairs on the side of the porch. Let's go down to the water," Gram said when they'd gotten the little kitchen sparkling. "We can sit in the sun and read until Ivy's father arrives."

"Should we leave her?" Nora nodded toward the living room.

Gram laughed quietly. "She made it from Tennessee to Florida. I think she can manage a walk down the dune to find us."

"You're right." Nora picked up her novel from the kitchen table. "Let's do it."

They gathered up a beach umbrella and two chairs and headed down the wooden walk over the dune. Gram held Nora's novel while Nora speared the beach with the umbrella and kicked a pile of sand around the base to steady the pole in the coastal wind. Then they set up their chairs and took a seat. Nora dropped her cell phone in a small pocket on the side of the chair, opened her novel, and dug her feet beneath the soft, powdery sand, the surface heat giving way to the cool compact earth beneath the top layer. Her book pages fought the wind, and she held them by the far edges to keep them from flapping madly. The sun beamed down on her legs, wrapping them in a balmy cocoon as the water lapped quietly in front of them. It was the perfect weather for their first day of vacation. While their plans for today had taken a bit of a turn, it didn't matter what she did in this place—anything was soothing.

She scanned the words on the page in front of her, but their meaning wasn't going in, so she tipped her head back and closed her eyes. She was too busy fretting over Ivy to read. What had the girl been thinking, driving through multiple states, down long country roads in the middle of the night? Did she realize how dangerous that could be? Especially in her old car. So many awful things could have happened. If she'd gotten stuck on the side of the road, she'd have tried to call home and everyone would've been asleep —and that was only if she could have got cell service. She might have even tried to call Nora, but her phone had been in the living room all night.

Nora shuddered, sat up, and tried again to focus on her book. Ivy was fine, and Blaze was on his way. But what would happen when he got there? She'd certainly find herself working Blaze and Ivy through their issues instead of relaxing on the beach like she should be doing.

When she surfaced from her thoughts, Gram was staring at her, her lips pressed together.

"Don't say anything," Nora said with an exhale. "I know what you're probably thinking."

"I'm not the one doing all the thinking," Gram returned. "You've been twitching over there since we sat down."

"Hey," Ivy called as she came over the dune.

Nora twisted around in her chair. "I thought you were asleep."

Ivy stepped up to them, her pajama bottoms rolled up to her calves, her white feet nearly camouflaged in the bright sand. "My phone buzzed and woke me up. I tried to fall back asleep and couldn't." She sat down on the beach next to Nora. She took down her hair from its ponytail, slid the holder onto her wrist, and tucked the flyaway strands behind her ears.

"Sorry again for just showing up like this." She fanned out her feet, making an arc in the sand. "I didn't have any friends to call in Nashville. The few people who are nice to me all know who my dad is, and I don't know if they care about me or if they only like me because my dad's a celebrity." She offered up her usual eye roll.

"Why didn't you try to call me first? It didn't look like you tried."

Ivy shrugged. "I wanted to get out of the situation. There was nothing you could've said on the phone that would have kept me there. I'm not spending every single day doing busywork."

Gram closed her book. "Can you tell us the whole story? What happened exactly?"

"Dad told me he had a plan for my summer. He handed me a sheet of paper with a calendar on it. Every single minute of my day was set already, and he hadn't even asked me. I balled it up and threw it at him."

"Do you think your response helped him to understand your point of view?" Nora asked.

"Definitely. I thought his idea sucked. I made that pretty clear." Ivy turned toward the water with a frown.

"Did you stop to wonder why he might be offering you the calendar?"

"Yeah, I told you already. He wants me out of the way so he can keep going with whatever crap he feels like doing. I'm pretty sure he never wanted a family. He made that clear when he left my mom. And now he has to deal with me. He's all nice to you because you don't get in the way."

"He isn't kind to you?" Nora asked.

Ivy folded her arms. "He isn't nice *or* mean. Just absent."

Nora pursed her lips and nodded, trying to show her

support for Ivy, but she was sure the teen had the wrong idea about her dad. "Okay, so what if you're right and he doesn't know how to be a dad? There's no manual on parenting, you know. He has to figure it out. And you have to figure out how to be his daughter. It's new for both of you. What if the calendar was his attempt to show you he's trying? He had to put all that together and organize it for you."

Ivy's tight lips relaxed, and her gaze dropped to the sand. "What are you gonna tell my dad when he gets here?"

"I'm not planning to make any accusations. We'll just talk it out. But I'll need you to be open to sharing your side too."

"In the meantime," Gram cut in, "you're at the beach. Take this time and relax a little bit. Do you like to read?"

"Sometimes," Ivy replied.

"Did you bring a book?"

Ivy shook her head.

Gram picked up her novel and lifted herself out of the beach chair. "I brought a bunch. Want to come up to the cottage and sift through my pile, see if you like any of them?" Gram turned toward Nora. "If not, we've still got a couple of hours before her dad gets here. Maybe we can take her into town to find a book she likes." Gram gestured to Ivy to follow her back to the cottage, leaving Nora on her own.

Was Nora out of her league with Ivy? The girl clearly needed someone to help her through her impulsive and defiant behavior as well as her grief. Nora wasn't equipped to do that. Nor should she have to work on her vacation. But if she didn't, without a trusted counselor, Ivy could land in serious trouble this summer. She could turn to drugs, the wrong crowd, she might do something stupid and deface property, or who knows what else she could get into.

Nora's cell phone buzzed from the pocket on her chair. She pulled it out to find a text from Blaze.

> They've closed a large part of the road, and the backup is unbelievable. It's a parking lot. My navigation says I've got another four hours. See you for a late lunch. Hopefully.

Nora responded and told him to be safe. She set her phone on the arm of her chair, got up, and went down to the water. The cool surf bubbled around her toes. She waded in until she was ankle-deep and put her hands on her hips, her plans of window-shopping with Gram and then floating out on this sparkling water slipping away. What would the day bring? Whatever it brought, she doubted it would be relaxing.

CHAPTER SIXTEEN

After Blaze texted that he was only twenty minutes away, Nora and Ivy hosed off their feet before climbing the back steps of the cottage. Gram held the railing, following their lead. Ivy had chosen one of Gram's books to appease her, and the three of them had read on the beach. After a while, Nora had actually managed to slip into the story and had finally calmed down from the morning's events.

When they got inside, Nora tried to run a comb through her hair, but the salty air had given it the consistency of straw. She twisted it into a bun and powdered her nose. She'd just added a little lip gloss when she heard the grinding of tires against the gravel outside.

Ivy and Gram were in the kitchen, and Ivy didn't seem terribly antsy to greet her father, so Nora opened the door.

Blaze got out of the car. Dark circles shone under his eyes and a twenty-four-hour stubble left a shadow on his square jaw. The hem of his wrinkled T-shirt hiked up when he slipped his hands into the pockets of his jeans.

"Hey," he said from his car.

"Hi."

He pulled a duffel bag from the backseat, shut the car door, and bounded up the stairs to reach her. A scent of cotton and spice floated toward her on the wind. She swallowed.

"I'm so sorry for this." He shook his head. "I'm mortified."

"It's all right."

But was it? Seeing him was 'all right,' but she really shouldn't feel glad to see him for the reason that was floating around in her consciousness.

Thoughts seemed to lurk behind his eyes. He took his hands from his pockets and raised them into the air. "I should've brought something for you—coffee or… lunch—to say thank you for spending the morning with my unruly daughter."

His little comment made her smile. "I've got both inside if you'd like some."

"Thanks," he said. "She doing okay?" He nodded toward the house.

"Yeah, she seems to be enjoying herself. She's in the kitchen with my grandmother."

He held up his bag. "I figured, if she wants to stay, since we're already here, I could find us a place. Maybe a change of location could help us connect. There's nothing a little mini golf and beach go-karts can't solve."

"That's a great idea."

Nora let him inside, and he followed her to the kitchen. Gram and Ivy were elbow-deep in cold-cuts and vegetables, making lunch. Ivy's hands stilled when Blaze walked in. Gram stopped as well.

"Hello," Blaze said to Gram. "Blaze Ryman."

"June Jenkins." Her eyes widened at Nora when Blaze turned his attention to Ivy, and she put the back of her hand to her forehead as if she would pass out from his attractiveness.

Nora gave her grandmother a look of warning, but she couldn't fault Gram's initial impression.

Ivy stood silently, not making eye contact, as Blaze dropped his bag on the floor and moved toward her.

"Want to tell me why running away was a better option than coming to talk to me?" he asked, his voice gentle.

"I told you, I don't want to do your stupid summer plan."

"You didn't need to make a seven-hour drive and miss a night's sleep to make your point."

"You wouldn't have listened," Ivy countered.

Blaze took a step toward her. "How do you know?"

"Because Mom told me all the time how *great* your listening skills were." She spit the words at him, her defenses obviously up by the rise in her shoulders.

"Fair enough. I didn't listen to your mom. I didn't do a lot of things right."

Ivy folded her arms.

Nora braced for an argument, but to her surprise, Blaze remained calm, his stare soft.

"But there are two sides to every story," Blaze said.

Ivy remained quiet, yet that defiant pout was front and center.

"I know you must be hungry, Blaze," Gram said, evidently trying to ease the tension. "I'm slicing up some fresh bread from the market, and Ivy and I laid out a tray of meats, cheeses, and veggies. There's fresh fruit over there." She shook a finger at a glass serving bowl. "Please, get yourself a plate."

"I don't want to waste any more of your time," he said.

"Nonsense," Gram said. "We'd love to have you."

"I don't want to eat up all your groceries either. Let me order us all lunch at least."

Gram waved off his proposition. "I think we can part with a sandwich or two." She handed Blaze a plate.

"All right," he relented. "Thank you. This looks delicious."

Gram offered Ivy a plate too.

As Blaze and Ivy each made a sandwich, Nora walked around the small counter. Trying to be inconspicuous, she took in his disheveled appearance, his old jeans and uncombed hair.

She reached across to get herself a plate. Was their meager lunch up to his standards? He wasn't always rich, she reminded herself. But the recollection of a gleaming sculpture in the entryway of his mansion made her wonder if he remembered.

Gram suggested they eat on the back porch. When they all got outside, she flicked on the radio, more oldies playing. Blaze turned his ear toward the source of the song.

"Do you hear that?"

"Hear what? The song?" Nora asked, taking a seat next to Ivy.

"That drumbeat."

Nora mentally sifted through all the sounds until she found the *thump, thump, thump* underneath the melody. "Yes, I hear it."

"What do you notice about it?" he asked.

Nora peered up at the porch ceiling, trying to figure out what he might be getting at. "What should I notice about it?"

"This is a slower song, but the underlying beat—"

"Is faster," Ivy said, finishing his sentence.

Blaze's attention landed on his daughter, the corners of

his mouth lifting. "Exactly. Why do you think they did that?"

Ivy scooted her chair up to the table. "Because the song is about a guy who's gonna tell the girl of his dreams he loves her, and his heart is probably beating out of his chest. The drumbeat is his heartbeat."

"You two can hear all that?" Gram asked. "Because all I hear is the song."

Blaze laughed. "That's what you're supposed to hear, but your subconscious will internalize the drumbeat, and if you've ever felt the nerves that come with telling someone how you feel, your brain will recognize it."

"I've always liked this song," Gram said. "Maybe that's why. I was the one who told my husband I was in love with him first, so I definitely know that feeling."

"You told Gramps you loved him before he'd told you?" Nora asked, picking up her lemonade and taking a sip of the tart, sweet liquid.

Blaze leaned back in his chair, focused on Gram.

"He was leaving for the summer to work with a logging company in the Tennessee Smoky Mountains. We hadn't been dating very long, but I was head over heels for him. I told him it wasn't a good idea for him to go, and he asked why. I said, 'Because I'm in love with you, and I can't manage a whole summer without you.'" She looked out at the Gulf with a satisfied smile. "I was so young—a summer felt like an eternity."

"Did he go?" Ivy asked.

Gram turned her attention back to the table. "Nope. He worked at the local diner that summer instead, and by August he'd proposed." She picked up her sandwich. "The moral of that story is: always tell someone how you feel, even if it's just the beginning."

Blaze gave Nora a flickering glance before focusing on his sandwich and taking a bite.

Was that a look? Maybe not. Why would he have looked at her just then? Nora took a gulp of her lemonade in an attempt to cool the heat crawling through her cheeks for even imagining such a thing. She glanced back over, and when she did he was looking at her again. Her heart began to take on the same tempo as the song that had started all this.

"It's a beautiful day," Blaze said, turning his attention to the view. "The tide's gentle."

"It's a green-flag day all day," Gram said.

"Green-flag day?" Ivy asked.

"I saw it on the news. It's like the stoplights, I think. There's green for low hazard, yellow for 'use caution,' and red for dangerous conditions. There's also a purple one as well."

Ivy wrinkled her nose. "What's the purple one for?"

"Dangerous marine life." Gram widened her eyes in mock dismay.

"We've come all this way," Blaze said, stabbing a piece of cantaloupe with his fork, "we might as well get a hotel room and enjoy the beach for a few days. What do you say, Ivy?"

Ivy lit up. "Can we?"

"Sure. If you promise to hear me out about the summer," he replied.

Ivy chewed on her lip. "All right."

"Thanks." He squinted out at the water. "There's something about the coast that makes everything melt away, doesn't it?"

"My thoughts exactly," Nora agreed.

Maybe after lunch they could all take a walk down the

beach like she'd wanted to do. That might be just the thing Ivy and Blaze needed to relax enough to air out their differences. And she didn't mind having Blaze there. His presence brought a little excitement.

Blaze yawned. "I'm gonna head back in the house for a minute and reserve a hotel room. The effects of a missed night of sleep are catching up with me."

"Of course," Nora said.

Yes, certainly he was tired. And Ivy probably was too. Blaze excused himself and went into the cottage.

"Are *you* sleepy?" Nora asked Ivy.

Ivy frowned and shook her head. "Not really. I probably should be, but being here gives me energy. It makes me want to sit barefoot and write in my journal."

It was good Ivy had somewhere to express herself. "Did you bring it with you?"

"Yeah, it's in my bag."

"You should go get it and take it down on the beach for inspiration."

"I will." Ivy picked up her sandwich and took a bite, a satisfied look on her face. She seemed calmer whenever she was in Nora's care.

"What kinds of things do you write in your journal?" Gram asked. "Songs? Inner thoughts?"

Ivy tucked a pink strand of hair behind her ear. "Whatever's on my mind."

Gram picked up her glass of lemonade and caught a runaway drip of condensation with her finger. "I used to keep a journal when I was a young girl."

"You don't anymore?" Ivy asked.

"I probably should, but life got busy there for a while, and I just didn't feel as though I had the time. I was busy being a wife and raising Nora's dad." She set her drink down and leaned forward. "I used to write about my plans for my life in my journal, but after I married Nora's grandfather, I was too busy making those plans to write them down. They were coming faster than I could document them."

"Why do you think that is?" Nora asked.

"Because I was happy. I didn't need to plan because I was too busy living a life I loved."

Ivy leaned back in her chair. "You're lucky. We're not all that happy."

"I wasn't always that happy either," Gram said. "I've had my share of worries over the years. We all do—the struggle is part of life. It's how you handle the struggles that make or break you."

Ivy drew inward, eating her lunch silently as if mulling over Gram's point. Gram seemed to have the same knack at connecting with Ivy as Nora.

Nora reached over and turned up the radio, the songs filling the air above the screech of seagulls and the swish-swashing of the tide. The heat had hit its crescendo, but the coastal breeze fought against it, sending a cool wave of air toward them. The day was positively perfect.

Just as they'd finished their lunch Blaze returned.

"Sorry, I took a quick catnap. I drifted off after I tried to find us a hotel room. I can't find a single hotel that has a vacancy. They're all booked." He turned his wrist over to reveal a large timepiece that probably cost more than the cottage. "It's already almost four o'clock. We're looking at a seven-hour drive, at best, and neither of us have slept." He ran his fingers through his hair.

"We could go into town and try to find a store with a tent," Ivy said. "Or we could sleep in the car."

Blaze rubbed the stubble on his chin. "We might have to bite the bullet and drive home—"

Nora and Gram both interjected at the same time. "No."

Gram deferred to Nora.

"It isn't safe to drive exhausted," Nora said, "and you'll also get caught up in Sunday traffic with vacationers heading back home." She stood up and collected the dishes. Her teaching contract had a clause regarding favoritism, bias, and the teacher's ability to justly evaluate or treat the student, not to mention the school's ethics policies. If she didn't tread lightly, having Blaze and Nora vacationing with them could lead to disciplinary action or investigation by the school or district. But sending them both off while they were exhausted wasn't right either.

"We're going to have to," Blaze said, helping her with his plate and Ivy's.

Ivy gathered up everyone's empty glasses.

"You all have two cars," Nora said, stepping inside and leaving the door open as the others followed. "You won't even be able to keep each other awake on the trip. I wouldn't be able to live with myself if anything happened." She set the dishes on the counter and peered down the hallway. She was in a terrible position, but there was only one option. "You could always... stay with us."

Blaze's eyes rounded. "Two more people in this tiny cottage? We'd be underfoot."

"It's just for a night," Gram offered.

"I can stay in Gram's room," Nora said. "It has two twin beds and, Blaze, you can take my room. Ivy can sleep on the couch. Then, tomorrow, we can all go our separate ways."

"I hate to crash your vacation." Blaze put his hands in his pockets and hung his head. "Ivy had an idea: we could sleep in our cars. It wouldn't be the first time I've done it."

"It just doesn't seem right when we have enough beds,"

Nora said. "It really isn't a terrible imposition. We'll all be asleep, and no one will even know the difference."

"You sure?" Blaze asked.

"Yes," Nora said emphatically.

A flash of happiness sprung into Ivy's eyes, the edges of her lips turning upward.

"One night," Blaze reiterated, holding a finger up to his daughter.

Nora took the dishes over to the sink. "Well, that's settled. Blaze, I'm sure you're still exhausted. Would you two like to have a rest?"

"I'm not tired," Ivy said. "I'd like to spend time on the beach and maybe write in my journal."

"I'll go with you," Blaze offered.

Gram held out her hands in an inclusive gesture. "Let's all go."

Ivy eyed her father. His presence added an additional layer to the atmosphere.

"I brought a swimsuit and a change of clothes," Ivy said. "Can I get changed real fast?"

"Sure," Nora said. "I need to rinse off these dishes anyway. The bathroom's just down there." She pointed down the hall.

Ivy got her suitcase and took it to the bathroom.

Blaze walked over to Nora's side of the counter and pumped some soap into his hands. "I can help. I'll wash, you dry."

Gram ran a paper towel under the tap, her gaze on Nora and Blaze. "And I'll wipe down the table outside." She squeezed the excess water into the basin and then left them alone in the kitchen.

Nora handed Blaze her dish rag while she rooted around in the drawer for a tea towel. Flashes of him on his social media trying on that fur coat came to mind unprompted. Was he really going to handwash dishes in their modest sink?

He turned the spigot to hot and ran his finger through the stream of water until it began to steam up. He rinsed the plate, then added dish soap to his rag, and scrubbed as if washing dishes was the most natural thing in the world for him.

"Thank you for letting us stay tonight." He rinsed the dish and handed it to Nora.

"You're welcome."

As Blaze washed another dish, she dried the one in her hand and peered through the glass door at Gram. This trip had been her grandmother's dream, and it had been interrupted, delayed until Ivy and Blaze could get back on the road. While Gram didn't seem to mind them being here, and Nora was glad to see them, she did hate that it was at the expense of quality time with her grandmother. All Gram's organizing had probably been a result of her restless energy to get here, and now she'd have to wait to really enjoy her vacation.

Ivy came out of the bathroom in a black one-piece swimsuit and a pair of jean shorts that looked as if she'd cut them herself, and she had a leather-bound journal tucked under her arm. "Ready."

"We're almost done," Nora said just as Gram came inside.

"I can jump in to make the dishwashing go faster," Gram said.

Ivy set her journal on the counter. "I'll help too." Even though sleep deprived, Ivy had a glow about her, as if the beach had already worked its magic on her soul.

Nora opened the drawer with the dish towels and

handed Ivy one. "Help your dad wash and then I'll dry and, Gram, you can put them away."

"Sounds like a plan."

Gram took the dried dishes that Nora had stacked beside her and began returning them to cabinets. Then, she assumed her position next to Nora. In a few minutes, they'd worked as a team to wash all the dishes and put them away.

Blaze took off his shoes and socks, setting them by his bag in the living room. Nora focused on getting the beach chairs to avoid the sight of his ruggedly casual appearance. They all left through the back door and headed toward the beach.

The loose sand near the house gave Nora's calves a workout as they trudged down to the shore under an electric-blue sky. A sandpiper chased the retreating tide back to the rolling edge of the Gulf. Nora covered her eyes with her hand and peered down the beach. There wasn't a thing in either direction except the occasional cottage. The shore was perfectly serene. She dropped the chairs into the sand and Blaze began setting them up.

"Should we take a walk?" he asked.

"Oh, that would be lovely," Gram piped up. "Nora and I had planned to take one this morning and we didn't get around to it."

Ivy kicked the sand. "Sorry."

Gram stepped over to her. "For what, dear?"

"It's my fault you didn't take your walk."

Gram threw up her hands. "We were meant to walk with you it seems! Look at this beautiful day. Now you get to share it with us."

Ivy smiled, relief evident. She scratched down something in her journal as she walked, and Gram paced slowly beside her, offering small talk. The wind made it difficult to hear what she said, but her comment had made Ivy feel better, which made Nora happy. Ivy had seemed to be in a brighter mood after being there a while, and she didn't want to ruin that. Having lost her own parents, Nora understood how important those moments of distraction from the real world were.

Blaze stepped up beside Nora, and the two of them padded along the wet sand just at the edge of the surf. He stopped and picked up a seashell at the water's break, the hem of his jeans darkening as the tide splashed against it. He turned the shell over in the palm of his hand then skipped it across the water.

"I shouldn't be glad that Ivy ran away, but I am," he said.

"Why's that?" Nora held up the hem of her sundress.

"I haven't been to this area since high school. Back then, I spent most of my time either sleeping or doing things I shouldn't like getting into my dad's beer supply. I was a stupid kid."

"Doing stupid things is part of life, right?"

He shrugged. "We came every summer, and never once did I anticipate enjoying this." He opened his arms wide. "I was too busy thinking about the next party or who was coming over that night to see what was right in front of me."

"You were young."

"Yeah, but even as an adult, I miss things that are right in front of me."

He started walking again, and she fell in step beside him.

"I'm not happy unless I'm chasing something, and it's brought me great success, but in doing that, I lose sight of the rest. I missed Ivy's entire childhood."

He looked over his shoulder. Ivy's journal hung from

her fingertips by her side, and she and Gram were deep in conversation.

"I should've fought harder for them, but how? I didn't know how to be a husband or father. I had no clue how to balance the hours I was working with giving them what they needed. And I still struggle with Ivy. I want to do better for her, but nothing I do seems to work."

Nora took in the honesty in his gray eyes, the gold flecks showing in the shadow of a beard on his jaw. "I wish I could relate to your work ethic," she said. "But I don't know what it's like to have that level of passion for something. I'm just an average person with no big talents."

"You're definitely not an average person," he said.

"I beg to differ."

"You have a way with Ivy that I can't match. An average person can't reach her like you can."

Gram had mentioned Nora's ability to reach people as her talent as well, but she didn't feel it. Perhaps it was because she didn't necessarily have an ability to reach people—it was just Ivy. But what did that mean for her after Ivy's senior year next year? What would her job be like without the girl?

"Who lives there?" Ivy called, jogging up to them, pointing to the cottage down the beach from theirs.

"No idea." Nora shielded her eyes from the sun.

A boy who looked to be around Ivy's age was leaning on the railing of the deck, facing the water.

"Maybe another renter," Nora said.

Ivy held her hair back and turned her face toward the boy. He smiled and waved.

Ivy waved back. "Let's turn around and walk back. Want to?"

For the first time since Nora had known her, Ivy looked bashful.

"I could do with a break," Gram said.

They walked back, settled in the beach chairs, and put their toes in the water. Ivy opened the journal on her lap. She twisted around to view the cottage down the beach and then began to write. Gram settled in her chair, and Blaze leaned back in his and closed his eyes. Nora continued to ruminate over how she hadn't done anything extraordinary in her life. Blaze might not have it all together, but at least he'd followed his passion. She didn't even know what she wanted to do if she did follow her heart.

Gram leaned over and chatted with Ivy about a song the girl was writing in her journal. The two discussed ideas and came up with rhymes, but the coastal wind made it hard for Nora to follow. Blaze, who still hadn't had more than a catnap, dozed off. Pretending to be listening to Gram and Ivy, Nora stole glances at him. His face was peaceful, that smile of his relaxed. The wind blew his hair back and forth.

The boy from the other cottage came down on the beach, pulling Ivy's attention from Gram. She closed her journal.

"I'm going to take another walk," Ivy said, getting up and brushing the sand off her bottom. She set the journal in her chair.

Blaze opened one eye but didn't stop her.

Ivy paced down to the boy and stopped, the two teens talking in the distance. They spoke for a while before she raised a hand in goodbye and headed back over.

"Meet a friend?" Nora asked when she'd returned.

"He's here for the week. His name's Jake." She looked back down the beach, her curiosity clear. "He seems nice. He was walking down to introduce himself."

Blaze roused and cleared his throat, sending a fatherly glance the boy's way.

Ivy eyed her father and then shook her head.

Seeming to notice his daughter's response, he changed the subject. "Should we call in some dinner?"

"That sounds like a great idea," Gram said as she hoisted herself out of her chair. She snapped it flat.

Nora followed.

"Can we get pizza delivered?" Ivy asked.

Blaze got up and closed his chair, slipping it over his arm by the built-in carrying strap. "At the beach? Why don't we order seafood from one of the local restaurants?"

Ivy's mood was delicate, as evidenced by the frown that had already slid back into place. Nora didn't necessarily want pizza, but the goal was to keep Ivy in good spirits so the teen and her father could rest up and head back home where their family counselor could manage the situation better.

"I could do pizza," Nora said.

Ivy threw out her knuckles and Nora gave her a fist bump.

"Pizza sounds good to me," Gram agreed. "We've got piña colada mix. Anything goes with that."

"All right, fine," Blaze said. "We'll get pizza. But if we do, I'm taking everyone out for breakfast tomorrow morning. The least I can do is treat you to say thank you."

"It's a deal," Gram said.

They stacked the chairs by the porch and rinsed off their feet before retreating to the cottage to order dinner. Gram immediately washed her hands and set in making everyone piña coladas. She even made a mix-only version for Ivy. Nora lit a few candles and set them out on the porch, and they settled at the table outside.

The pizza came, and Gram topped off their drinks as Blaze helped Nora divvy up slices. Gram whispered something to Ivy, making the girl laugh, and Blaze shimmied around Nora to hand his daughter some pizza. Anyone looking on would think they were a regular family, there for a vacation. And Nora had to admit she was enjoying having them there.

LATER THAT NIGHT, Ivy had plopped onto the sofa with her phone and fallen asleep, and Gram had retired to her room. Blaze and Nora were out on the porch swing, one final piña colada in hand. Stars filled the darkening sky as the final remnant of sun cast a light blue glow on the horizon. The humidity was replaced by a cool breeze, and the white sand nearly glowed in the moonlight.

"It's like the world stops when you're out here," Blaze said, leaning back in the swing, his long legs moving them gently in time with the lapping of the waves. "I haven't even thought about anything back home."

"I know what you mean."

They sat next to one another, his spicy scent wafting over to her on the wind. As he rocked the swing, the side of his thigh brushed her knee, sending tingles through her limbs. He scooted his leg away and grinned at her before taking a drink of his cocktail.

Nora now felt comfortable with him there, but also off-kilter because he was so personable. She wasn't quite sure how to define the feeling he gave her; she just knew her other students' parents didn't evoke that response in her.

"Sorry again for crashing your summer vacation," he said, his cheeks pink from the alcohol.

"I'm really not all that disappointed that you did, honestly."

He met her gaze, questions in those stormy eyes.

"It's been nice to have you all here. And I'll help you and Ivy in any way I can."

They fell into silence as they finished their drinks to the song of the waves. Blaze's eyes seemed to become heavy, and he closed them before stretching.

"I'm going to have to crash," he said, with a yawn. "I got a second wind earlier, but I'm going down."

"I can't believe you stayed up as long as you have."

He stood and Nora hopped off the porch swing as well. As he looked down at her, she was keenly aware it was just the two of them out there.

She swallowed. "Let me show you your room."

On their way, Blaze stopped in the kitchen. He took his glass and her drink from the counter where she'd set it and rinsed them in the sink. He added some dish soap and washed the glasses. She wanted to find something interesting to say, but him standing there, barefoot and washing dishes, had dissolved all rational thought. She shouldn't have had rum in the last two drinks…

While offering Blaze and Ivy a place to stay had seemed a fine idea earlier, now that it was quiet and just the two of them were awake, the situation felt very different, personal. Perhaps it was all in her head.

To avoid the situation, she went in and checked on Ivy. She covered her up with a blanket from the edge of the sofa and then lingered in the living room for a tick until the water turned off in the kitchen.

"You didn't have to wash the glasses," she said after she returned to the room.

"I'm earning my keep."

The glitter of humor in his eyes was intoxicating, so she focused on the task at hand, leading Blaze down the short hallway to the room where she'd slept last night. At least she'd made the bed.

"Here you go." She went into the room and pointed to the adjoining bathroom. "There are towels under the sink."

"Thank you."

As she turned to leave, he lightly tapped her bare shoulder, his touch stealing her breath.

"Good night."

She forced out a response. "Good night. See you in the morning."

On her way out, she squeezed her eyes shut and took in a deep breath to try to clear her head as she let herself into Gram's dark room, her heart pattering.

Gram was already asleep, so Nora clicked on the small bedside light to find her way to the en-suite bathroom to wash up. When she crossed the room, a piece of paper with obvious letterhead peeked out between the pages of Gram's book on her bedside table. Quietly, Nora padded over to it, opened the book, and squinted to make out what the paper was. It looked as if it might be a hospital letterhead, but the words were blurred in the dark. Probably just a full-page receipt from her appointment the other day that she was using as a bookmark.

She smiled at her sleeping grandmother. That would be just like her to repurpose an old sheet of paper instead of buy a bookmark. She never spent any money on herself. This trip was the first time she'd done anything like that. Nora made a mental note to surprise her with a beachy bookmark. She'd sneakily get one when they went shopping in town.

CHAPTER SEVENTEEN

The hearty aroma of freshly brewed coffee tickled Nora's nose, rousing her from sleep. She opened her eyes to bright sunlight streaming through the window. Gram's bed was empty. Nora pushed the blankets off her legs and got out of bed. She padded into the bathroom, brushed her teeth, washed her face, and drew a comb through her hair. Then, she put on some powder and lip gloss and slipped on a pair of shorts and a T-shirt.

When she went into the kitchen, Gram was sitting solo at the table with a cup of coffee and her novel.

"Morning."

Gram looked up from her book. "Good morning."

"You the only one up?"

"Ivy just went out on the porch. I told her I'd join her after my coffee."

Nora nodded and stretched her arms over her head. She moved to the coffeemaker and poured herself a mug, then took it outside to say good morning to Ivy.

The girl was at the table, bent over her journal, her pen

moving a mile a minute, a glass of orange juice and her phone beside her.

"Whatcha doing?" Nora asked, taking a seat.

Ivy looked up. "Finishing the song I was writing."

"It seems you've picked up the pace with your songwriting. Have you written more recently?"

Ivy shrugged.

"You seem to enjoy it."

Ivy didn't answer.

Nora wrapped her hands around her mug. "Are you okay?"

"Sure." Ivy went back to writing a line, but then scratched it out.

"I wonder what time you and your dad are taking off today," Nora said. "We probably have time for breakfast out like your dad suggested. That might be nice."

"Oh, I'm not going home with him."

Nora blinked. "What?"

"I thought about it all night, and I'm tired of making excuses for him."

"What do you mean?"

Ivy rolled her eyes. "Never mind. You'll just give me some mumbo jumbo about how I need to listen to him and do what he says."

"What do you mean by 'making excuses for him'?" Nora scooted her coffee out of the way and leaned into Ivy's space to get her attention. "Tell me. I'll try to help."

"I didn't give you the full story of why I ran away."

Nora waited for her to divulge whatever was bothering her.

With a sigh, Ivy picked up her phone and opened one of her social media apps. She scrolled for a few seconds until she got to a video of a young guy. She turned the phone around for Nora to view it.

"Who's that?"

"Alex Byron, lead singer of Phiz. A new pop band."

Nora pursed her lips. "I don't understand. What does this have to do with why you ran away?"

Ivy hit play on the video and slid the phone over to Nora.

"Tell me, who is the most influential person in your life?" the interviewer asked.

The young man leaned back in his chair with a smirk on his handsome face, and brushed his golden hair out of his eyes. "Definitely my producer, Blaze Ryman."

"Really? Why's that?" the interviewer asked.

"No matter what's going on, he stops everything to help. He gives me the best advice. He's like a father to me."

The clip ended. Ivy reached over and snatched her phone.

"I saw it before I left home that night." She clicked off the screen. "I ran away because I was angry that Dad puts so much effort into his musicians, but he'd rather send me away to camps and activities all summer."

Nora could understand why that video would hit a nerve.

Ivy stared at her journal. "I've been trying to write music to win him over, but I shouldn't have to do that."

Nora's heart sank for the girl. Didn't Ivy enjoy songwriting? Was she truly only writing music to find common ground with Blaze?

"Why are you still writing music this morning, then?"

"I'm trying to reach him, to make him want me. Because he never has."

Nora folded her hands, unable to drink her coffee under

the weight of Ivy's admission. "I think you need to tell your dad all this."

Ivy's mouth dropped open. "Are you kidding? No way." She closed her journal. "Sorry I said anything. Let's just drop it."

"Why don't you want to open up to your dad?"

"Because I don't want him to have to try. I want our relationship to be as easy as it is with him and Alex Byron. So can we let it go, please?" She stood up. "Your coffee's probably getting cold. And I'd love a cup. Let's go inside."

When they entered the kitchen, Gram had a look on her face that let Nora know she'd overheard their conversation through the screen door. She sent an empathetic nod over to Ivy as the girl poured herself a mug of coffee. Nora shook her head, having no idea what to do.

"Good morning," Blaze said, coming into the kitchen in his wrinkled T-shirt and jeans from yesterday, his disheveled hair and thick stubble oddly attractive.

"Morning," Nora said. "I was just going to make some more coffee. Would you like one?"

"I'm happy to make it," he said, joining his daughter. "Don't work on my account. Please, relax." He gestured toward the table.

Nora lowered herself across from Gram.

"Hey, squirt," he said, coming up beside Ivy and pouring himself a mug of coffee.

Ivy cut her eyes at him. "Squirt? Really?"

"I was just being funny. Did you wake up on the wrong side of the sofa?"

Ivy pouted and took her coffee to the table, as she mumbled, "He's got jokes this morning." She dipped her head and scrolled on her phone.

"I'd like to make good on my offer to take everyone out

to breakfast," he said, sitting next to Nora. "I'm thinking we could all go out, and then Ivy and I could head home after."

Ivy looked up from her phone.

"You don't have to rush off," Gram said, giving Nora a wink. "You both drove all the way to Florida. Why don't you two stay for a few days. We have plenty of room."

Nora held her breath. If they stayed, she'd be in a terrible position. Didn't Gram realize that? Not only would she be riding the professional line longer than expected, but their staying would infringe on Nora and Gram's vacation. This trip had been Gram's doing, and Nora wanted her to have every chance to enjoy it.

"I'm sure they need to get back to their lives, Gram," Nora said.

But Ivy's face lit up like a Christmas tree. "Please, Dad. Can we stay?"

"We don't want to be an imposition," Blaze said. "Ms. Jenkins is trying to have a vacation, and we're in the way."

"Your father is just being polite, which I do applaud," Gram said. "We'd love to have a little excitement around here."

Nora might have to assign Ivy to a new counselor next year to avoid any conflict of interest, but the look on the girl's face and Gram's insistence that they stay was making her question her resolve. Even if Ivy had a different school counselor, Nora would still be able to see her and offer advice if Ivy asked for it. And while they were at the cottage, they could be professional.

She cut in. "Blaze, could I talk to you out on the porch for a minute?"

Ivy's eyes widened, and she sat straight up in her chair, but Nora offered her a look and discreetly shook her head to let the girl know she wouldn't mention Ivy's earlier admission to Blaze.

Blaze followed Nora. She shut the main door to keep their voices from filtering into the kitchen.

"This week could be an opportunity for you and Ivy to be together with nothing in the way. We're here for two weeks. You can stay one and then my grandmother and I will still have a week to ourselves."

Blaze cocked his head to the side. "You want your work to spill over into your vacation?"

"Helping the two of you doesn't feel like work."

He stared at her, looking as if he was trying to make up his mind. "If I say yes, you have to let me do something to say thank you. I'll buy meals, take us out for excursions—whatever you want. I can also pay you for a portion of the rental. It's the least I can do."

"Well, Gram took care of the rental, so paying for the cottage is between you and her, but I'll take you up on the rest."

He broke into a smile. "Done."

Just then, Ivy opened the door and poked out her head. "Are y'all done talking about stuff? I'm starving."

"Let's all get ready for breakfast," Blaze said. "Ivy, do you have enough clothes for the week, or do we need to take you shopping?"

A plume of excitement visibly rose within Ivy. "We're staying for a *week*?"

"It looks like it."

Ivy squealed and ran back inside.

"I guess it's official," Blaze said. "You can't seem to get rid of us."

As much as she told herself otherwise, Nora was perfectly fine with that.

CHAPTER EIGHTEEN

At breakfast, Ivy ran into Jake, the boy from the next cottage down, on the sidewalk in front of the shops, and the two of them spent most of the meal chatting. After, they decided to walk around the village together.

"You have my credit card on your phone?" Blaze asked Ivy.

"Yeah."

"Get yourself something special."

"Okay," she said. "Thanks."

"I'm full as a beached whale," Gram said, patting her belly. "Breakfast took it out of me. Think we could swing by the cottage and drop me off for a rest?"

Blaze peered down the sidewalk at Ivy, who'd tucked her baggy shirt into her shorts and checked herself out in the reflection of one of the shop windows. Jake said something to her. She turned toward him and laughed.

"I'd like to stay in town and shop," Nora said. "I could be available for Ivy while you take Gram back to the cottage." This would be the perfect opportunity to get Gram that new bookmark.

"All right," Blaze said. "Be right back." He offered an arm to Gram.

Gram took Blaze by the bicep, and they walked toward his car while Nora popped into a nearby shop.

The door bells of the beach boutique jingled when Nora entered. She perused the whitewashed wood tables full of cups, mugs, towels, and other souvenirs in pastels and bright pinks. She picked up a set of coasters with hand-painted sand dollars and set them back down. Then she flicked through the stack of coffee-table books about the villages along the Gulf Coast.

She browsed the many wares before stumbling upon a display of book-themed items and admired a quilted book-sized bag in the turquoise and deep blues of the water. It was so lovely that she decided the splurge was worth it to surprise Gram. She also found an array of bookmarks, so there was sure to be one that would be perfect. She thumbed through a few with landscapes of sea grass, the white sandy beaches, and the signature stripes of the Gulf before finding one with a watercolor of a pink beach umbrella and two white Adirondack chairs. She could almost imagine sitting there with Gram.

She plucked the bookmark from the others and went up to the cashier to pay. The woman slipped her items into a shopping bag and topped them with tissue paper that was almost too pretty not to keep. Buying a gift for Gram made her feel festive. What would her vacation have looked like so far if Ivy hadn't shown up? Nora and Gram would have taken their walk on the beach and probably popped into a few shops before Gram got tired and wanted to return to the cottage. Funny, they'd still done the same things, just with more people along. She didn't mind having them there.

It was actually kind of nice. She just hoped Gram felt the same.

Feeling productive, Nora stepped out into the sunshine. Strolling tourists and others on brightly colored beach cruisers dotted the sidewalks. The scent of salt and savory dishes from the outdoor grills filled the air. The relaxed and happy atmosphere grabbed hold of Nora. She walked along the sidewalk, the gift bag swinging in her hand. Her breakup with Carson and her year at school seemed like a lifetime away. She couldn't imagine a better way to start her summer.

A little while later, after lots of window-shopping, Nora's phone pinged with a text from Blaze, telling her he was stopping by a beach shop at the end of the village to pick up Ivy and then he could come get Nora and drive her to her car if she told him where to meet her. She texted back with her location, and he said he'd be there as soon as he could.

It was a beautiful day, and she could easily walk to her car, but taking a ride with Blaze was something she might not ever get to do in her lifetime. How many famous producers asked to give her a ride in their Maserati?

While she waited, she walked across the street to the ice-cream shop with the pink-and-white-striped awnings and a line of color-coordinated Adirondack chairs under it, keeping one eye out for Blaze's car. She popped inside to take a peek at the offerings. As she considered the flavor selection and wall of topping options, Blaze's voice at her ear made her jump.

"Anything good?"

She turned around with a gasp.

"Sorry," he said. "I didn't mean to startle you."

"You were quick," she said, trying to still her pattering heart. "Where's Ivy?"

"She texted that Jake's taking her back to the cottage."

"Does she know Jake well enough to let him drive her back?"

"No, but I can see where she is on my app, and she's already almost home. I'm going to talk to her about jumping in a car with someone without asking, but I doubt it'll go over well, since she was willing to drive through multiple states on her own. I'm sure she thinks she can handle herself." He peered down at his phone. "Looks like she made it."

"I'll text Gram to let her know." Nora fired off a quick message.

Nora's phone pinged immediately with a return text. "Gram says Jake and Ivy are with her." She "loved" the comment and slipped her phone into her back pocket.

"Wanna get some ice cream?" he asked. "It's on me. Part of my promise if you let us stay." He flashed that grin of his.

"All right." She waved a hand at the wall of toppings. "The offerings are a little overwhelming, wouldn't you say?"

"Definitely." He held up a finger and walked over to the cashier, who'd already noticed him. Did she know who he was? "Excuse me. What's your bestselling ice cream?"

The young girl looked around as if to make sure he was actually speaking to her. Then she responded with, "The Crashmasher." She pointed to the word written in curly script on the menu. "It's big enough for two."

"Want to share it?" Blaze asked.

Sharing ice cream with the parent of a student wasn't really in Nora's job description, but Blaze's charm was chipping away at her determination to keep things all business.

Oh, what the heck. She was on vacation after all, and it was just ice cream.

"Okay."

Blaze paid for the order, and they got a table. The girl behind the counter was typing madly on her phone. She definitely recognized him. When they called his name, the girl at the counter beckoned him over, showing him her phone. Then she offered him a napkin and a pen, and Blazed signed his name while the other worker with their order chattered on.

Nora gasped when he turned around with their treat.

"How are we going to eat that?" she asked, as he set down the fishbowl-sized ice-cream concoction.

"I have no idea."

"Did the girl at the counter recognize you?" she asked, pulling a napkin from the small box-holder on the table.

"Yeah. She's a fan of the new country singer Micky Lawson, and she saw me in his stories."

He handed her a spoon and then waved over one of the staff. "Can you tell me what's in this exactly?"

The girl hurried over excitedly. She pointed to the bottom filling. "That's a layer of our toffee cake, a play on 'coffee cake,' but instead of the cinnamon topping, it has toffee bits." Her bright pink nail moved to the second layer. "And this is our signature bourbon-vanilla ice cream with mini peanut-butter cups."

Blaze playfully bit his knuckle in fear over the glass trough of a bowl, making Nora laugh.

"On top of that," the girl continued, "you have three layers: crushed toffee, caramel, and chocolate crumble. It's all crowned with butter-cream ice cream, whipped cream, and edible gold sprinkles."

"Thank you," Blaze said.

"No problem." The girl went back to wiping down tables and snickering with her friend behind the counter.

He pulled out his phone. "Speaking of stories, I should take a video of this and put it on mine. I'm lacking content at the moment. People are going to wonder if I've been kidnapped." He gave her a wink. Tipping the bowl toward him, he took a close-up of the giant sundae with the window behind it, blurred palm trees in the background. Then he held up the screen so Nora could see. He posted the clip with the caption: *Currently out of office.*

"This dessert is quite an unexpected adventure," Nora said, digging her spoon into the sugary decadence and taking a bite.

He flashed a devious grin. "We all have to live out of our comfort zone every now and again, right? When I go to the gym, my trainer says, 'Don't lift weights for you. Lift weights for yourself in twenty years. He'll thank you.'"

She savored the creamy chocolate flavor of the first bite, then said, "I will definitely have to test my limits, for the sake of my future self." She scooped another bite.

"If you really want to test your limits, I saw something on the way to meet you that might be fun."

She licked a drip of vanilla off the back of her spoon. "What was it?"

"I really want to do it while I'm here, but I don't want to do it by myself."

She stared at his handsome face, wondering what he was up to. "What is it?" she asked again.

"Trust me and face your fears?" he said.

"I should be fearful of whatever it is?" She dipped her spoon back into the bowl, careful to stay on her side of the ice cream.

"Nah. But I think you're fearful of surprise."

Why would she be fearful of surprise? What about her outward persona had made him think that? Did she appear on the outside as predictable as she felt on the inside? That, in itself, was terrifying.

"Fine. I'm cool with surprises."

"Great." He sat back with a satisfied look.

"How long will we be? I'll let my grandmother know."

He got back on his phone. "Let me check…" He typed a few things, scrolled, and typed some more.

She leaned over to see what he was doing, and he pulled the phone out of her view. "No, no. It's a surprise, right?" He worked on the phone a bit more. "There. Got us tickets, and we need to be there by noon. It'll take about two hours. I'll text Ivy to ask if she wants to go with us," he said, typing again on his phone.

He got a response right away. "She said she'd rather stay with Jake." He pursed his lips. "I'm going to need to spend some time with this kid. He's becoming a regular fixture. I'm asking if Jake wants to go too. The more the merrier."

Nora dipped her spoon into the ice cream and lifted another sweet bite. What was Blaze up to?

His phone pinged again. "Ivy said they don't want to go, so it's just you and me."

Nora's curiosity was definitely piqued. She texted Gram that she and Blaze would be out until a little after two, and to let her know if she needed anything.

Gram texted back:

> I couldn't be happier. Enjoy yourself. Ivy, Jake, and I are on the beach.

Blaze offered to drive to their mysterious location, so after they ate as much ice cream as they could manage, they walked to his Maserati. She'd never been in a car that nice before. The headrests of the leather seats were embroidered with the car's logo, for goodness' sake. He revved the engine and pulled out of the parking spot. She couldn't feel a single bump on the smooth ride to their destination.

He pulled to a stop at a brightly painted hut about fifteen minutes down the road.

"Bike rentals? Are we taking a bike ride?"

Blaze threw his head back and hooted. "A two-hour bike rental is not my idea of getting us out of our comfort zone. Give me a little credit."

"But we're going in there?" She pointed to the yellow-and-orange bike-rental office.

"Yep."

She tucked Gram's gift into the floorboards, got out of the car, and they strode up to the bike shop. Blaze opened the door, and they went inside.

The man behind the desk greeted Blaze. "You must be Mr. Ryman, here for your twelve o'clock adventure for two."

"Yes, sir."

"Excellent. I'll get the captain, and we'll have you on your way in just a second." The man disappeared into a back room.

"Adventure?" Nora asked, a little nervous suddenly. "Adventure" could be underwater shark diving or something similar.

"Don't worry. You're safe with me." He produced an evil laugh, his humor breaking her slight apprehension.

What could be the worst that would happen at a bike-rental place? There weren't any cliffs around or anything. He'd said they weren't biking. Was he kidding? If they were biking, it would be down the beach and back, most likely. But the clerk had said "captain." Maybe they were taking a boat ride. Given that the Gulf was incredibly calm, that might be nice.

"All right, Mr. Ryman," the man said, walking through the small room. "If you two could follow me."

They walked out the back of the building where a boat bobbed against the dock. A portly man with tanned skin and a younger man with sunglasses and bare feet headed toward them, carrying two life vests.

Yes. A boat ride! How wonderful.

"My name is Captain Jimmy, and this is my assistant, Randall. We'll be driving your boat."

"Blaze." He reached out and shook Captain Jimmy's hand and then Randall's. "And this is Nora."

"Hello," Nora said.

"Ladies first." Randall handed Nora a life vest. "You'll want to tighten it so it's snug. I don't anticipate you getting in the water today, but in case of emergency, we want your vest fitting well."

As she clipped the buckles, Captain Jimmy reached over and tugged the straps, tightening them before handing the other vest to Blaze. Randall left them and took a seat at the wheel of the boat.

"Hop aboard, and I'll get you fitted."

Fitted?

Blaze stepped onto the boat deck and reached out his hand to Nora. She took it to steady herself as she climbed on. He peered down at her and smiled as he let go.

"All right," Captain Jimmy said, grabbing a wide set of straps all woven together. "Nora, we'll get your harness on first."

She turned to Blaze who gave her an encouraging nod.

Captain Jimmy patted the cushioned bench. "Have a seat right here, and I'll have you step into it."

Nora complied, wondering what she was stepping into, both figuratively and literally.

Captain Jimmy laid the strap on the floor of the boat and asked her to put her feet in the openings. Then he slipped it up to her calves. "Now you can stand up and shimmy it into place."

He helped her slip the harness up to her hips and then asked her to sit back down. "I'll thread this strap through your life vest to get you all secured. Then we'll work on your hubby."

"Oh, he's—"

Captain Jimmy yanked the harness, tightening it and causing her to lose her breath, although she wasn't sure if she'd already stopped breathing when he'd said Blaze was her husband. Couldn't the man tell they weren't together? She peered over at Blaze, who was grinning at her, clearly amused. His chiseled jaw and straight, white, perfect teeth, those gray eyes—she swallowed and focused on the belts around her body.

Captain Jimmy held a belt from her harness. "Once you're up in the air, this strap will be like this." He lifted it. "Feel free to relax and hang on to this if you want to."

"We're going in the air?"

Captain Jimmy's bushy brows pulled together. "That's usually how parasailing works."

Parasailing?

"How high are we going?" she asked as the captain assisted Blaze with his harness.

"About 300 feet in the air. It doesn't sound like much, but with the right wind, you can see the curvature of the earth."

He said it as if seeing the roundness of the planet was a good thing. Other than in the safe confines of an airplane,

Nora's feet had never left the ground. Her mouth dried out. She was about to dangle from a few straps hundreds of feet in the air?

Blaze's sudden warm grip on her hand yanked her attention away from her fear of heights. Now she was worried about that invisible personal-work line she'd been trying so hard to keep drawn between them. She'd shared an ice cream and now she was clasping the hand of her student's father.

His breath at her ear, he said, "Don't worry. We'll do it together."

Get fired?

"Let's get you two in the chute and ready to fly," Captain Jimmy said.

Nora's knees wobbled as she walked to the back of the boat, and Blaze tightened his hold on her hand.

"Have you ever done this before?" she asked, unable to let go of him.

"Nope."

Captain Jimmy yanked on a tether at the back of the boat, and a multicolored parachute plumed out over the water. "Come on up and I'll clip you in."

They stepped up on the platform at the back of the boat, and the captain helped them get into position. Then he asked them to lean back, and he adjusted their seat. Nora's fingers trembled slightly, and her heart pounded as she held on to the straps. Captain Jimmy directed them to sit and stretch their legs out straight just as Randall fired up the boat engines.

As the boat moved, the parachute filled with air. Nora and Blaze lifted slightly off the platform as if they were in two backyard swings. Then, when the boat gained speed, *whoosh*, her stomach dropped, and they sailed into the air. Nora laughed at the feeling despite her trepidation.

"This is incredible," Blaze said, while they floated higher and higher.

Nora's whole body shook, their feet dangling high above the earth, the boat getting smaller under them, but a wave of exhilaration also filled her, and she couldn't stop smiling. It was terrifying and thrilling in equal measure.

She had a view of the entire horizon from up there. She could see all the way down to the high-rises of Panama City Beach, miles away. The wind whipped around them. Was this how birds felt?

"Look!" Blaze pointed down to the deep-blue water beneath them.

Two dolphins arced in unison above the water.

Nora gasped and then reached over him to point out two more.

He turned his head toward her, uniting with her in the excitement, and locked into her gaze. They shared a moment of solidarity, both experiencing this magnificent feeling together. He wrinkled his nose playfully as if he'd guessed they were thinking the same thing.

Never, in a million years, had she thought she'd have this much fun on her vacation. And, as crazy as it sounded, she owed it all to Blaze and Ivy.

CHAPTER NINETEEN

When they arrived at the cottage, Gram and Ivy were on the porch swing, reading. To Nora's surprise, Ivy was wearing a simple linen sundress. She'd pulled her hair back, and with the brown roots that had grown out around her face, she almost looked like a different child.

"Did you get a new dress?" Blaze asked.

Gram looked up from her book and bobbed her eyebrows happily, clearly as surprised by Ivy's choice as they were.

"Yeah. I used to wear dresses sometimes, and I was admiring it in the beach shop. Jake noticed me looking at it. I said I hadn't worn a dress like this in a long time. He told me he thought it would look good on me."

"He's a smart cookie," Nora said. "He was right."

"Where were y'all?" Ivy asked.

Nora plopped down at the outdoor table. "Parasailing." She gave Blaze a conspiratorial grin.

"You got my dad to parasail?" Ivy asked.

"It was his idea," Nora countered.

Ivy's eyes rounded. "Living on the edge, Dad?"

Blaze chuckled, sitting down next to Nora. "Exactly. Speaking of living on the edge, you might want to consider that you don't know Jake very well. You shouldn't have ridden home with him before you knew him better."

While Blaze's comment seemed generally lighthearted, it clearly hit a nerve for Ivy.

"You don't trust my judgment?" Ivy asked.

"You don't know him. You might have asked my thoughts on the matter before you took off with him."

"You haven't been there to tell me what to do my whole life, and you want to start now? I had to take care of myself while Mom worked, and she trusted me to do that. You haven't trusted me once."

Gram turned her book over in her lap.

"That's not true. I trust you," Blaze said.

"So much that you want to fill every hour of my summer with something so I'm not left to my own choices?"

"I was trying to keep you from being bored."

Ivy crossed her arms. "You were not. You were trying to keep me from doing something I shouldn't."

"Why do you think that?" he asked. "*Were* you planning to do something you shouldn't?"

"See? You assume it!"

"Ivy, I only asked because you brought up the subject."

Nora interjected, "Hang on, hang on. Before things get heated, let's—"

"No!" Ivy tossed her book to the side and got up from the swing, the thing nearly rocking Gram right off.

Gram grabbed the ropes and steadied the bench with her feet.

"It's already heated," Ivy said, tears brimming in her eyes. "This is why I came here to get away from you. You don't treat me like a person. You treat me like a kid."

Blaze raised his arms, looking helpless. "You *are* a kid."

"I'm going to be eighteen by the end of the summer. And I've been on my own since I was little. I'm practically an adult. But I'm forced to go to this stupid school and follow everyone's rules when I'm fine on my own."

Ivy angrily wiped a tear with her wrist, her lip quivering. "You don't even know your own daughter! Mom did! I miss Mom!" She bounded down the stairs, over the dune, and out to the sand, where she sat down and hugged her knees over the balloon of her dress.

"What am I supposed to do with that?" Blaze asked.

Nora knew what it felt like to lose her mother. Her heart ached for Ivy. "She's got a lot of pent-up grief, and by the sound of things it seems she might not have had a lot of limits living with her mother. I'm sure Candace had to work quite a bit as a single mom."

"That was her choice. She wouldn't take my money."

"I know, but now Ivy has to navigate the effects of that choice. We're going to have to tread lightly around her. She's hurting."

He got up and stretched his arms across the railing, peering out at his daughter. "I want to help her and parent her, but she won't let me. How am I supposed to be her dad when she blows up any time I ask for a bit of compliance?" He shook his head, his gaze on his daughter. "Should I go down and try to talk to her?"

"You could," Nora said, "but I wonder if the message might be better received from an innocent third party. I could try."

"Okay." He stepped back and folded his arms. "I'll stay up here." He turned to Gram. "You can fill me in on this Jake kid."

Nora walked down to the beach and sat next to Ivy. Tears streamed down the girl's face, her eyes red.

"I'm sorry you've been thrust into this whole new place. You didn't ask for any of it," Nora said.

Ivy sniffled, her bottom lip still quivering.

"And you must miss your mom terribly."

All the strength left Ivy's face. She crumpled against Nora's shoulder and sobbed. Nora put her arm around the girl and squeezed her tightly.

"I don't know how to be this new person," she whimpered.

"You don't have to be a new person. You just have to find your way in different surroundings."

"I don't want to live with him," she cried. "Mom never had anything good to say about him, and I trust her more than anyone."

"I understand, but as your dad said, there are two sides to every story. He doesn't know how to do this either. But, together, the two of you could figure it out. You've just gotta give him a chance."

Ivy sat back up and her chest filled with air, but she didn't respond.

"I mean, he took me parasailing!" Nora exclaimed. "You said it yourself—he doesn't do that kind of thing, right? He's trying."

"He's trying to make you like him so you'll take his side instead of mine."

"I see the situation differently."

"Well, we'll agree to disagree." Ivy wiped another tear.

"Look, I'm not asking for miracles. But why don't you try to hear him out. Push yourself not to flinch at the first disagreement. When he asks something of you, talk to him.

He's willing to listen, and I think he wants to do right by you."

"I'll hang out, but I'm not promising anything." She squeezed her eyes shut and wiped the remaining tears away.

The rest of the afternoon, Ivy played card games with everyone and kept the peace. But she was quiet. When dinnertime came, the atmosphere wasn't jovial enough to warrant a night out. Blaze offered to bring back some seafood to cook. With everyone in agreement, he ran out to pick up a few dishes and returned as quickly as he'd left.

"Want to help me make dinner?" he asked Ivy when he got back.

She didn't say yes, but she seemed to be considering it.

"I promise it'll be a better experience than last time." A smile played at his lips.

"We won't have Cappy's to bail us out if we screw it up," she said, making a tiny joke, but still careful in her response.

He retrieved containers from the bag and set them on the counter as Gram and Nora pulled plates and glasses down from the cabinets.

"We can do this," Blaze said. "Do we have a frying pan? I bought scallops."

"Fancy." Ivy waved her fingers in the air, but didn't smile.

"Fancy and easy. The guy at the market said you literally just cook them in butter."

"I can help too," Gram chimed in. "What else did you get?"

"Peel and eat shrimp—also easy. Are you sensing a theme?" He reached into the bag and took out a bottle of wine. "The guy said this goes really well with seafood."

"Do I get a glass?" Ivy teased, squinting at him.

"No, but you do get this." He pulled out a bottle of lemonade and set it in front of his daughter.

"Fair enough." Ivy opened the lemonade and took a big drink of it, her shoulders not quite as slumped as they had been during the card game. "So what am I actually cooking?"

Blaze handed her a Styrofoam box. "Crab cakes."

"How do I do that?"

"The same way we do the scallops—just plop them in butter. We also have asparagus, mixed veggies, and we have gumbo."

By the time they sat down to dinner, Ivy and Blaze were at least able to hold a conversation.

"Jake said I have the coolest name he's ever heard," Ivy said as she cut a scallop in half.

"I came up with your name," Blaze said, holding a half-finished glass of wine. "Did your mom ever tell you how we thought of the name Ivy?"

She shook her head.

"There was this old house down the road from the little shack we were renting at the time. It was two stories, white brick, with a chimney on each side of the house, and ivy arched over the rounded front door. It was the most extravagant place we'd ever seen. We named it "The Ivy," and we used to say that one day things would go our way, and we'd have our own Ivy."

"You named me after a random house?" Ivy asked.

"Wait. It gets better, I promise."

"I hope so."

Gram laughed.

"When we got pregnant, things were already going sideways with us. I was working around the clock. But there was one day when all the craziness seemed to stop. I met your mom for her doctor's appointment, and we got to hear your heartbeat. We both cried. I leaned over and gave your mom a kiss, and I promised myself I'd do whatever I could to make things better between us."

"That promise didn't work," Ivy said under her breath.

"Your mother's and my marriage was an impossible situation, given our maturity levels at the time, Ivy. But that day was different. The doctor asked if we wanted to know the sex. We said we did. He announced we were having a girl. I told your mom that nothing else mattered but you, and that you were our Ivy. It was just like finding the perfect lyric to a song you're trying to write. I put my hand on her belly and said, 'Let's call her Ivy.'"

Nora sat behind her glass of wine, falling for the man who sat across from her. He was so much more than the guy on the social media posts. He was kind and real, and she couldn't take her eyes off him.

"Mom never told me that story," Ivy said with a frown. "I wonder why."

"I don't know," Blaze returned. "But I'm happy to tell you now."

"THAT WAS SUCH a lovely story Blaze told tonight," Gram said as she came into the bedroom to get ready for bed.

"It was."

Gram set her book on the nightstand.

"I almost forgot," Nora said. "I bought you a surprise today." She went over to her suitcase and pulled out the gift bag from the boutique. "It's been in Blaze's car, and back in the rental, so the bag's a bit beat-up." She handed the gift to Gram.

"What's this for? It's not my birthday."

"It's just to be nice. And to say I'm glad you convinced me to come on this trip. I really needed it."

Gram took out the quilted book bag and held it up by the strap. "Oh, my goodness, this is beautiful! Thank you, dear."

"I thought you could use it to carry your book to the beach."

"I will."

Gram was about to set the quilted bag down when Nora stopped her.

"There's one more thing in there."

"Oh, there is?" Gram reached into the bag and fished around for a while, pulling out the bookmark. She held it up in the lamplight. "That's lovely."

"I noticed last night you were using that hospital paper to mark your page, so I thought you could do with an actual bookmark. You deserve it."

As Nora said the words, she tried to figure out why she'd seen a flash of what looked like fear across Gram's face when she'd mentioned the word "hospital."

"Are you okay, Gram?"

Gram slipped the bookmark into her book. Then she gave Nora a wide smile. "I'm fine, honey. I was just thinking how you're so right: I should treat myself more." She set the bag and her book on the bedside table and climbed under her covers. "You're such a dear for thinking of me," she said before clicking off the light. "Sweet dreams."

"Sweet dreams."

Nora got into bed and stared at the dark ceiling. Had

Gram acted weird just now? Or had she imagined it? It had been a long day. Perhaps they were both just tired.

CHAPTER TWENTY

By the time they all got out on the beach after breakfast the next morning, the sun was already intense. Seagulls soaring overhead were dark shapes against the bright orange light. Nora adjusted her sunglasses and self-consciously tightened her cover-up around her torso, not comfortable bearing all in her new bikini in front of Blaze. The personal-professional line wasn't just blurred at this point, it was nonexistent, and she had to maintain some professionalism. She settled into the chair next to Gram while Blaze set up two more for himself and Ivy.

"Hey, Ivy!" Jake jogged down the beach toward them from his cottage. When he reached them, he brushed his floppy hair off his forehead, and waved at Ivy.

"Wanna paddleboard?" He tossed a thumb over his shoulder toward his cottage where two brightly colored boards jutted out from the sand.

"Yeah." Ivy dropped her journal into the empty chair Blaze had set up for her. Then she turned to Blaze and under her breath mumbled, "I'm gonna hang with Jake."

"Okay," he said.

Gram sat down next to Nora and opened her book, setting her new bookmark on the arm of the chair. Blaze slipped his sunglasses on and leaned back in the sun. Soon, Ivy and Jake were balanced on their boards, their paddles moving slowly in the quiet surf.

"Looks fun," Blaze said.

Nora squinted at Ivy and Jake. "I wonder if it's harder than it seems."

"You could give it a try," Gram suggested. "The rental information said there's equipment in the storage room under the porch." She waggled her eyebrows at Nora when Blaze wasn't looking.

Nora stifled a grin. Gram had seemed to be herself all morning, so Nora was pretty sure she'd misread her grandmother's expression over the hospital paper last night, to her relief.

Blaze leaned forward. "Want to try it?"

"Are you serious?" Nora asked, ignoring Gram's googly eyes behind her.

"Why not?" He stood up. "June, do you know if the storage door is unlocked?"

"The key is in the dish on the counter by the fridge."

"Be right back."

When Blaze left for the cottage, Nora turned to Gram. "I wasn't planning to take off my cover-up. I'm Ivy's teacher. I don't think it's a good idea to prance around in my swimsuit."

"If you were on vacation, and Blaze was in the cottage next door, he'd see you in your swimsuit."

"But he isn't. He's sleeping in our house. What would my school officials say?"

Gram shook her head. "Your school officials need to

loosen up. You're a grown woman. And you're doing nothing wrong. It's not like you're dating him or anything."

"What if I fall off the thing? That could be embarrassing."

"Or fun," Gram countered.

"Speak for yourself. I'll make *you* go out on that thing," she teased.

Gram chuckled. "I would if I could."

Blaze returned with a board under each arm. He dropped them and released the Velcro straps holding the paddles onto each board.

"Wanna jump on one?" he asked Nora.

Parasailing was adventure enough, and at least with that she was fully clothed...

"Stop thinking so much." He tossed a paddle toward her, the long thing landing with a thud on the sand. "Just do it."

Blaze grabbed the hem of his shirt and yanked it upward, and all Nora could see were biceps and pecs. He draped his shirt over the chair, then he picked up his board and paddle and carried them down to the water.

Nora took a second to regain her composure.

Jake and Ivy paddled closer to him. Blaze adjusted the height of the paddle and took the board past the break of the waves. Then he climbed up on it and sat on his knees.

"Come on!" he called up the beach to her.

"Go on. Don't leave the poor man hanging," Gram said.

With a deep breath, Nora stood up from her chair. She dawdled, fiddling with the tie of her cover-up, still deciding. She pulled the tie loose.

Blaze waved her in again.

She tentatively shimmied off her cover-up, revealing her

bikini. She picked up the board, dragging the back end of it in the sand as she paced down to the water, feeling exposed.

Ivy waved from her board, unfazed by Nora's attire, wobbling before she found her balance again. She and Jake moved in unison.

Blaze was still bobbing in the water on his knees. "Make sure your paddle's the right height. Jake just said it should be six inches above your head."

"Hey there." Ivy paddled over. She helped Nora steady the board. "Climb onto it, and I'll show you how to paddle. Jake just showed me, and it's easy."

Nora got onto her knees, and the board seemed stable.

"You're gonna want the board to be moving when you try to stand up," Jake said, "so use your paddle to come out to us."

Nora and Blaze started paddling.

"Now, turn so the wind is behind you. This way." The boy pointed in an easterly direction.

Nora complied. She and Blaze were both managing, and it took so much focus to keep her balance that she forgot all about her exposed body. She tried to get up on her board while Blaze was busy doing the same. Quickly, she placed her feet wide on either side of the board's handle and stood up, swaying slightly. She shifted her weight on her toes to maintain stability.

"Look! Ms. Jenkins is a natural," Ivy said.

Blaze finally hopped to his feet, lost his balance, and pivoted off the board and into the Gulf. He surfaced, shaking the water from his hair and wiping his eyes. "How are you doing that?"

Ivy giggled and Nora stifled her amusement.

As he climbed back up on the board and got onto his

knees, Nora turned her gaze to her paddle to avoid gawking at the water glistening off his rounded muscles.

"I went slowly, got the board moving, and then placed my feet carefully. I'd take a wide stance. It seems to help with balance."

He tried again, pushing the board forward with his paddle.

"Now gently place your feet where you want them. One at a time," Nora instructed.

Blaze worked slowly and rose to a standing position. "Hey, there we go," he said.

Ivy and Jake paddled out further while Nora and Blaze hung back.

"How did you figure out how to get up on your board so quickly?" Blaze asked.

"I don't know," Nora replied. "I just felt it."

"I like that," he said, his eyes on her. He paddled up next to her board. "Moving on feeling is how I live my life. It might not be perfect, but it's gotten me this far."

"Maybe I should move more on feeling. You're certainly convincing me this week."

There was a fondness in his eyes when he looked at her that she couldn't deny. And it scared her to death because she probably shouldn't even be out here with him, let alone feel the way she was feeling about him.

WITH THE SUN now below the horizon, Blaze and Nora were relaxing in the secluded quiet of the porch, while Ivy scrolled through her phone on the sofa in the living room. The sun had completely disappeared, producing a mass of stars in its wake. Gram had turned in for the night, and

Nora had decided the clear skies were too lovely to sit inside.

Blaze came out onto the porch, carrying two glasses of wine.

"Ivy's asleep," he said, handing Nora a glass. "So I guess we're the lone survivors of the day." He sat down next to her on the porch swing.

"I guess so," she said before taking a sip of the crisp, sweet wine. The humidity had worn off, leaving a light breeze. "It's so nice tonight. I'll bet it's room temperature down by the water right now."

"Why don't we take our glasses and go for a walk on the beach?" Blaze asked.

"That sounds wonderful."

They descended the long staircase from the porch to the sand below and followed the wooden path over the dune to the beach. The sand was soft on her bare feet. The gentle rhythm of the waves and the slight buzz from the wine made her forget everything but the moment with Blaze.

"This is nice," he said. "The last few days have made me realize I don't slow down enough."

"I feel the same way. I've never taken a long vacation like this."

The water shushed toward them and bubbled over their feet.

"I've been on a lot of trips, some even for vacation, but I didn't rest. I stayed busy and filled every minute." He peered over at her, the moonlight glimmering off the glass of wine hanging by its rim from his fingertips. "I think I know why."

She held her hair back to keep the wind from blowing it into her eyes. "Why?"

"Because I didn't have anyone to share it with." He

stopped and faced her. "Taking this walk is more interesting than anything that could fill my schedule. I enjoy talking with you."

He started walking again, and she followed.

"Why?" She couldn't help but ask, given the incredibly fascinating people he hung out with.

"I find what you have to say fascinating. And you don't want anything from me. You seem as happy as I am just walking and drinking a glass of wine." He held up his glass and took a sip.

"I find you pretty fascinating too," she admitted, glad for the darkness to hide the heat that rose in her cheeks. "I've never met anyone quite like you."

"I hope that's a good thing?"

Amusement swelled in her chest. "Yes. It's a good thing."

"How am I different from other people you know?"

She splashed in the water with her next step, sending a sprinkle onto her shins. "You don't seem to follow rules."

He laughed. "I follow rules."

"Not right-or-wrong rules. Those unwritten rules that we have to get good grades, go to college, get a nine-to-five job with a 401(k) and still come home and work until we fall asleep. You don't do that. I wonder what it was within you that ignored all that and followed your passion."

He frowned. "I don't know. A typical life never occurred to me."

"That's what makes you intriguing. Eighty-five million of us in this country don't know what you inherently know: how to survive outside the traditional workforce. We find something we don't hate doing that kind of fits our talents. Many of us don't even really understand what our true talents are. But for you, it's so easy. You move through the world just knowing."

The corner of his mouth lifted as he seemed to consider the idea.

"I don't even know what my talents are, or if I really have any," Nora admitted.

"Of course you do. You might not have found them yet, but everyone has talents. Personally, I think your talent is connecting to people."

"I should rephrase my statement. I haven't found my *passion*. I know I'm good at connecting with people, but I haven't found that thing that makes me whole. I watched you in the recording studio, and you lit up like a lightbulb. Your talent and passion work together, and you're unstoppable."

To her surprise, he took her hand and stopped her. He guided her down to the sand and she sat next to him, facing the water.

"We're going to figure this out," he said.

"I doubt we'll do it tonight," she said lightly.

"Probably not, but we can try." He tipped his head back, his gaze moving up to the stars. "If money were no object, and you didn't have to work, what would you want to do?"

"Probably travel the world."

He looked at her. "No wonder you haven't found your passion."

"What do you mean?"

"Well, you had every answer available to you, and you chose world travel, so that means traveling interests you. And have you traveled the world?"

"No."

"Then how will you find your passion?"

She chuckled. "So I'm supposed to quit my job, leave

my grandmother, and travel the world just in case it's my passion?"

"You don't have to do it all at once. You've made a good start. You've ventured to Florida for these two weeks, the southernmost state in our country. Next trip, push yourself a little farther."

"What about Gram? She might not be able to travel so much."

"Well, when you decide to travel, call me, and I'll check in on her."

She laughed at his little joke, but he put his hand on her shoulder, the gesture silencing her.

"That wasn't meant to be funny. I'm serious." He looked out at the water. "I haven't been great at doing things for others, and I'd do that for you."

"Thank you," she said, the rest of her words unavailable in that instant. His kindness and candor had muddled her mind.

They continued to chat for a few minutes more before Nora suggested they return to the cottage and head in for the night. They stood up and brushed the sand off them. As they walked together, a strange sort of solidarity hung between them, and she wondered where it might go in the morning.

They rinsed off their feet in the outdoor spigot, and then he offered to tackle the kitchen cleanup if she took care of the porch.

"We'll tag team it," he said.

While Blaze was inside, she couldn't shake how normal he seemed when he was out of his element. He was nothing like his public persona. All those glamorous photos, wearing designer suits with his arm draped around the biggest stars seemed miles away. She gazed in through the window at him rinsing dishes at the sink, as she collected the remaining glasses. But this side of him wasn't his real life. In a matter of days he'd be back in the studio or on a plane, off to find the next big star.

"I can't find that metal cork stopper we were using for the wine bottle," Blaze said when she came inside, "I hope I didn't throw it away." He went over to the trash can and peered into it.

"There's mostly paper in there anyway. I can wash it if you did." She set all the glasses next to the sink. "I'll just have a quick look." Nora stared into the trash can, moving a few things around. "Are you sure it's not on the counter?"

Blaze paced the kitchen, quietly lifting things and moving knickknacks. "I don't see it." He bent down and checked the floor.

"We can do a better job of looking in the morning. I'm going to wash up, and then I'm heading to bed. It's been a nice evening."

"Yes, it has." He stood terrifyingly close to her, looking down at her as if he wanted to say something. "Well, good night." He disappeared down the hallway and into his room.

She wanted to throw caution to the wind and see where things went with Blaze this week, but her rational side stopped her. Moving past where they were would open up a whole lot of issues. And even if she wasn't Ivy's school counselor, the beach atmosphere was such a departure from their normal lives. It was magical here. She couldn't begin to imagine herself in Blaze's real world. She wouldn't fit into it. Not to mention the fact that Ivy needed to grieve her mother and establish normalcy with her dad before introducing a new dynamic. Leaning into her growing feelings for Blaze was a bad idea on every level.

She shook off her thoughts and focused on reality. She figured she'd check the trash for the metal wine stopper one more time.

Nora lifted the empty paper plates that sat on top of the pile, trying to see if she could locate the stopper. She moved a napkin out of the way and noticed the familiar hospital letterhead. It wasn't like Gram to throw away a receipt. She kept them for five years for taxes; she had files of them. Nora pulled out the paper to view it in the light and scanned the wording.

RECOMMENDATION: Ultrasound-guided left breast biopsy of indeterminate mass at the 1– 1:30 position...

BIOPSY? *Mass? So it isn't a receipt...* Nora checked the date; it was months ago. Gram hadn't said anything at all.

Nora folded the paper and put it into her pocket. Then she fished around a little more for the wine top. Unable to find it, she washed her hands and went into the bedroom with Gram. As she got ready for bed in the bathroom, her mind was going a hundred miles an hour. Why hadn't Gram told her? Gram's behavior had been different lately: the beach trip, seeing Gramps in her dreams, organizing everything, treating herself to that cinnamon roll when she usually wouldn't...

Nora *had* been right—she'd seen fear in her grandmother's eyes when she'd mentioned this paper. Had Gram tried to hide it by burying it in the trash? Had she already had the biopsy? Was Gram facing something and had yet to break the news to Nora?

IT HAD TAKEN Nora ages to fall asleep after seeing the hospital letter to Gram, and just as she'd gotten deep into slumber, she was aware of something tapping her.

"Nora."

It was barely a whisper, so quiet she wondered if she was dreaming.

"Nora."

Gramps's voice sounded younger than it had in life. Was he here to give her a message about Gram? Did he have the answers?

Then the tapping became a hand jostling her.

"Nora."

She opened her eyes and blinked to adjust to the darkness. In the moonlight, she made out Blaze's face over her and sat up. He took her hand, quietly leading her out into the living room where Ivy's sofa bed was empty.

"Where is she?" Nora asked, still trying to wake up.

"I have no idea." He held up his phone. "Her location isn't coming through, and she's not answering my texts." He ran his fingers through his hair, pacing the room. "I got up to have a glass of water and saw she was gone."

"Have you looked outside to see if she's on the porch?"

"Yes. I've been outside, around the house, down the beach to that kid's cottage, and all around their property. All their lights are off. Her car's still in the driveway."

"Hm. Then maybe she decided to take a walk?"

"In the dead of night on a secluded beach?" He lunged over to the back window and looked outside then shook his head and checked his phone. "What the hell is she thinking?"

"Let's get in the car and see if we can find her. Gram's here if she comes back before we do. I'll leave a note."

While Nora searched the drawers for a pen and paper, Blaze darted off to his room and returned with his car key. She found a small pad and scribbled down a quick note on the counter for Gram in case she woke up.

Blaze took her hand, that unifying element between them surging.

"Let's go."

They climbed into Blaze's car, and he pulled onto the dark country road. He put the windows down, calling Ivy's name as they drove, parallel to the coast.

"She can't just leave whenever she feels like it," Blaze said.

"We don't know if she's done anything yet."

"She absolutely has. She got upset with me, and now she's running away like she did when she came here. She can't run from me every time I try to be her parent." His jaw clenched before he barked Ivy's name out the window.

He handed Nora his phone. "My passcode is 3954. Can you check the Family Monitor app to see if her location shows now?"

Nora opened Blaze's phone, the device large in her hand. All those videos and stories—this was what he'd recorded them on. It had probably been in his pocket while he mingled with the rich and famous. She opened the app and clicked on Ivy's name.

"It located her." She held out the phone to Blaze. "Turn left in about a mile."

"Keep the screen open so we won't lose her if we drive out of cellular range."

"It's good to know she didn't intentionally turn off her phone," Nora said.

"Yeah, but she hasn't responded. That's on her."

The engine revved as Blaze hit the gas, only slowing down to make the turn. He peered over at his phone and then squinted in front of them. "This is a public beach access," he said, parking the car next to the only other vehicle in the parking lot and getting out.

Nora followed, stepping close to him in case there were anything amiss. They walked up the steps and down the long boardwalk to the beach. In the moonlight, a couple was lying on a blanket in the sand. Nora recognized the oatmeal-colored sundress.

Just then, Ivy popped up, her eyes wide as she scrambled to her feet. She awkwardly reached down and picked up her phone as Jake roused.

"I fell asleep," Ivy said, as Jake got to his feet, groggy.

"Get to the car," Blaze said in an even but forceful tone.

"I didn't mean to. I just—"

"GET to the car!" He turned to Jake. "Is that your ride in the parking lot?"

"Yes, sir." Jake's gaze was on the sand.

"I suggest you get in it and we'll follow you home."

"Yes, sir."

"I'll see you tomorrow," Ivy whispered as Jake passed her.

When they got to their cars, Ivy slid into the back of Blaze's. "Can I explain?" she asked as Blaze slammed his door and started the engine.

He gripped the shifter and Nora put her hand on his in an attempt to defuse his anger. The slight slump in his shoulders was a start.

"Jake texted and asked if I could go out to the beach with him to talk. I knew after the way I acted earlier, that you probably wouldn't let me go. Plus, you wouldn't let me meet up with him that late anyway. I didn't think talking on the beach was a big deal, and you all were sleeping, so I wouldn't disturb you. I'm sorry. We were just talking, and we laid back to watch the stars and fell asleep."

Blaze didn't answer, he just drove. Was that fear in his eyes?

At least Ivy was safe. But it was clearer to Nora than ever before that Blaze and Ivy needed guidance beyond anything she could provide.

CHAPTER TWENTY-ONE

The rest of the drive was quiet. Blaze drove to Jake's house to make sure he got in safely. Then he drove Nora and Ivy back to the cottage. The minute they parked, Ivy jumped out and ran inside.

Nora lingered, waiting for Blaze. His hands were still gripping the top of the steering wheel. Then he dropped his forehead onto his knuckles and closed his eyes.

"You know, she didn't run away tonight," Nora said quietly. "*Tonight*, she was being a typical teenager. Sure, she shouldn't have gone out, and she should face a consequence for not telling you, but she was asleep on a blanket on the beach with a new friend. There are worse things she could've been doing. I understand, though, why it was so scary."

He sat up, his chest filling with air. He breathed out slowly. "When Ivy ran away from home to come here, I was completely panicked." Letting go of the steering wheel, he turned to her, looking utterly exhausted. "But once I knew she was with you—and after I had the long drive to calm down—I was able to show up and not lose it." He shook his head. "I can't keep it together when all her offenses continue to stack up and fill my mind every minute. I don't know how to parent her by myself."

Nora reached over and took his hand. He peered down at their intertwined fingers, unsaid thoughts in his eyes.

They sat together in the car, without any further explanation. Nora sent silent support with a little squeeze. A couple of times, his lips parted as if he wanted to say something, but then he closed them again. Given the night's drama, she didn't press him. He had a lot on his mind.

"We should probably go inside," he finally said.

"Okay." She let go of his hand. Just as they got out of the car, Nora pointed to the orange-and-pink horizon. "Look. Sunrise."

He slipped his hands into his pockets and turned his face toward the orange glow. Then he looked down at her, those gray eyes full of deliberation. Without divulging any of it, he nodded toward the front door of the cottage.

When they entered, the savory scents of bacon and eggs mixed with the buttery sweetness of pancakes and syrup. Ivy sat, slumped, at the bar and pushed her eggs around her plate with her fork.

"Good morning," Gram said as Nora and Blaze sat down at the bar beside Ivy. "I got your note and figured since the sun had risen and you were yet to be home, that at the very least I could have breakfast waiting for everyone." She took the pan off the heat and scraped the eggs into a serving dish. "I made Ivy's favorite: pancake sandwiches. She told me the other day she likes those."

Nora tried to smile, but given the situation, it probably came out as more of a grimace. "Ivy's a ball of excitement. How are the rest of you?" Gram asked.

"I think we need to get on the road and head home," Blaze said.

Ivy snapped up. "What?"

Nora wanted to stop him, but this was his decision. It was probably better anyway. She was a school counselor, not their family therapist. While she wanted him to stay for personal reasons, that probably wasn't a good idea either. They had nowhere to go from here.

Ivy folded her arms. "I'm not leaving."

"You're leaving if I tell you we are." Blaze's voice was controlled, his eyes on her with laser focus.

Ivy turned to Nora. "Ms. Jenkins, tell him we can stay."

"If your dad says it's time for you to go, then it's time."

Rejection flashed across the girl's face.

"Everyone at least eat first," Gram said.

Ivy picked up her plate and stomped out to the porch. Through the door, she faced the water and wiped a tear away angrily.

"You've barely slept," Nora said quietly to Blaze. "You know how hard it is to go all day when you haven't had enough rest. Why don't you at least give it one more night and then you can go first thing in the morning?"

"So Ivy can get her way?"

"You and Ivy will have the same issues tomorrow morning that you have now," Gram cut in, "but you'll have a good night's sleep and a few more meals under your belts." She slid a plate of stacked pancakes with drizzled syrup, eggs, and bacon his way. Then she set a mug of black coffee next to it.

Blaze took his plate to the table and sat down, his attention on Ivy through the back door. Nora shot Gram a worried look. She shrugged as if to say she didn't have an answer, and went to make Nora a plate while Nora poured herself a cup of coffee.

With a heavy heart, Nora took her plate over to Blaze and sat down. "Life's not like those happy love songs, is it?"

He looked up from his pancakes. "No, it's not. It's damn near impossible." He stabbed a bite of pancake. "What do you do when you're in an awful situation? How do you calm down?"

She picked up her coffee. "I suppose I find a quiet spot and read a book or something similar where I can lose myself for a while. Then when I come back to the problem, I've given my mind a rest, and I can try to tackle the issue with a wider perspective."

He nodded. "You're right. I usually write songs or put together melodies."

"Ivy likes to write songs too," she offered. "She's a lot like you."

He ate silently, but he was definitely thinking over his next move.

Nora picked up her plate. "I think I'll go out to the porch with Ivy."

He didn't answer.

Nora went outside.

"Mind if I sit with you?"

Ivy didn't answer either.

She sat down across from the girl. "I'm trying to convince your dad to at least wait until the morning to go home."

The girl frowned. "I haven't made a single friend since I moved to stupid Nashville, and the minute I find a friend here he makes me leave. He doesn't care whether I'm happy. He just wants me to fit into *his* life."

"He does care. He cares so much that he stayed up all night last night trying to find you, terrified."

Ivy pouted.

"I know your mom gave you a lot of freedom. And you're right that your dad doesn't know you as well as she did. You need to get to know him and show him who you are. And the more you can prove to him that you're capable and worthy of his trust, the more he'll let go. He's never had to be your parent before, and he's scared to death that he'll do the wrong thing by you."

"Shouldn't he know? Isn't he the grown-up?"

"Sure. But there's no instruction manual on how to raise a teenager. You could offer a little insight." She offered Ivy a small smile.

Ivy stared out at the water, not budging.

Nora pointed to the horizon. "The horizon seems like the edge of the world from here, doesn't it?"

Ivy nodded.

"The world just keeps going no matter what. Isn't that amazing?"

Ivy eyed Nora, clearly wondering what her point was.

"The world will continue whether you and your dad get along or not. Life continues to move forward. And at the end of the day, he's all you've got, and you're all he has."

Movement at the door caused Nora to turn. Blaze was in the doorway.

"She's right, you know." He sat down next to Ivy. "I don't know what the heck to do, but I've been around for a few more spins of the earth..." He waggled a finger at the horizon. "I can help with giving you my perspective. But you've gotta let me."

"I don't like it when you yell at me. Mom never yelled at me."

"Did you drive across three states in the middle of the night without telling her?"

Ivy shrunk back, defeated.

"I'll bet you were a different person for your mom than you are for me."

Ivy twisted in her chair and squared off in front of him. "Why didn't you try?"

Her question seemed to come out of left field for Blaze.

"What do you mean? I'm trying like crazy."

"For Mom? You chose work over her. Why didn't you love her enough to try?"

His shoulders fell, and his forehead softened. "I tried the only way I knew how at the time. I was the breadwinner, so I worked all hours to provide for you two. Balancing work and family was an impossible task for a young kid that didn't really know how to be a father."

"Why didn't you come see me?"

"She wouldn't let me. And because I wasn't there, I thought I'd be more of a nuisance than a help. I saved up all the child support your mom wouldn't take. It's in an account in your name. I sent you gifts every year for your birthday and Christmas, and they were returned unopened. She didn't want me in your life, and I didn't think I was a good enough father to push back. She knew more about being a good parent than I did."

Ivy's lips parted in shock; this information was evidently new to her.

"Your mom and I both made mistakes. I don't think there's a clear winner in either of our battles. But we both wanted nothing but the best for you. I wasn't there for you growing up, but I can be here for you now. You just have to let me."

Ivy didn't say anything, but that defiant frown had melted away.

With Blaze offering that kind of honest reaction, Nora could only guess that they'd eventually figure out where to go from here.

AFTER GETTING ready for the day, Ivy came out of the bathroom, and Nora had to stifle a gasp. The teen had on another sundress, this one white cotton, and she ran her fingers through a head of shiny auburn hair, the deep color making her gray eyes sparkle.

"I bought some wash-in hair dye when we were in town yesterday."

"The color suits you," Nora said.

"My gosh, you look gorgeous!" Gram padded over to her and tussled the ends of Ivy's silky hair. "Who knew that stunning babe was under all those baggy clothes." She winked at Ivy, making the girl's cheeks flush.

"I asked Jake to help me pick out the hair color and the dress."

"He knows what looks good on you," Gram said.

Ivy wrinkled her nose at Gram and curtsied. "Did you know, he lives close to us? He's from Brentwood."

"Who's from Brent—" Blaze stopped on his way into the kitchen, his mouth hanging open. "What supermodel swallowed my daughter?"

Ivy chewed on a smile. "I wanted to try this hair color. It's just a wash-in, but if I like it, I can get the permanent version."

"You look beautiful," Blaze said.

Ivy's cheeks flamed. "Thank you."

Blaze took a seat on the sofa. "So Jake is from Brentwood? Is that what I heard?"

"Yeah, we only live about thirty minutes from each other. It's like it was meant to be."

"Are you two an item?" Gram asked, picking up her novel from the coffee table.

"Kind of. We exchanged numbers, and he said he wants to see me again. He's a junior at Brentwood Academy, Dad. It's a private school."

"Yeah, I know it. Not too far at all."

"Do you think I could go to school there?"

"We could look into it." His gaze fluttered over to Nora.

"Can we please stay today? Jake was going to take me into town. We're going to get lunch, and then we're going book shopping in Seaside. He's leaving tomorrow too. He has summer baseball practice. He's on the elite team."

Blaze stared at his daughter. "Only if you promise me you'll never scare me like that again."

Ivy gave him an honest look. "I promise."

"All right. Keep your phone on so I can get in touch with you if I need you, okay? And tell Jake I'm sorry I flew hot on him."

Ivy smiled. "I will." She picked up her big sack of a bag, looked down at her new dress, and abandoned it. Then she walked out the front door.

"Well, how about that?" Gram said.

"One boy can cause a change in my daughter that I've been hoping would happen for an entire year?" Blaze said.

Nora laughed. "That's the way with teenagers. But if you think about it, Jake seems to be a great influence on her. He's driven—he's on the elite baseball team; he's thoughtful —taking her out to see the stars at night and book shopping; and he's got a great sense of style." She winked at him. "Ivy hasn't connected with a single person until now, but when she does, it's someone like Jake. She might just be on her way to being all right."

While Blaze seemed to agree, and it looked as if things were moving in a good direction, he didn't look relieved. A niggling worry crawled around at the back of Nora's mind: if Ivy left Oakland High, that would mean no more meetings with Blaze. And she wouldn't see Ivy again either. And Ivy had become the light in her day.

THAT AFTERNOON, Nora, Gram, and Blaze sat on the beach under the umbrella. After a while Gram reclined her chair and fell asleep.

Nora put down her book. "It's hot. I think I'm going to get in the water and cool off," she announced. She didn't want to admit it, but she hoped Blaze would go down to the water with her.

"Sounds good," he said, his eyes on a magazine he'd brought down from the cottage.

Nora chewed on her lip, lingering for a tick, but when he didn't look up, she stood, slipped off her cover-up and padded down to the surf.

The cool Gulf splashed and gurgled around her as she waded in. Gently, she laid her palms on the sparkling surface. Through the clear water, she could see all the way down to the white sand under her toes. The coastal wind tickled her wet skin, giving her goosebumps. She bent her knees and dipped down until the salty water was at her shoulders then picked up her feet and ebbed and flowed with the pull of the tide.

Out of the corner of her eye, she could see Blaze was

still reading his magazine. There was a time when she'd worried about being in front of him in a bathing suit. Now that she finally felt comfortable, he hadn't even looked up. Something was eating at him, but it wasn't her place to ask.

The rest of the afternoon and evening went about the same way. Ivy stayed with Jake, and Blaze kept to himself for the most part. Nora was quiet as well, spending time with Gram. With everything that had happened with Ivy, they hadn't had a chance to talk about the letter Nora had found in the trash, so she struggled to make conversation. With nothing else to do, she had lost herself in her book most of the day.

For dinner, they'd all made sandwiches and leftovers. Blaze turned on the TV, the local news and weather filling the empty void of conversation. A couple times, throughout the evening, Gram sent Nora a questioning glance, but Nora just shrugged discreetly.

Ivy walked in around eight thirty. "Hey."

Gram smiled, and Nora waved as Blaze greeted her.

"We should probably make sure we've got all our things packed," he said. "And then we should head to bed to get a good night's sleep before we go tomorrow."

"Yeah," Ivy said.

He waggled a finger at her. "No leaving the house tonight, do you hear me?"

"I won't," she replied. "Jake's getting his rest, too, so he can make the drive back. He and I are going to follow each other home."

"That sounds like a plan. We'll leave first thing in the morning."

"I can make you some breakfast sandwiches and put them in the fridge," Gram offered.

"Don't put yourself out. We can grab something on the road," Blaze said.

Gram tutted. "Nonsense. I'll make you something. Maybe a pancake sandwich." She winked at Ivy.

Ivy flashed a smile, oblivious to Blaze's about-face. "Thanks, June."

Blaze stood up from the sofa and stretched. "Well, I'm heading to bed. Thank you both for having us."

"It was no problem," Nora said.

Real life had crept in before Nora had even finished her vacation. But Blaze's aloof behavior was probably for the best. They needed to keep things professional. She'd already found herself having feelings for him, and that was the last thing she needed.

CHAPTER TWENTY-TWO

When Nora walked into the living room the next morning, Ivy's blankets were folded neatly, the pillow stacked on top. Through the window, both Ivy's and Blaze's cars were also gone. She hadn't even gotten a chance to say goodbye.

Feeling heavy, Nora needed a cup of coffee. She went into the kitchen and loaded the coffeemaker. She leaned on the counter, her mind full of so many thoughts all at once: the fun she'd had with Blaze, the struggle with Ivy, the promise of Ivy's new friend, and then to Blaze's abrupt change... Had she done anything to cause it? She combed back through their time together, but she came up empty.

As the heady aroma of coffee filled the air, she tried to clear her mind and focus on the vacation that, for all intents and purposes, was starting today. Although, she didn't feel she could settle in until she got to the bottom of that hospital letter.

She went into the fridge to find the cream and noticed the sandwiches Gram had made last night were gone. She was glad Blaze and Ivy had taken something to eat with them.

"Morning—oh, thank you," Gram said, making a beeline for the coffee.

"Good morning, Gram."

The quiet atmosphere made Nora uneasy. She hadn't realized how much she'd enjoyed Blaze and Ivy's banter until it was gone. She wasn't ready to confront Gram just yet. She needed to get her head straight first.

Gram pulled a mug down from the cabinet. "Did you get to say goodbye to the Rymans before they left?"

"No. They were gone before I got up."

"I slept like a rock. I didn't even hear them leave." Gram spooned some sugar into her coffee.

"I didn't either. I wish I had. I'd have liked to have seen them off." Nora tried to ignore the weight on her chest when she thought about not seeing either of them until school started at the end of the summer. And if Ivy and Jake carried on, and Ivy decided to attend Brentwood Academy, she might not ever see them again.

"Blaze sure was quiet yesterday," Gram said, sitting down at the island with her mug. "Did something happen between you two?"

Nora shook her head, still confused by his behavior. "No. All I can think of is that he was too busy worrying about Ivy to be his usual self."

"Hm. Well, let's not allow it to spoil the rest of our trip. Try to let it go so you can enjoy yourself."

Nora brought her coffee over and set it on the counter next to Gram's. She wouldn't be able to enjoy herself until she knew what was going on with her grandmother. With a deep breath, she pushed forward. "There is, actually, something else…"

Gram's eyebrows pulled together. "What is it?"

Nora took a seat. "I found that hospital letter in the trash."

The same look of fear she'd seen in Gram's eyes when she'd first mentioned it, flooded her grandmother's face once more.

"Wanna tell me what's going on?"

Gram stood up and squared her shoulders. "Let's sit on the porch."

Nora had hoped her grandmother would say that they'd cleared her, and that the letter was just an old piece of trash she'd used as her bookmark, but she hadn't. She wanted to sit outside. That wasn't a good sign. Nora's heart pounded as she followed Gram to the swing and lowered herself beside her.

"They found a suspicious lump," Gram said, facing the Gulf, the breeze blowing her gray hair off her face. "I went for an MRI about a month ago so they could see it better. They sent the images off for a second opinion, and I was waiting until after vacation to call them back for the final word."

Nora's heart fell into her stomach. "Why did you wait? If there's an issue, we should get this taken care of sooner rather than later."

"If it is something of concern, I'm not sure I can go through that kind of surgery. From what they told me, it's pretty invasive, and then there's radiation and probably chemotherapy, and I'm no spring chicken. The last thing I want to do is spend the rest of my years in pain."

Tears pricked Nora's eyes.

"I didn't tell you for this very reason." Gram lifted her chin as if in defiance to the possible cancer that had invaded her. "There's no need to worry until we actually have something to worry about."

"What are the odds that it's not cancerous?" Nora asked, blinking away her tears.

Gram shook her head. "I don't know. But until they say for sure that it is, I'm going to operate as if it isn't. There's no sense in losing wonderful days like this out of fear. You can't spend your time worrying over things that can't change."

Nora gripped her mug and pulled her knees into her chest, rocking the swing. "It's hard to turn off the fear."

Gram gave her a fond look. "But you *have* to or you'll drive yourself crazy." She held up her mug. "Let's enjoy our coffee and then go shopping like we'd planned to do when we first got here."

"Okay."

Gram got up. "But first I'll wash all the sheets and change the beds around."

"You don't have to do that."

"I'd like to." Gram gave her a smile and went back inside.

Nora wiped a tear away and took a long sip of her creamy coffee, trying to let it soothe her. But she'd been faced with a new dilemma that hadn't surfaced from her subconscious until now: Gram wouldn't be with her forever. What would her life look like when Gram was no longer in it? She hadn't wanted to think about it, and she didn't want to now, but there was a possibility she'd face that question sooner than she'd like.

In everything she did, she'd chosen the safest route; she hadn't even tried to figure out her own passions or who she was without Gram. And now, where did that leave her?

Those same questions hung in her mind all day, even while she shopped with Gram. It was difficult to enjoy perusing seashell trinkets and hand-painted pottery when she had life-changing events on her mind.

The days carried on, the weekend came and went, and the next week she and Gram continued as if nothing was wrong, when in Nora's mind, everything was wrong. After spending time with Blaze, she felt as if she didn't even know herself. And how was she going to have time to find herself when she had to deal with Gram's possible diagnosis?

Or the fact that she'd fallen for Blaze?

She *knew* they would never work outside of that one week at the beach, and she'd still allowed herself to be swept off her feet by his charm. She couldn't just insert herself into Blaze and Ivy's lives. And even if she wanted to, Blaze had left without even a goodbye, and he hadn't said anything about staying in touch, or messaged her since.

This vacation hadn't been nearly as restorative as Nora had hoped. In fact, it had been the opposite.

CHAPTER TWENTY-THREE

Nora sat behind the wheel of the packed rental car and took one final look at the cottage as the afternoon sun cast its orange glow. "Well, that's it."

"Maybe we'll come back next year," Gram said, her elbow out the open car window.

Nora offered a courtesy smile, but she was still worried about what next year might look like. As Nora pulled out of the drive heading for the airport, her mind full, Gram's attention had already flitted off to her phone, seemingly not having a care in the world.

The windy beach road looked different from the night she and Blaze had driven down it in the dark. She sifted through her memories of him: the ice cream they'd shared, their parasailing adventure, walks along the beach, their long talks out on the back porch... Had she overromanticized it all? But he had looked at her with such fondness, and he'd initiated a lot of their outings. Then it was as if, suddenly, he'd changed his mind. How had things gone so wrong? Had she done anything or said anything to cause this? She was just being herself. But maybe she wasn't enough...

She forced her focus onto the drive. He'd probably decided what she had known all along, but had forgotten thanks to his charm: that they shouldn't be together. That was that. She was going to try to get on with her summer and not think about Blaze anymore. Just like Gram had said, there was no sense worrying about things she couldn't change.

Gram's phone pinged, pulling Nora from her thoughts. She glanced over and saw Gram fire off a text. She never got on her phone.

"Who in the world are you texting on a Sunday?" Nora finally asked.

"Ivy."

"What?" Nora pulled up to a stoplight and looked over at Gram. "Why?"

"We exchanged numbers while you and Blaze were off parasailing. I've been checking in on her to see how she's doing."

"How is she?"

"She says she met with the counselor, and she's not too bad." Gram typed a line more and clicked off her phone. "I'm surprised Blaze hasn't filled you in."

"I still haven't heard from him."

"And why haven't you reached out to him?"

"Because he doesn't seem to want me to. And it just makes more sense not to."

Gram sighed. "I've been holding my tongue, because your life is your own, but if you want an old woman's opinion, you need to let go of the rules you set for yourself. They're unnecessary boundaries. Give in to your feelings for once. I saw the way you two looked at each other."

Nora put on her blinker and merged onto the highway toward the airport.

"What are you talking about?"

Gram folded her hands in her lap. "Would it really be the end of the world if you dated the father of a student? I'm sure you could get Ivy onto the caseload of the other school counselor if you were up front with the Oakland staff."

"That's the least of my worries, Gram. There are plenty of other reasons nothing will happen between Blaze and me."

"What in the world could they be?"

"Well, for one, I'll never fit in with his lifestyle. Is he really going to take the school counselor to red-carpet events with all those famous people?"

"That fancy lifestyle has built up around him, but that's not who he really is," Gram said. "That was pretty clear during our time together at the cottage. I have it on good authority that Blaze has been down in the dumps since he and Ivy got home."

Nora glanced over at Gram. "Why? What did Ivy say?"

"Exactly that. She said he seems to be moping around whenever he's at the house."

"I doubt very seriously that his mood has anything to do with me."

Gram pursed her lips and shook her head. Nora flipped on the radio and turned up the music to avoid any further conversation. She had enough on her plate with Gram. She didn't need any further discussions about Blaze.

But the rest of the drive to the airport, she wondered what *had* changed his mood.

BY THE TIME they got home from the airport that evening, Gram was exhausted.

"My back is killing me," she said. "I didn't realize what a toll travel can take on a body." She rubbed her shoulder. "But I'm glad we did it."

Nora dropped their bags inside the apartment. "Me too."

After Gram retreated to her bedroom to unpack her things and run a bath, Nora went into her room, shut the door, and flopped onto her bed. With all the travel and everything on her mind, she'd been through the ringer. She buried her head in her pillow and relished the smell of home.

Everything had been so much easier before she'd gotten involved with Blaze—if "involved" was even the word for what they'd been. He'd filled her head with all that talk about following her passions, and now she was unsettled and unsure of her direction. He'd wooed her with his charm and gotten her in a muddle when he'd evidently gotten bored with her and decided to move on. While she certainly couldn't imagine what Ivy's mother had been through, she'd had a tiny taste of how Blaze could blow through her life and upend it.

The sweet moments between them were what confused her most. He'd been so kind and personable, that even she—who'd sworn off a relationship with him from the beginning—had fallen for him. She needed to get a read on him. And there was only one way to do that.

She pulled her phone from her back pocket and impulsively dialed Blaze's number. He answered right away.

"Hi," she said, gathering her thoughts.

"Hey."

His tone was heavy, but the sound of his voice was music to her ears. Nora swallowed and centered herself.

"My grandmother's been in touch with Ivy and said you all had your first session with the new counselor. I wanted to see how it went." She closed her eyes and lay back on her pillow.

"It went fine."

"I'm glad to hear that. And how's Ivy? Has she spent any more time with Jake?"

"She's good. She and Jake are an item, I think."

"It's so great that she's made a friend." She was already concerned with what a breakup would do to Ivy's fragile state, but it wasn't her place to fret over it. "And how are you?"

Silence buzzed down the line before he finally answered, "Fine."

That was two fines in one very short conversation.

"That's good." Her words came out in nearly a whisper. She shouldn't have called. She should have taken the hint at the cottage. Blaze didn't want to talk to her anymore. She hadn't been all that helpful with Ivy, and he had better things to do in real life than hang out with her. She swallowed against the lump in her throat. "I was just... checking in. Glad everything's okay." She gritted her teeth when her voice broke on the last word, tears welling in her eyes.

"I'm sorry," Blaze said.

She cleared her throat. "For what?"

"I didn't want to hurt you. I'm no good at this."

"Good at what?" she pressed.

"Nora, I care about you too much to screw this up. And given my history, I'm bound to."

Screw what up? They'd have to have something for him to be able to screw it up. Her heart hammered in her chest, her pulse rising. He felt it too? She'd tried to ignore her feelings for him, push them away, but they were right on the surface.

"You deserve someone who'll give you everything, and I don't think I'm that guy."

She didn't know what to say, and her emotions had welled up unexpectedly, robbing her of a good response, so she sat there, silent.

"Well, I have to go," he said.

"All right," she managed.

"I'll see ya."

He hung up, and Nora dropped the phone onto the bed beside her. A tear rolled down her temple onto the pillow. A page had turned in the story of her life and, stupidly, she'd thought the rest of the book was planned out. But that new page was blank. She wiped her tears and cleared her throat again, and got up to see if Gram was done with her bath and still awake. Maybe she could take her mind off all this.

Thank goodness, her grandmother was watching TV.

"Are you okay?" Gram said from the sofa when Nora plopped down beside her. "Your eyes are red."

"I'm just tired."

"If you're tired, go to bed. That's what I figured you were doing."

"I'm tired, but I can't sleep."

"What's on your mind?"

Loaded question. Nora crossed her legs and pulled a throw pillow into her lap. "My future."

"Oh, that's deep. No wonder you're wired. Don't you want to save that for the morning?"

"I probably should, but I can't stop thinking about it." She leaned on the pillow and squeezed her exhausted eyes shut, then opened them when the sting was too much to bear. "Blaze said something when we were together, and it's bugged me ever since."

Gram clicked off the television. "What's that?"

"He asked me what I was passionate about, and I didn't have an answer for him. Do you know what you're passionate about?"

"I was passionate about your grandfather. And I'm passionate about family."

Her answers were quick and decisive, only serving to make Nora feel more inadequate.

"I don't have anything."

"Well, the good news is that you're young enough to figure out what lights your fire."

"I don't think my job is my passion."

"But you've spent an awful lot of time outside of school helping Ivy. I'd think that would be a sign of passion."

Nora chewed on the inside of her lip, not wanting to say what had entered her mind.

"Right?" Gram pressed.

"I think I'm more passionate about Ivy than I am about my job."

Gram smiled. "She's easy to be passionate about. I really enjoy her company."

"I do too." A wave of sadness overtook Nora. "But I don't think I'm needed anymore, so what do I do with that passion? Now, when I go to work, I won't feel the same. I'm already dreading going back if Ivy isn't there."

"Lots of people don't love their jobs."

She looked into Gram's eyes. "But shouldn't we want more for ourselves?"

"Of course we should." Gram laughed. "But in our limited time on this earth, we'll have lots of battles, and we'll have to choose which ones are worth the fight. Is this newfound apathy over your job worth the upheaval of finding something else? Only you can answer that."

"I don't know." Nora shook her head. "I don't feel like I know anything anymore."

"You're too young for a midlife crisis," Gram teased. "You have time to figure it out."

"And how am I supposed to do that?"

"Think you'd like to paint? Buy canvases. Think you'd like to garden? Get yourself a basil plant and see how you do. Maybe cooking is your thing. Take a class. Just lean into what you like."

"Blaze said to think about what I would do if money were no object, and I said I'd like to travel the world."

Gram closed her eyes and cooed. "That would be a dream, wouldn't it? To wake up in a cozy bed and breakfast in the Cotswolds, with rolling hills of green as far as I can see and rain beading on my window, as I sit by candle light... Mmm."

"That would be incredible," Nora said. "But I have responsibilities."

Gram's gaze shifted downward. "And what if you didn't have those responsibilities? Would you go then?"

That lump formed again in Nora's throat. There was only one way she wouldn't have those responsibilities, and she didn't want to think about it. "I would choose the responsibilities over travel, but even if I had no responsibilities, what would I buy a ticket with—my good looks?" she teased. "Because that wouldn't get me much."

Gram brightened. "Oh, phooey." She slung a pillow over to Nora in mock disgust. "You could buy a thousand tickets with your looks."

"You find me the ticket salesman that agrees with you, and we're off to Europe."

Gram laughed, the sound like windchimes. It was so nice to hear her laugh.

Nora could easily slip back into worry over her grandmother, but she decided to stay in the moment. *Don't ruin this.*

But Gram sobered. "You know what I'd like to tell you about your life?"

"What?"

"Enjoy the moments when you don't know what's next. Be excited about them."

"Why would I be excited when I have no plans?"

"Because those moments are the slip of time before God reveals your next big journey."

Gram's words tingled down her spine. "I love that." She moved the pillow to the corner of the couch. "You're so right. I shouldn't worry so much."

"There's nothing really to worry about. Your future is going to happen. I'll be gone one day, and—God willing—you'll get old. Those are the only two real absolutes. The rest is entirely up to us."

"I love you, Gram."

"Love you too, dear."

Before Nora climbed into bed, she texted Blaze.

> I know you don't have it all figured out, and I don't either. But I'm happy being friends.

She didn't get a response and, eventually, she fell asleep.

CHAPTER TWENTY-FOUR

Gram's words were still going around in Nora's mind when she woke up the next morning, and she decided this was the first day of the rest of her life. She browsed the website on her laptop as she sat at the kitchen table with her cup of coffee.

"What's that you're looking at?" Gram asked, puttering into the kitchen.

"Travel destinations. Places I'd like to visit."

"Already? We just got back," Gram said with a laugh as she made herself a coffee and sat down next to Nora. "Where were you interested in going?"

"So many places. I looked up the Cotswolds. That's definitely on my list. And so are London and Paris. I'd like to go to this island called Paros in Greece, Bora Bora, and, of course, New York... I'm making a list."

"Oh, I hope we go to all of them."

"I have no idea if we'll actually go to any of them." She added Montana to her list.

"But you're writing them down. That's a start."

"Yeah. I have no money now, but maybe if I make this

list and create the intention of going, somehow, I'll make it happen. I'm not sure with work, though. We'll have to plan a trip each summer or something."

"Gramps is up there with The Big Man. If anyone can talk Him into helping you make your trips happen, it's your grandfather." Gran grinned.

Nora closed her laptop. "Have you heard from Ivy today at all?"

"She texted me to tell me she's decided to attend Brentwood Academy. She's been heavy with that Jake boy. Other than that, she's been too busy to text an old woman."

Nora gripped her mug. "Brentwood?"

Gram nodded.

Nora let the fact that she wouldn't see Ivy next school year sink in.

"You okay?" Gram asked.

"I suppose so." Truthfully, she wasn't sure if she was okay or not. Would she find a way to catch up with Ivy to see how she was doing? "I hope she's able to have a good summer."

"What about your summer? Have you heard from Blaze?"

"I called him last night, but things were awkward. And then I texted him right before bed, but he didn't come back to me."

"He's the first man you've had any interest in since Carson."

"Being with him feels different from other people. I felt something for him," she admitted. "He said he cares about me."

"That's a start."

Nora shook her head. "But he said, 'You deserve someone who will give you everything, and I don't know if

I'm that guy.' Something's holding him back. And I think I know what it is."

"What, dear?"

"I'd get in the way of his life."

"You think?" Gram asked, not looking convinced.

"I'm willing to put money on it."

"I'll bet he's stewing over you right now," Gram said.

"Oh, really? Let's put that theory to the test." Nora opened her laptop once more. "We'll go to his social media and see if he's posted anything." As she pulled up his page, she sent a silent wish into the air that he'd mention something that would give her an inkling as to his thinking—even if it was cryptic. She hoped to see him contemplating his life and wondering what was next, the way she was. She clicked on his story and held her breath.

His handsome face filled the screen.

"Back in the studio today, working with an incredibly talented band."

That familiar voice made her skin tingle.

Blaze's camera turned around, giving her a glimpse behind the glass wall of a beautiful woman with headphones on, singing into a mic. Her hair was pulled back in a messy ponytail, and she was stunningly gorgeous, without a bit of makeup on from the looks of her milky skin. She winked at the camera, and Nora was left to wonder if that little wink had been at Blaze and not the viewers.

Feeling deflated, she clicked through to the next story, perking up when she saw Blaze and Ivy together. Ivy had a silly grin on her face and a loaded burger between her fingers. Brightly colored words on the screen said, *Pickle burgers are great, but pickle burgers with this one are the best burgers!*

Nora smiled, glad they were back at Cappy's together. Maybe one day, she'd go with Gram.

The video kept looping, showing Ivy's smile over and over, and Nora couldn't deny she missed the girl.

She clicked to a third story to see Blaze diving into his pool. He came up from the bright blue surface and shook the water from his hair.

"Working on a record is hard work. Time to play," his overlaid voice said. His triceps bulged as he hoisted himself out of the pool, retrieved a towel, and wrapped it around his fit waist. Then he seized the camera and turned it around. The band from earlier filled the loungers around the pool, the lead singer in a fringed bikini. She fluttered her manicured fingers in a little wave at the camera before Ivy came out of nowhere and did a cannonball into the pool, splashing them all.

"He seems to be having a great summer," Gram said.

"Yeah." She peered into her coffee, the surface of it cloudy as the temperature had cooled. "Looks like he isn't missing me at all."

Not like I'm missing him.

Gram set her hand on Nora's arm, commanding her attention. "What's meant to be will be."

"You talk to Gramps still, right? Get him to do a little persuading up there, like you said."

Gram chuckled. "I'll tell him." She clapped her hands. "Now. Enough of this wallowing. We need to go get groceries. There's nothing in the house to eat."

"I'll go. Do you want to write down what we need?"

"Sure."

Nora gathered her laptop and destination wish list and went into the bathroom to brush her teeth. After, she washed her face and combed her hair, fretting the entire time over what to do with her life. She channeled Gram's explanation about the moments where she didn't know what was next: *"... those moments are the slip of time before God reveals your next big journey."*

Nora was a linear thinker, so the idea that nothing would come of her feelings for Blaze was a difficult pill to swallow. Why had she fallen for him if she was supposed to do something else? And, clearly, he had feelings for her—he'd said so, himself: *"I care about you too much to screw this up..."* What was the point? The random nature of the situation drove her crazy.

Despite what he'd said, Blaze seemed to be able to go on more easily than she could, which made her feel inadequate. Did she have so few life experiences that she couldn't rebound as well? That idea only brought her back to the fact that she didn't even really know who she was anymore. She peered over at the list of travel destinations she'd made. Would she find that paper decades later only to realize that the list was a dream life she'd never been able to manage?

She slipped on her jean shorts and a T-shirt, balled up the paper full of dreams, grabbed her keys, and went into the living room to see Gram. On her way in, she tossed the paper in the kitchen trash can.

"The grocery list is on the counter, dear."

"Okay, thanks." Nora grabbed it and headed out the door.

When she got to the market, she sat in her car, watching people go in and out. How many of them knew what they were supposed to do with their lives? Before her beach trip, Nora had thought she knew. Did Blaze have so much pull on her that he could change her outlook on life in a week? How was that possible?

Perhaps that was why things hadn't worked out. Maybe

he wasn't supposed to be hers, but rather her wake-up call to figure out her real purpose in life. She still couldn't help but care for him, though. He'd been the first person since Carson to make her feel something again.

She opened her phone and clicked her way to his stories once more. To her surprise, there was a new one. He had his arm around Ivy as they sat out by the pool. Then Jake poked his head through the two of them and made a face, before putting Ivy in a pretend headlock and saying, "She's all mine."

Blaze offered a playfully stern face and said, "Excuse me? I think she's ours."

Ivy giggled and kissed both of them on the cheek.

Nora clicked off her phone, her heart in her stomach. In her memory, even with the stressful moments, their week together had been like a dream, and she'd stupidly imagined it would continue after they got home.

Brentwood Academy. What would next school year look like without Ivy? The reality of it only clouded Nora's decision about what to do with the rest of her life more.

They all looked so happy... It was as if God had said, *"Yes, Nora. That's exactly right. They weren't meant for you."*

She dropped her phone in her lap and put her hands on the steering wheel, panic taking over. She hadn't wanted to even allow the thought, but it was squirming around in her mind, not letting go of her this time. Gram *had* to be okay. If she wasn't, Nora didn't know how she'd manage. Gram was her grounding force, and without her, Nora would be completely lost.

NORA DROPPED a heavy bag of groceries onto the counter and went out to the car to get another.

"I'll help," Gram said from the balcony. She climbed the one flight down the stairs to the bottom floor and walked out to where Nora was unloading. She peered into the back of Nora's car, which was full of groceries. "Planning for the apocalypse?"

"We didn't have anything, so I bought everything. I got supplies to make those biscuits you like to bake; I got tons of casserole ingredients; we can make summer salads; we can bake sugar cookies..." She lifted a bag onto each hip as Gram pulled another sack from the backseat of the car. "I also got three different kinds of coffee; I figured we could try matcha lattes—I bought that too. And I got lots of different kinds of syrups—the organic ones."

Gram stared at her, but didn't say anything.

"I also thought, since we did all that organizing before the trip, that it would be a great time to redecorate. I might dip into my savings and spring for a new sofa. We need one. I also have some ideas to spruce up the kitchen."

"All this happened while you were at the grocery store?"

"Yeah, I just got to thinking. You know how we took the beach trip because you said you weren't getting any younger?"

"Yes."

"Well, why don't we live our lives that way? Until now, I've spent every calculated minute doing the things I was *supposed* to do. And look what that got me: a relationship with Carson that was a disaster because I chose to date someone who looked good on paper, and a lifetime of nothing much. Let's live in the slip of time before God reveals our next journey, like you said. We should be in the moment, and in this moment, I want to redecorate our apartment, light some candles, and sit with you on a new sofa with some delicious home-cooked food."

What she didn't say was that she wanted to spend every moment with Gram because she didn't know what the future held.

Gram smiled. "I like your thinking."

"What I do with my life is up to me. Blaze taught me that," Nora said as they climbed the stairs.

"He did?"

She opened the door and held it for Gram with her foot. "Yep. He focused on making his business a success and he did it. I thought maybe I should take a page out of his book and see where it gets me."

"Sounds like a plan."

She did like a plan.

CHAPTER TWENTY-FIVE

Gram and Nora spent the next week nesting. They went to the furniture store and picked out a new sofa, and Nora had decided to repaint the kitchen and living room. She immersed herself in her plans, shopping and picking out new rugs and knickknacks.

Gram stepped out the front door to get the mail from the apartment's wall of boxes and came inside. She'd been getting the mail all week. While they hadn't spoken about the letter from the hospital, Nora was willing to bet Gram was as on edge as her, waiting for the MRI test results, even though Gram hadn't said so. Nora certainly had been quietly worrying.

"Anything good?" Nora climbed down from the ladder.

"Just junk." Gram lumped the pile on the counter. "You've been working hard."

Nora put her hands on her paint-speckled hips, and assessed the second coat of cheerful cream on the wall. "This brightens the kitchen so much."

"It will go lovely with the tweed rug you got and the

new dishes," Gram said before making a cup of coffee and taking it into the living room.

Nora stayed back and squinted at the wall, imagining it behind her new décor.

The blue and teal pottery-style dishes had been an impulse-buy, but they'd reminded Nora of the Gulf, and she thought it was only fitting to change to the color scheme since it was those two weeks that had made her look at life differently. She'd realized she'd been going through her days on autopilot, not stopping to smell the roses, and Blaze and Ivy had been the shake-up she'd needed. She had still thought about both of them since being home, but she didn't spend too long dwelling on them. This era was about her, and finding what made her happy.

"Look at this," Gram said, holding out her phone. "Ivy just sent it to me."

Pulling herself from her inner turmoil, Nora peered around Gram to see Blaze and Ivy doing a choreographed dance in unison to a pop song.

"It's got four hundred thousand likes," Gram said. "Ivy says that's a lot."

Nora smiled. "It is a lot."

Gram grinned down at the screen. "Look at those two. They seem to be getting along."

"That's wonderful," Nora said. They got their happy ending after all. Well, Nora was going to do her very best to find hers.

"Blaze looks handsome," Gram said.

Nora folded the ladder and leaned it against the wall. "He always looks handsome." A flash of those gray eyes when he smiled at her floated into her mind.

"Has he texted at all?"

Nora shook her head. "Ivy hasn't either. I think my season in their lives is finished."

"That's a shame. They're both lovely."

"I know. I miss them," she said honestly. "It's only been a couple weeks, but it feels like a lifetime since I've seen them."

"You should call."

"It was awkward last time I tried. And Blaze and my conversation ended on my text, which he never replied to, so I think it's best if I let it go."

"No life ever changed for the better by taking the easy way out."

Nora bristled. "I didn't. I texted him, and he didn't text back."

"Then text him again."

"I'd assume he's not in the market to date a psycho," she teased.

Gram put her hands on her hips and cocked her head to the side. "Texting someone twice does not make you a psycho. Maybe he's not sure what to say."

"Well, neither am I." She picked up her paint roller and rinsed it in the sink. "Look, I know you're just attempting to be helpful, but I've tried very hard to move on, and I was getting good at it. Bringing Blaze up takes me right back to our time together, and there's no need to go backward."

"I'm sorry. I won't mention it again. I guess I just thought you two were great together." She put up her hands. "But it's not my business. Your life is yours."

THE REST OF THE DAY, Nora set in, redecorating the apartment.

"I put all your books on this shelf," she said to Gram as she filled the new bookshelf that divided the small living and kitchen spaces.

She filled the shelves with their books and topped them with a lamp, an aloe vera plant, and a small Boston fern. She'd added cream-colored seat cushions to the dinette chairs, and set a tall dried floral arrangement in the center of the table to give it some height.

"That chandelier is stunning," Gram said, coming in to see her progress.

With her landlord's permission for both lighting and wall color changes, Nora had switched out the lighting above the table to a chandelier made of wood and brushed nickel.

"I think it looks so much more current. I never really put a bit of myself into the apartment until now. It feels like it has a little personality."

"You could go into interior design," Gram said from across the room as Nora added a wide-weave throw to the back of the corner chair in the living room.

"I got most of the ideas online," she admitted. "And decorating isn't my thing. I just wanted to make us a space we could enjoy." She fluffed the new gauzy curtains at the sliding doors to the small balcony.

"It's definitely beautiful, but are you sure you're doing this for us?"

Nora slid the last book onto the shelf and stood up. "What do you mean? Who else would it be for?"

Gram squinted at her as if trying to see through to her inner thoughts. "I just want to make sure you aren't using this little project to avoid anything."

"What would I be avoiding?"

"You tell me." She pulled out a chair at the table and sat down. "If Blaze had been—"

"Nope." Nora waved her hands in the air, stopping the conversation. "I'm not talking about Blaze. I'm trying to build a life I can be proud of. And I've made a good start. Now, I'm going to get a shower, get ready for the evening, and we're going to make a fantastic dinner, light the candles, and dine at our newly decorated table."

"All right," Gram said.

Nora went into her bedroom and shut the door. Why was Gram so bent on bringing up Blaze? Was it because she worried about her own future and didn't want to leave Nora alone? Blaze was wonderful, but he'd made his point with his silence. And Nora would do her best to be ready when and if she had to go at it alone. But she didn't want to think about life without Gram right now.

She turned on the shower to let the water heat up. While she waited, she went into the bedroom and plopped down on the bed. Her phone sat on the side table. Just to torture herself, she picked it up, opened her social media app, and searched for Blaze, clicking on his stories.

"Ivy and I are going out tonight. Should be fun," he said as he held the phone toward his reflection in a full-length mirror.

He had on an attractively tailored pair of trousers and a button-down that showed off his pecks more than it probably should. His hair was combed and his face shaved. She closed her eyes, wishing she could be with them.

The sound of Ivy's voice brought her attention back to the phone, and she realized the video was still going.

"I'm excited about tonight." Ivy did a little spin to show off her denim dress and boots.

She looked positively radiant. How much she'd changed from the girl who'd slumped in Nora's office.

"Got the tickets, Dad?"

"Yep. Got 'em!" Blaze said from the background.

From the look of their outfits, they were probably going to a country music event. She was glad he was taking Ivy. It was nice to see them doing things together.

Nora rolled her head on her shoulders and tossed the phone on her bed. She missed them. She shouldn't have peeked into their life. It was just a reminder that she didn't fit in it, and given how great they seemed to be all of a sudden, neither of them would require her services anymore. Perhaps the new counselor was just what they'd needed. And with Ivy going to Brentwood Academy next year—something Blaze hadn't even bothered to tell Nora—she was effectively out of their lives forever.

With a heavy heart, she went into the bathroom, undressed, and stepped into the shower. She closed her eyes. The warm stream pelted her face. She stood, motionless, as if the water could wash away her thoughts. Had Gram been right? Was all the decorating and cooking just a subconscious attempt at blocking out the hole Ivy and Blaze had left in her heart? She'd opened her vacation home to them, and neither had even texted to say thank you. It didn't seem like them at all. Could she have done more to change the events that had unfolded?

She continued to ruminate over it as she put on her makeup and did her hair. She didn't have anywhere to be tonight except for her apartment, but this new version of herself wanted to put in the effort. She was worth it. Even if no one else could see it yet. In a way, she'd learned that from Blaze as well. While she hadn't been able to keep seeing him—and he'd warned her of that—she'd turned the head of the biggest producer in Nashville, even if only briefly. So she had to have some redeeming qualities.

She sat on her bed. *Gramps, are you really around like Gram says you are? I need a favor.* She peered around the room, looking for a sign, but nothing was amiss. *If you're really here, could you talk to The Big Man for me and give me some direction? I'll do whatever I'm supposed to do. What's next for me?* She stared at the dancing dust particles in a stream of sunlight until they blurred in front of her.

Still unsure of her direction, and with no sign from Gramps, she got up from the bed. She slipped on her pale blue sundress and painted her toenails to match. Then she went into the living room to spend the evening with Gram.

Gram had the pile of junk mail next to her. She quickly folded a piece of paper and tucked it into her book.

"What's that?" Nora asked.

Gram slipped the book under her arm. "Just a sales flyer. I'm using it as a bookmark."

"Where's the bookmark I got you?" she asked, suspicious, her heart pounding like a snare drum.

Gram smiled. "In my other book."

"Gram..." Nora gazed at her.

"What?"

"What's on the paper?"

"I said it's *nothing*." She wrinkled her nose at Nora. "You look lovely. What do you have planned for tonight?"

Nora assessed Gram's demeanor. She didn't have that panicked look as if she'd gotten terrible news. Perhaps the paper was, in fact, just a flyer.

"My plans are to hang out with you. Let's find something really delicious and exotic to make tonight for dinner," Nora said, coming over and taking her hand to help her out of her chair.

With the book still pinned under her arm, Gram gripped Nora's hand and got up. She gathered the mail, and followed Nora into the kitchen. On her way, she set the pile of envelopes and magazines on the bookshelf, along with her book.

"Are you sure you want to make something now?" Gram looked at her watch. "It's barely five o'clock."

"Well, if we make something, it might take us an hour or so." She took Gram's hands again and gave her a twirl, making Gram laugh.

"What's gotten into you? You're all dressed up, suddenly a five-star chef…"

"I just want to seize the day."

Nora eyed the paper in the book over on the bookshelf, but decided to let it go for one evening. If Gram did have bad news, they couldn't fix it tonight, so she'd like to have one more evening of normalcy. She opened the pantry and started browsing the ingredients they had left, but she stopped.

"I have to be honest with you, Gram. I thought about Blaze and Ivy before deciding to make this big dinner tonight. Do you really think I'm avoiding my feelings?"

"Oh, honey, I don't know. I just want you to follow your heart."

It was tough to follow her heart when neither Blaze nor Ivy wanted to reach out. "You're right," she said, deciding to push forward. She didn't know what she was doing, but she couldn't just stand by and sulk. "My heart says the chicken casserole I saw online the other day sounds delicious."

Gram took her phone off the table and began typing. "What's in it?" she asked, her eyes on the screen.

"Oh, no need to look up a recipe. I printed one." Nora opened one of the drawers by the sink where she kept the potholders. "I stuck it in here." Nora waved the paper in the air. "See? I've got it."

Gram let out a breath of air, and set her phone down while Nora scanned the ingredients and checked them against their inventory. Gram seemed weirdly on edge all of a sudden. Maybe she wasn't up for a big dinner? Did she feel all right?

"We don't have cherry tomatoes, basil, or dry mustard." Nora closed the cabinet. "You know what? I could change into my pajamas, and we could order a pizza with all the toppings, pour ourselves a glass of wine, and veg out in front of the TV instead."

"I don't think you should bother."

She turned to face Gram, confused by her behavior. "Why? We could wait if you're not hungry. We need to eat dinner at some point, though, right?"

Just then, the doorbell rang.

"Who's that?" Nora asked.

Gram shrugged and shook her head, but the shift in her gaze told Nora that something was amiss. She stared at Gram, but Gram only nodded toward the door.

"You gonna get that?" Gram asked.

Nora opened the door to find Blaze and Ivy in the outfits they'd had on in the video. Had they stopped by on the way to their concert? Ivy held two large bags in her arms. They were taking groceries?

"June might have texted me to tell me you were planning dinner at your new table," Ivy said, flashing her a smile. She moved past her into the kitchen and greeted June. "Your apartment is so pretty!"

"Let me show you what Nora's done," Gram said, taking the bags from Ivy and setting them on the counter. She and the girl walked into the living room.

Nora offered Blaze a questioning look.

He took her hand and guided her out onto the balcony, shutting Ivy and June inside.

"I'm sorry I haven't called…" He ran his thumb over her knuckles. "I wanted to get this just right."

Nora held her breath, unsure of what he was going to say. She dared not anticipate something wonderful because the letdown would crush her if his message wasn't what she hoped for.

He let go of her and took a step back as if collecting his thoughts. He took a deep breath. "Being with you changed my entire way of thinking."

She leaned back against the doorframe. *I know what you mean.*

"I used to think that following my passion meant that I had to shut everything else out, that I had to spend all hours of the day following it. But you showed me I was wrong."

"Really?"

"It isn't worth as much unless I have someone to share it with." He took her other hand this time. "I got home and tried to work. As I did, something funny would happen, and I'd want to tell you. Or after work, I'd be beat, and I'd want to come home and talk to you to decompress, the way we did in the evenings at the beach, and you weren't there."

Happiness bubbled up. "I had no idea."

"I've never needed anyone. But a relationship isn't just about me. I had to be sure I knew how to give you what *you* needed. That stared with learning how to be a full-time parent to Ivy. I couldn't bring you into our life until I got a handle on that." The corners of his mouth turned upward. "What I hadn't expected was mine and Ivy's mutual adoration of you to unify us."

No one had ever told Nora anything so heartfelt before.

"The other night, I got up the nerve and admitted how I felt about you to Ivy. I wanted the life I had at the beach. I missed it. Ivy was so excited. It took everything I had to keep her from telling June what I'd said."

Nora shook her head. "Our life at the beach wasn't real life."

"It was more real than anything else I've experienced lately."

They looked into each other's eyes as the warm summer breeze blew against them.

"It was a pretty amazing handful of days," he said.

Her heart pattered, every nerve ending on alert. "Ever since you left the beach, I couldn't get you off my mind."

His gray eyes sparkled. "Oh, yeah?"

She nodded.

"I don't know if I'm any good at this," he warned. "My last try crashed and burned."

She grinned. "Mine too."

A look of seriousness slid over his face. He waggled a finger between the two of them. "This feels different, though."

"It does to me too." She took in a steadying breath. "But how will we manage in the real world, once we both go back to work?"

"Well, the one thing Ivy taught me was that the best way to manage is to do it together. I think we can face anything that way."

"That's a great answer."

A moment of buzzing uncertainty hung between them.

"So..." Blaze said.

His adorable hesitation had her stomach doing somersaults.

"So," she said with a smile.

"Want to go out on a date sometime?"

Nora chewed on a smile. "I'd love to."

"Ah, I can't handle this new dynamic between us." He paced in a circle and then arrived back in front of her.

"New dynamic?" she asked, but she felt it too. She just wanted to hear his side to see if he could verbalize what was pinging around inside her.

"I've told you how I feel about you, and that changes everything, so now I'm in this strange space where I don't know how to act with you. Do I hold your hand? Do I put my arm around you?"

She laughed. "You can do both if you'd like."

His movement stilled, those eyes falling upon her. Blaze took a step into her space. She tipped her chin up toward him as he moved in.

"I just want to do this the right way," he said, his voice a whisper. He took her hand. "So you're all right with this?"

"Mm-hm."

He let go of her hand and pushed her hair behind her shoulder with a finger. "And that?"

"Yes," she said, trying to breathe.

He leaned in and softly whispered in her ear, his spicy scent intoxicating her. "This okay?"

Never before had she felt anything like this. They were barely touching each other, but the energy between them had the intensity of a bolt of lightning.

"Ahem."

They pulled apart when Ivy appeared at the door. "Y'all can make out later. We have dinner to prepare." She flashed another grin in their direction and held the door open, beckoning them inside.

Blaze looked like a kid who'd been caught with his hand

in the cookie jar. With a chuckle, he nodded for Nora to go in first.

"What are we cooking?" she asked him, still trying to slow her pounding heart.

Gram's delighted gaze darted between them.

"Mac and cheese, and burgers. I figured I'd stick to what I'm good at," he replied.

She laughed. "That sounds delicious."

"I did get us a bottle of Dom Pérignon."

Gram's eyes widened, and Nora sucked in a breath.

"It's an eight-hundred-dollar bottle," Ivy whispered into Nora's ear.

Blaze pressed his lips together and shook his head at his daughter. "The price doesn't matter. We need to celebrate, so I brought a good champagne." He took the bottle from the counter.

Ivy giggled and went over to Gram, who was opening cabinets and asking where the champagne flutes were.

"Telling each other how we feel doesn't require an eight-hundred-dollar bottle of champagne," Nora said quietly to Blaze. "You know you don't have to impress me. You do that all by yourself."

"We have more to celebrate," he said, popping the cork off the bottle as Gram pulled three champagne glasses from the cabinet. He poured them each a glass and handed one to Nora. Then he took her over to the table. "Please." He offered her a chair and she sat.

Gram and Ivy took a seat with Nora, Blaze lowering himself across from her, their champagne fizzing in front of them.

"What's going on?" she asked.

"Well, remember I said I've managed to take a little time

off this summer. I still have to work, but a lot of it can be done on my laptop and not in the studio."

"Okay." What was he getting at?

Ivy leaned in, her face alight. "This was my idea, by the way."

"What was?" Nora asked, looking back and forth between Blaze and Ivy.

Ivy wriggled her shoulders enthusiastically. "I fired my counselor."

Nora's shoulders fell. "Oh, no. Not a good fit?"

Ivy shook her head. "No. I wanted a way to spend time with Dad. And I don't think I need a counselor at all. I feel better when I spend time with *you*—something me and Dad agree on. I'm better at managing the loss of my mom when you're there. You make me feel like things will be okay."

"That warms my heart, Ivy," Nora said.

"Dad and I have done a lot of talking, and I've decided that to honor my mom, I do want to do charity work. But I've changed how I want to do it." She waved her hands at her father as if to usher in Blaze's explanation.

"What are you up to in the next few weeks?" he asked. "Do you have any plans?"

Nora consulted Gram, who was grinning from ear to ear, her eyebrows bouncing excitedly.

"I don't have any plans that I'm aware of."

"Great, because you, me, Ivy, and your grandmother are traveling first class to New York."

Nora tried not to spill her champagne. "What?"

"I've got a day planned at a food bank," Ivy said. "You can help me if you want. After that, we can tour the city."

"Then we're flying to London for more charity work of Ivy's choosing, where we'll spend a little over a week, because I've allotted enough time to visit the Cotswolds.

After that, Paris and Greece." Blaze pulled a wrinkled piece of paper from his pocket, smoothed it out, and slid it over to Nora.

She recognized her handwriting. "My travel list."

"I can dig through the trash, too, you know," Gram said.

Nora scanned the many places she'd listed. "Gram, you had a hard time with a short flight to the beach. Are you up for this level of travel?"

"I can manage. I hear there are some lovely little cafés where I can rest while you all run around the cities."

Nora's skin tingled with the idea of traveling the world. But then that folded paper in Gram's book over on the shelf next to them came into view.

"We should really stay until we hear that second opinion about your test results," she told Gram.

"Well, I told you a little fib." Gram reached over and took her book from the bookshelf. She pulled out the piece of paper and held it up. "I wanted to share the news tonight, over champagne. They got the final results back and the mass is noncancerous. They're going to keep an eye on it, but they don't expect anything to come of it."

Nora got up and threw her arms around her grandmother, a lump in her throat. "That's wonderful news."

"Maybe Gramps actually does have some pull with the man upstairs." Gram winked at Nora.

It was then she realized she'd just asked for Gramps's help to show her where to go next in her life. And there she was, with a first-class ticket to her future. Maybe he did have some pull, indeed.

"So do you want to go?" Blaze asked.

"Absolutely."

Ivy clapped her hands. "I'm so excited! Dad wouldn't let me text you or anything until he had this straight. I can't tell you how hard it was to stay quiet." She held up a finger. "Hang on! Let me get a Coke."

Ivy ran into the kitchen. There was a crack and a fizz, and she came back in with a can of soda. "To people who feel a whole lot like family." Ivy raised her can.

"And to the future." Blaze held his glass in the air.

Nora and Gram raised their champagne together and clinked glasses with Blaze and then Ivy.

"You didn't have to do all this," Nora told Blaze, feeling a bit overcome by the gesture.

Blaze took her hand. "I've spent a lot of my life finding my own way. Now it's time to support others while they do the same. My focus is on you and Ivy. This trip might not give you the meaning of life, but it'll be one step forward for the *three* of us."

Tonight, another page had turned in Nora's life story, but this time, the blank page in front of her held nothing but excitement.

EPILOGUE
ONE YEAR LATER

"Ivy. Ryman." The announcer's voice boomed through the microphone, Ivy's name echoing through the entire field at Brentwood Academy, where they all sat in lines of white chairs.

Nora fanned herself with the paper program as she sat between Gram and Blaze, beaming, while Ivy walked across the stage in her cap and gown. Her auburn hair fell in loose waves down her back, and coupled with her heels and a gold bracelet she'd borrowed from Nora, she looked more like a young woman than a girl.

Nora had been able to watch Ivy blossom this school year. Having quit her job at the high school, Nora had taken a position as an online social and emotional learning coach. She taught workshops and courses on social-emotional skills, like controlling emotions, resolving conflicts, and developing resilience. The job allowed her to help kids while also having the flexibility to travel and spend time with Ivy and Blaze.

Ivy shook the announcer's hand as he handed her a diploma. Then she turned, a wide smile on her face, and pointed at Blaze before pumping her fist in the air. Gram blew her a kiss, and Blaze and Nora stood up and cheered. Jake whooped from his seat up front, among the other graduates.

How far Ivy had come.

After, they headed back to Blaze's for the cookout he'd planned in celebration of Ivy's graduation. She'd finished the top of her senior class at Brentwood, and she'd already gotten acceptance letters from three universities. She was still trying to decide where she wanted to go.

Over the last year, Blaze and Nora had gone on more trips. For these, Ivy and Gram had opted to stay at home. Ivy appreciated the freedom Gram allowed, and Gram enjoyed sunning herself by the Rymans's swimming pool.

Blaze had surprised Nora with a trip out west to Montana, ticking that off her list, and they'd spent a week in Bora Bora—her favorite spot yet. He'd been right: the trips hadn't shown her the meaning of life, but every excursion had opened her up to a new way of living and all the possibilities she had with Blaze.

When they got to the pool area, a chef had already begun to prepare the barbeque for the party, but that wasn't the highlight. Ivy nearly fell over backward when she saw the band setting up in the corner.

"Is that..." She pointed at the lead singer.

"Yep. I pulled a few strings at work."

Blaze and Nora had been in cahoots about getting Ivy's favorite band, Slim Rocket, to play at the party. They were an up-and-coming group, discovered by Blaze and adored by his daughter. Their latest single, "When We Crash," was climbing the pop charts, and it was only a matter of time before they were a household name for every teen in America.

Jake stepped up behind Ivy and wrapped his arms around her waist. "Whoa, is that Slim Rocket? Your dad is so cool."

Ivy giggled and tossed her black graduation robe and hat onto one of the loungers. She wrapped her arms around Jake's neck. "We did it!"

"We did." He gave her a big hug. Then he raised his arms in the air. "Party time!"

Gram did a little jig, making them all laugh.

The heat settled upon them as the kids began to change into their swimsuits and jump into the pool while the band played.

Over the last year, while Ivy still dealt with grief over her mother, she had really grown into herself. She'd gotten involved in the after-school music club, and she'd even sold her car. As a graduation gift, Blaze told her he'd buy her a new reliable car so she could get around at college. She'd settled on a red BMW convertible on the condition he drive with her to the beach with the top down.

To Nora's delight, Blaze agreed instantly.

The Next Day

"I thought Ivy was headed to the beach today with all her friends to celebrate graduation," Nora said, as she stood in Blaze's entryway.

In her final year of high school, Ivy had made tons of friends. She had bonded with one girl in particular named Natalie, who'd also lost her mother. The two girls were inseparable and were headed to the beach together, along with a group of their extended social circle.

Which was why Blaze's request didn't make any sense.

He'd told Nora they'd planned to continue the celebration, and had asked her and Gram to come over this afternoon.

"She is. But she's pushed her trip back till tomorrow."

Nora sharpened her hearing. "Is there another band out back?"

Blaze held up his hands. "Guilty. It's easy to do, given my line of work, and so much better than a DJ, don't you think?" He led them across the shiny marble floors toward the back of the house.

Nora looked over at Gram for any additional explanation, but Gram just shrugged.

"When did you plan this?" Nora asked as they followed him.

"I'd originally thought to have another party later in the summer, but when I told Ivy about it, she insisted we have it now. Since she and Natalie both got early acceptance to Vanderbilt, they're moving into an apartment together after they come back from the beach."

Blaze opened the back doors, and the place was full of people—many of them Blaze's friends. But not all of them. Nora's old colleagues from Oakland High were there too. Kim rushed over.

"Hi!" Nora's friend gave her a big squeeze.

"Hi." Nora looked over at Gram again, but got another shrug. "What are you doing here?"

"Blaze and Ivy invited us to the party."

Ivy came over and draped an arm around Gram's shoulders. "I hope I invited everyone," the girl said. "I asked the chemistry teacher, Mrs. Edmunds—she came." Ivy pointed across the pool area. "And she said I should ask Mrs. Rodgers, the orchestra teacher. She's at the bar. And my old P.E. teacher, Jill Bryson. Then, I just told them to invite anyone they thought might want to come party with you."

"Thank you," Nora said, still a little confused by all the hoopla.

While she was surprised that Blaze would move a bash of this size up a couple of months just for Ivy, she did love that he was attempting to follow his daughter's wishes. They'd really bonded this summer.

"Get a drink," Blaze suggested. "We've got everything you can imagine at the bar."

Nora and Gram went over to the bartender and got themselves a soda. When they turned around, Blaze had disappeared. Nora and Gram wandered through the crowd as everyone chatted happily, danced, and socialized.

Then suddenly, the band stopped, and the crowd quieted as Ivy took the microphone. The girl looked so much more like a woman, standing there. She was poised, confident, radiant.

"You know, it's funny how life can hit you out of the blue," Ivy said, her voice echoing through the yard. "Death, change, new friends... You can find yourself in an unfamiliar place or fall in love out of nowhere." Ivy winked at Jake who was standing at the side of the makeshift stage.

"I've learned that it's the things that come out of nowhere that are often the things that change our lives. A lot has happened for me over the last few years. Many of you know that. But there's one more thing that would really round out my childhood before I embark on the next stage of my life." Ivy stepped aside.

The band played a low drumming sound as if waiting for a big reveal.

Then Blaze took the microphone.

"Ivy's not the only one who had life hit her out of the blue. I've spent the last year doing all sorts of things I never thought I'd do: I took vacations with my daughter; I traveled the world; and I met someone who completely changed me." He held out his hand, drawing everyone's attention to Nora. "Nora, would you come over here with me?"

The crowd whooped as Nora joined Blaze.

"You've upended the life I thought I wanted and showed me something better than I could've ever imagined. Will you..."

Nora stared at him, her breath still in her lungs.

"... help me take Ivy to college and get her settled in?"

"Of course," she said with a laugh.

"And will you..."

She eyed him, silently questioning what he was about to say.

"... travel to more places with me?"

She grinned at him. "Yes."

"And will you..." This time, he got down on one knee, and all the kids went wild. "Be my wife?" He opened a baby blue jewelry box, revealing a stunning solitaire diamond on a platinum band.

Tears of joy welled in her eyes. "Yes."

He slipped the ring onto her finger—a perfect fit—as everyone clapped and hooted.

He stood up, and Nora threw her arms around his neck, as his lips met hers. All the cheers faded. Nora was lost in that moment with the man who took her breath away every day, not just this one.

Then, a new set of arms were around her. Ivy gave her a big squeeze. "He wanted to show me the ring before I left for the beach to get my opinion, and I couldn't go until it was on your finger. With everything else we're celebrating, we couldn't leave this until later."

While onlookers and friends clapped Blaze on the back and congratulated him, Gram took Nora's hand.

"My eyes! I'm blinded by that rock on your finger. Holy cow." Gram squeezed her eyes shut and then laughed. "It's absolutely beautiful."

Nora wiggled her finger, the stone catching the light and sparkling. "I can't believe it."

"Do you think you'll keep your online job now that you'll be Mrs. Blaze Ryman?"

The truth was, she didn't know. She was starting to love the surprises life brought her when she didn't have a plan. There was nothing better than those things, as Ivy so eloquently said, that came out of the blue.

A LETTER FROM JENNY

Hello!

Thank you so much for picking up my novel, *Out of the Blue*. I hope it whisked you away to a beachy destination and (if you have them) made you want to run and hug your teenagers.

If you'd like to know when my next book is out, you can **sign up for new Harpeth Road release alerts for my novels here:**

www.harpethroad.com/jenny-hale-newsletter-signup

I won't share your information with anyone else, and I'll only email you a quick message whenever new books come out or go on sale.

If you did enjoy *Out of the Blue*, I'd be so thankful if you'd write a review of the book online. Getting feedback from readers helps to persuade others to pick up my book for the first time. It's one of the biggest gifts you could give me.

Until next time,
   Jenny

ACKNOWLEDGMENTS

In every book I write, I have to thank Oliver Rhodes, for the risk he took on me at the very beginning and the time he spent on the process to teach me how to be an author. He also paved the way for my journey into publishing by his strong example. I am forever grateful.

To Randi Smith, Sierra Allred, and Emma Sherk, I am delighted to have had your eyes on this novel. Your insight was invaluable. Becky Philpott, thank you for your suggestions; Lauren Finger, thank you for shining up this story and getting it ready for a crop of new readers; and Charlotte Hayes-Clemens, I'm so happy to have had your eyes on the final version. To my cover designer, Kristen Ingebretson, you are the best of the best! Thank you for all the creative discussion around branding my novels.

And last of all, a heartfelt thank-you must go out to my husband, Justin, and my kids, for managing when I told them that I was adding yet another book to my list. They carried the load as I worked tirelessly to fit this extra novel into my schedule. They are an amazing support and my whole world.

Printed in Great Britain
by Amazon